SLOW RIDE

erin mccarthy

BERKLEY SENSATION, NEW YORK

THE BERKLEY PUBLISHING GROUP
Published by the Penguin Group
Penguin Group (USA) Inc.
375 Hudson Street, New York, New York 10014, USA
Penguin Group (Canada), 90 Eglinton Avenue East, Suite 700, Toronto, Ontario M4P 2Y3, Canada
(a division of Pearson Penguin Canada Inc.)
Penguin Books Ltd., 80 Strand, London WC2R 0RL, England
Penguin Group Ireland, 25 St. Stephen's Green, Dublin 2, Ireland (a division of Penguin Books Ltd.)
Penguin Group (Australia), 250 Camberwell Road, Camberwell, Victoria 3124, Australia
(a division of Pearson Australia Group Pty. Ltd.)
Penguin Books India Pvt. Ltd., 11 Community Centre, Panchsheel Park, New Delhi—110 017, India
Penguin Group (NZ), 67 Apollo Drive, Rosedale, Auckland 0632, New Zealand
(a division of Pearson New Zealand Ltd.)
Penguin Books (South Africa) (Pty.) Ltd., 24 Sturdee Avenue, Rosebank, Johannesburg 2196,
South Africa

Penguin Books Ltd., Registered Offices: 80 Strand, London WC2R 0RL, England

SLOW RIDE

A Berkley Sensation Book / published by arrangement with the author

PRINTING HISTORY
Berkley Sensation mass-market edition / October 2011

Copyright © 2011 by Erin McCarthy.
Excerpt on pages 287–289 by Erin McCarthy copyright © by Erin McCarthy.
Cover art by Craig White.
Cover design by Rita Frangie.
Interior text design by Kristin del Rosario.

ISBN: 978-0-425-24396-1

BERKLEY SENSATION®
Berkley Sensation Books are published by The Berkley Publishing Group,
a division of Penguin Group (USA) Inc.,
375 Hudson Street, New York, New York 10014.
BERKLEY SENSATION® is a registered trademark of Penguin Group (USA) Inc.
The "B" design is a trademark of Penguin Group (USA) Inc.

PRINTED IN THE UNITED STATES OF AMERICA

10 9 8 7 6 5 4 3 2 1

continued . . .

OCT   2011

HEIRESS FOR HIRE

"If you are looking to read a romance that will leave you all warm inside, then *Heiress for Hire* is a must read."
—*Romance Junkies*

"McCarthy transforms what could have been a run-of-the-mill romance with standout characterizations that turn an unlikable girl and a boring guy into two enjoyable, empathetic people who make this romance shine." —*Booklist*

"Amusing paranormal contemporary romance . . . Fans will appreciate Erin McCarthy's delightful pennies-from-heaven tale of opposites in love pushed together by a needy child and an even needier ghost." —*The Best Reviews*

"One of McCarthy's best books to date . . . *Heiress for Hire* offers characters you will care about, a story that will make you laugh and cry, and a book you won't soon forget. As Amanda would say: It's priceless."
—*The Romance Reader* (5 hearts)

"A keeper. I'm giving it four of Cupid's five arrows."
—*BellaOnline*

"An alluring tale." —*A Romance Review* (5 roses)

"The perfect blend of sentiment and silly, heat and heart . . . Priceless!" —*RT Book Reviews* (4½ stars, Top Pick)

"An enjoyable story about finding love in unexpected places, don't miss *Heiress for Hire*."
—*Romance Reviews Today*

continued . . .

A DATE WITH THE OTHER SIDE

"Do yourself a favor and make a date with the other side."
—Rachel Gibson, *New York Times* bestselling author

"One of the romance-writing industry's brightest stars . . . Ms. McCarthy spins a fascinating tale that deftly blends a paranormal story with a blistering romance . . . Funny, charming, and very entertaining, *A Date With the Other Side* is sure to leave you with a pleased smile on your face."
—*Romance Reviews Today*

"If you're looking for a steamy read that will keep you laughing while you turn the pages as quickly as you can, *A Date With the Other Side* is for you. Very highly recommended!"
—*Romance Junkies*

"Fans will appreciate this otherworldly romance and want a sequel."
—*Midwest Book Review*

"Just the right amount of humor interspersed with romance."
—*Love Romances*

"Ghostly matchmakers add a fun flair to this warmhearted and delightful tale . . . An amusing and sexy charmer sure to bring a smile to your face."
—*RT Book Reviews*

"Offers readers quite a few chuckles, some face-fanning moments, and one heck of a love story. Surprises await those who expect a 'sophisticated city boy meets country girl' romance. Ms. McCarthy delivers much more."
—*A Romance Review*

"Fascinating."
—*Huntress Reviews*

For my father

Even after ten years you are greatly missed.

PROLOGUE

TUESDAY Jones stared at the minister in front of her, watching his mouth move, but unable to process what he was saying. The sun was hot on her arms, the breeze flapping her skirt, heels sinking into the soft grass, while her mother wept quietly beside her. None of it seemed real. It was like her entire body and her brain had been dipped in analgesic, and she was completely numb as she watched them lower her father's casket into the ground.

This wasn't supposed to happen. He was supposed to beat cancer, be one of those miraculous stories of triumph.

Instead, he was dead just three months after diagnosis, and Tuesday couldn't believe it was real.

She hadn't cried. She couldn't cry. It was like all of her emotions were locked inside her, frozen solid.

It even took her a second to realize when her sun hat was

lifted off her head by a gust of wind. She actually stared at it blankly as it tumbled past her mother's legs.

Only when it appeared her grieving mother was going to give chase did Tuesday react. "I have it," she murmured to her mother, squeezing her hand as she moved across the grass.

If it had been up to her, she would have just let the hat fly away to God knew where. She didn't care about the hat. She didn't care about anything.

A man a few headstones over bent down and caught her hat.

"Here you go," he told her, holding it out with a wisp of a smile.

"Thank you."

"My condolences." He nodded toward her father's funeral, now complete.

Her family and her father's friends were murmuring to each other, standing around in small groups. Tuesday swung her head back to the man in front of her. "Thank you. The same to you."

He nodded.

When Tuesday just stood there, staring at him without even really being aware of what she was doing, he cleared his throat.

"I guess you were close with him?"

"Yes. It's my father." And she couldn't go back. She knew it was weird and awkward that she was just standing there staring at this man, intruding on his grief, but she knew that if she turned, if she walked across that grass and had to face her mother, she would lose it. Which she couldn't do. She needed to keep it together for her mother, who was beyond devastated. Her mother had lost her life partner and she was walking around in a haze. Tuesday needed to be strong.

"I'm sorry," he said.

"And you?" she managed, determined to force normal conversation from her mouth, to focus on this man standing in front of her in a white dress shirt and black pants. As long as she concentrated on being normal with him, she could hold the tears, the hysteria at bay.

"My cousin." His thumb jerked behind him. "My mother." He pointed to the left. "My kid brother." His finger stayed in the same direction, then slowly fell to his side. "It does get easier with time, I promise."

And suddenly Tuesday lost it. The lip started to tremble, then the tears sprang out, while the low, deep sobs burst forth from her chest. She fought for control, but grief was winning. His eyes went wide, then suddenly his arms were around her, holding her.

"Shh, it's okay, let it out. Stop fighting it."

So she did. She let the sobs wrack her body, let the tears stream onto his gray-striped tie and shirt, even as she held her arms awkwardly at her sides, unable to wrap them around him. He had a muscular, solid chest, and arms that held her with gentle yet strong confidence. He smelled like aftershave, and his deep voice was soothing as he murmured in her ear over and over.

When she finally got a rein on her crying, and was able to step back, too upset to even feel embarrassed that she had sobbed on a stranger, he reached out and wiped her cheeks with callused fingers. "Everyone needs a good cry now and again."

Tuesday sniffled, using her arm to wipe her nose like a little kid.

"I'm Daniel, by the way."

"Tuesday."

"I think you should get back to your family, Tuesday," he told her. "Take care of yourself. Again, I'm sorry."

He squeezed her hand in good-bye, his green eyes flooded with sympathy before he turned and left.

Tuesday glanced down at the headstone he had been standing over. Peter Briggs. The stock car driver, killed in a wreck a few years earlier. His cousin, he'd said.

She watched Daniel walking across the grass, a slight limp to his gait, and she knew immediately who he was.

Daniel "Diesel" Lange.

Pete Briggs's cousin and a driver of considerable reputation and success until his car had kissed the wall head-on, leaving doctors and officials alike wondering how the man was still alive. He'd suffered a broken neck, a punctured lung, and a shattered leg, but he had survived, though he had retired.

A good ol' boy, Tuesday's father had called him.

And her dad's favorite driver.

As she made her way back to her mother, she found herself glancing up at the sky, like she could somehow see her dad there.

Her father's favorite driver had been standing ten feet away during his funeral. She thought her dad would have appreciated the irony of that.

It was the first peaceful thought she'd had all day.

CHAPTER
ONE

GRATEFUL that her toast as maid of honor was behind her, Tuesday also appreciated that her orange bridesmaid dress looked remarkably better under the muted ballroom lights than it had earlier in the day. Heading for the bar—because one glass of champagne clearly wasn't enough—she veered at the last second to the dessert table. She was supposed to meet Evan Monroe, the man who had been smart enough to marry her best friend, Kendall, and throw her a big old wedding reception four months after their impulsive elopement. When Evan had commented during dinner that women couldn't do shots of whiskey, Tuesday felt it was her duty, orange dress and all, to stand up for her gender.

But first she wanted a piece of cake.

To coat her stomach for the liquor.

Or maybe just because she liked cake.

She had to admit she was feeling weird-happy for Kendall, but also like she still wasn't totally enjoying herself. Like she couldn't. Yet for the first time in the three weeks since her dad had died, she didn't feel like she might burst into tears at any given moment, so that was progress. Baby steps. Little tiny almost nonexistent baby steps, because there was nothing easy about losing her father. Death sucked. Grief sucked.

On that very unpleasant thought, she grabbed a piece of cake from the assortment and crammed it into her mouth.

And discovered that she had chosen the damn coconut slice, one of her very least favorite flavors ever. There was good, there was bad, and then there was coconut. Her mouth automatically opening in horror, she looked around for a napkin, the flavor invading and offending every single one of her taste buds. Feeling like she might gag from the texture, she worked the cake forward with her tongue, debating just chucking it out of her mouth and into her champagne glass.

A hand shot out in front of her mouth and Evan said, "Just spit it out."

She only paused for a second before depositing the vile waxy coconut hunk into Evan's hand. "Oh, my God, thank you. Coconut. Ick. That was so freaking gross—"

Tuesday forgot the rest of her sentence when she looked up and realized that it wasn't Evan next to her. It was Diesel Lange. Retired driver. The man she had cried on at her father's funeral.

And the man she had now just spit chewed-up cake into his outstretched palm.

Oh. My. God. She felt heat flood her face as she stared at

him, trying to think of something, anything to say. "Sorry," was the best she could manage. "I thought you were Evan."

It was a lame explanation, but how did you really explain regurgitation onto total strangers?

His eyebrows furrowed. "Why would you think I was Evan?"

"Because I was meeting Evan." Tuesday licked her lips, still tasting the coconut, still feeling like an ass. "I don't usually just spit out food into random people's hands, you know." Food she realized he was still holding. "God, that's so gross, I'm sorry."

She reached out and grabbed the cold, mushy, spit-filled blob off his hand. It left a slimy smear across his skin. "Crap, sorry." She was tempted to lick it off, but figured that would make it worse. A lot worse. She didn't imagine any man wanted a woman to just lick them at a wedding reception.

Then again, maybe men did.

The oven her face had become burned a little hotter.

But he just gave her a lopsided smile. "Quit apologizing. I'm the one who stuck my hand out. I don't like coconut either, so I'm glad I could help. The texture makes me want to hurl."

She felt slightly better, or at least she would when that saliva trail across his hand was gone. First she'd snotted on his dress shirt at the funeral, now she'd spit on him. Classy.

"Let me get you a napkin." Which now that she was glancing around, she saw they were plenty on the corner of the table, but they were blending into the tablecloth, which had created this moment of horror for her. "Here." Grabbing several off the top of the stack, she scrubbed at his hand with it. "I can't believe I spit on you."

His other hand reached out and stilled her, wrapping loosely around her wrist. "Stop. A little saliva never killed anyone."

"I don't have any communicable diseases, just so you know." Oh, God, did she really just say that? Tuesday downed the rest of her glass of champagne.

Diesel burst out laughing. "That is good to know. But I wasn't worried."

Then he just . . . looked at her. Tuesday wondered if he remembered who she was. Wondered if she was supposed to acknowledge that she had cried on him. But what if she said something and he didn't recognize her? She glanced ruefully into the bottom of her empty glass.

What was the most disconcerting of all was that she had never been the type of woman who worried about things like this. She was no stranger to voicing her opinion, and she had never lacked for confidence. You couldn't be missing either if you wanted to be successful in the field of sports reporting. So why she was standing there wide-eyed and mute like an anime cartoon girl she did not understand. That shit had to stop.

"I was meeting Evan at the bar. I should head on over there," she said. "Come with me and I'll buy you a drink."

"It's an open bar."

She grinned. "I know. But it's the thought that counts."

He smiled back, a crooked smile that sent a shiver racing up her spine. *Hello.* She'd just felt the first jolt of sexual interest she'd had in months. It had been instantaneous when the corner of his mouth had risen slowly and slyly, and Tuesday cleared her throat, suddenly unnerved. He was tall, with shaggy dark blond hair and some short facial hair that she felt the urge to touch to test its softness.

She knew he was single.

And she knew herself well enough to know that she needed to get the hell away from him as soon as possible.

But he held his arm out for her. Like a gentleman does to escort a woman somewhere. "Lead the way, Tuesday," he told her.

There was no way to avoid slipping her own arm through his without being totally rude, so she did, clutching the empty glass in her free hand, and trying not to look up at him. He had used her name. Did that mean he did remember her or he had just heard her name announced as maid of honor at the beginning of dinner?

But she was Tuesday Jones, damn it, and even though she hadn't felt stronger than a wet napkin the last few months, she at least needed to thank this man. "By the way," she told him, forcing her head to lift to look at him, "thanks for letting me bawl on you in the cemetery. I appreciate you tolerating the crazy girl."

He sidled a look down at her that she couldn't read. It was sympathetic, yes, but there didn't seem to be any pity in it. It was something else, another emotion, but then again, maybe it was just the light playing off his pale blue eyes.

"No problem. I'm glad I could be there for you. Your dad was a good guy, and I'm really sorry for your loss."

Tuesday drew up short a foot from the bar. He knew her dad? Well, duh, of course he knew her father. Over the years her dad had probably interviewed him a dozen times. Her brain wasn't firing at full neurons lately. "Thanks," she murmured, setting the champagne glass down on the bar before it slipped from her sweaty palm.

"What the hell took you so long?" Evan asked, grinning from ear to ear as he swaggered over to them, his tie askew. "Change your mind, wimp out on me?"

Her emotions were swirling close to the surface, thoughts of her father's extensive career as a sports journalist suddenly thrust in front of her by Diesel Lange, and she wiped her hand down the front of her pumpkin-colored dress. Who thought of pumpkins in August? It made no sense. But the orange color scheme was what Kendall had wanted, and Tuesday guessed maybe it was supposed to be more tropical than fall foliage.

Evan's grin started to slip. "Are you okay?"

No, not really. She was feeling far from okay. And that feeling like she might cry at any given second had returned full force. "Yeah, of course I am. Bring it on, Monroe." She turned to Diesel. "Do you want to do a shot with us?"

He shook his head. "No, thanks."

Why was he looking at her like that? Those eyes just bore into her, like he was seeing something she didn't want anyone to see. Tuesday was intensely aware of how close he was standing to her, how tall he was even though she was five foot eight. There weren't a lot of men who towered over her, but he did. He had a presence, too, that seemed to surround her, that made her want to both lean on his chest for comfort, and strip him naked and get thrown against a wall.

Neither of which were appropriate to do at the moment.

"Don't be a wuss." Evan tried to hand a shot glass filled

with whiskey to Diesel. "It's my wedding and I never see you anymore, so I say you owe me."

"Seriously, no thanks. I take pain meds and trust me, it ain't a good combination." Diesel shrugged. "I'll take a Coke though."

Tuesday thought about the limp she had seen Diesel use at the cemetery. For some reason, she had assumed that's all it was, that there wouldn't actually be pain anymore. It had been at least two years since his accident, if she was remembering correctly. But if he limped, she imagined it was because he was in pain.

Yet he always looked so calm.

Suddenly confused, her emotions pinging in multiple directions, Tuesday turned to the bartender. "Can we get a Coke, please?" She took the shot of whiskey Evan was holding out to her. God knew the last thing she needed was to throw back some Jack, but the truth was, she felt a little afraid of the direction her thoughts and feelings were going in. Maybe the liquor would take the edge off.

"Are you sure your wife doesn't want a shot?" Tuesday asked Evan.

"Are you kidding? Kendall can't hold her liquor. She's not drinking at all tonight because she doesn't want to wind up trashed and doing the worm on the dance floor in her wedding dress."

Tuesday sniffed her drink. "So that's what you have me for, right? I'll be the one making an ass out of myself in a few hours."

Evan grinned. "We can only hope."

Unfortunately, given the way she was feeling, Tuesday

thought that might not be that far from the truth. For a split second, she hesitated. Maybe the whiskey was a bad idea on top of the champagne. But then Evan lifted his glass and tossed it back and she was just competitive enough that she had to follow suit, taking it cleanly and quickly. As the burn raced down her throat, she tried not to wince.

Diesel raised his eyebrow, his soft drink lifted to his lips. "You don't play around."

No, she didn't. And she wasn't going to let this night descend into melancholy for her. It was Kendall and Evan's wedding, for crying out loud. New beginnings, a celebration of hope and love and the future. She needed to shake the sadness off.

"Hell, no," she told him. "You have to take drinking seriously, you know. You want to dance?"

He shook his head. "No."

It was amazing how fast alcohol could loosen her limbs. She ought to be worried, but the truth was, she was glad the knots in her shoulders had unfurled just a bit. "What? Well, that's just rude. Why wouldn't you want to dance with me?"

"I can't dance."

"Pfft." She looked at Evan. "He can't dance, and he does it anyway."

"I can so dance. I own that dance floor. If Lange won't dance with you, I will."

Tuesday would rather spend more time with Diesel, but he was shaking his head. She ought to be offended, but there was something about the way he looked at her, she just couldn't believe it was that he didn't want to be with her. There was that something . . . there was a word for it but she was starting to suspect she was drunk because she couldn't figure out what it was.

"Okay. Let's polka."

"But they're playing Donna Summer," Evan protested.

"Perfect. We'll polka and hustle at the same time. It's all about creating your own path, my friend." Tuesday leaned over the bar. "Another champagne, s'il vous plaît." Oh, yeah, she was drunk. Busting out high school French was always a sure sign of that.

"See you later," she said to Diesel, taking her drink from the bartender. "Stay away from coconut."

Did that make sense? She wasn't really sure, but he just nodded. "Have fun."

"Always." Not exactly true, but if she stated it often enough, maybe it would become true.

Fun. Yeah. That's what she was having.

Tuesday grabbed Evan by the arm and went to prove it.

DIESEL watched Tuesday head out onto the dance floor with no small amount of regret. He had thought about her a few times since her father's funeral, wondered if she was okay, felt compassion for that grief he knew all too well. She was a gorgeous, vibrant woman, a daughter her father had spoken very proudly of, but she had Diesel curious. He suspected that she was very close to the edge of cracking at this wedding, and he didn't imagine that a shot was going to prevent that from happening.

Dancing was probably good for her though. Leaning on the bar, Diesel discreetly bent his knee to ease the stiffness in it. It was really giving him hell today for some reason,

13

prompting him to take the pain meds he usually avoided before he'd left for the wedding.

"Hey, what's up?" Ty McCordle sidled up to him. "What are you drinking?"

"Coke."

Ty raised an eyebrow. "Boy Scout, huh? I need a beer myself."

Diesel fought the urge to sigh. He hated explaining himself. He hated admitting that he couldn't do certain things like dancing or drink. Not that he had ever danced before his crash, but hell, he would like the option. Now he couldn't, plain and simple. It was annoying. But it was what it was. No sense whining about it.

"So Evan finally took the plunge. Have to say I didn't see that coming." When Diesel had been driving in the Cup series with Evan, he had always thought of him as a perpetual bachelor. Unlike some of the other guys, he'd never had a serious girlfriend.

"Did you know he and Kendall were an item ten years ago?" Ty took his beer from the bartender and took a sip. "Guess they were supposed to be together all along."

He shouldn't say anything, shouldn't draw attention to himself, but Diesel couldn't resist. "Do you know Kendall's maid of honor?"

"Sure. She's Tuesday Talladega, the blogger. Bob Jones's daughter. She actually just asked me to do an interview about her father, give some memories of him. She's arranging some kind of cancer benefit in his name."

"Really?" Diesel thought it sounded like a great idea, and a positive way for her to channel her grief. Unlike whiskey.

He watched her doing maneuvers on the dance floor that

seemed to defy gravity, her hips swiveling and her body dropping down between her bent knees. He coughed into his palm. Jesus, he had just felt a kick of lust, his junk jumping into a semi-erection faster than he would have thought possible.

Not cool. He was supposed to be showing her sympathy, not a tent in his suit.

"Wait a minute." Ty nudged him. "You got the hots for Tuesday, don't you?"

He hadn't thought about it that way. He had thought he'd been feeling sorry for her pain and loss. But at the moment, as she booty-grinded on the dance floor, he thought maybe there was something a little more primal drawing him to her than just sympathy.

"I don't know Tuesday."

"That wasn't the question."

"No, I don't have the hots for her. I just feel bad for her because she lost her father." And maybe he was a little attracted to her. And technically, that could probably be called the hots.

"Uh-huh. Whatever." Ty slapped him on the shoulder. "I know that look, buddy. You should go dance with her. Dancing is the gateway to sex, you know."

"No, thanks." He wouldn't even if he could. Wasn't his style. "And why is it whenever a guy is in a relationship, he's always trying to fix his friends up with whatever single woman is standing around? Jefferson was trying to pawn me off on Kendall's cousin."

Ty grinned. "Because we don't want single friends reminding us of our lost freedom."

"Is that what it is? Then sign me right up." Diesel hadn't

had a serious girlfriend in almost four years and he had to admit, he missed knowing he had someone to go to the movies with, or say, a wedding reception. But most men bitched about being trapped. It was just expected. Standard guy talk.

"Aside from being with the woman I love, the best thing is regular booty." Ty cleared his throat. "Can't beat that, man, I'm telling you."

Diesel wasn't even sure he remembered what sex with a partner felt like. It was safe to say he hadn't been getting out much. "Hell, I'd settle for irregular booty."

"Well, there it is, waiting for you out on the dance floor." Ty gestured to Tuesday. "She's looking for donations of items for a silent auction for the cancer benefit. You should donate something, like an engine rebuild or some of your vintage parts. It'd give you a good excuse to talk to her, and it's for a good cause."

Diesel had been rebuilding vintage stock cars and selling them since his accident. It kept him busy and gave him something to do with his hands. He liked the idea of somehow helping Tuesday's cause. "Yeah, I could do that." In fact, he could actually donate a completely rebuilt car. That would bring in a shitload of cash. "I'll talk to her about it after she's done dancing."

Which didn't look like would be happening any time soon. Tuesday was breaking it down with a guy who was at least a hundred and twelve. He was just shuffling in front of her in awe, a shit-eating grin on his face while she shimmied all around him.

There was no denying that Diesel would give anything to stroll out there, grab her, and kiss the stuffing out of her.

In fact, if he were totally honest, he wanted to throw her down on the nearest table and lift her ugly orange dress.

"She's a live one," Ty commented. "Good luck with that." He grinned. "Sucker."

Diesel was about to remark that Ty was the one planning the wedding of the decade with his fiancée Imogen, but just as he opened his mouth, a pack of kids hell-bent on hitting the chocolate fountain went flying by him. Or three of them did anyway. The fourth plowed right into Diesel, the impact causing his knee to buckle as the boy tried to shove back off of him.

"Sorry!" he said without a backward glance, his shirttail untucked and floppy hair bouncing as he ran to catch up with his friends.

For a split second, the pain was so bad Diesel thought he might puke. But the sharp biting agony settled down into a standard throb and he took a deep breath. It was cool. He was cool. No big deal.

Ty was looking at him in concern, but much to Diesel's relief, didn't actually say anything other than, "Punk kids. We were never that rowdy."

"Yes, we were," Diesel said, but his words were ground out through clenched teeth. "I'll catch you later, I'm going to hit the head."

"Sure. Good seeing you, man."

"You, too." It was sheer willpower that allowed Diesel to walk across the room to the exit with only a slightly more exaggerated limp than normal. He didn't want to draw attention to himself, but he needed to get the hell out of there and sit down for a minute.

Fortunately, the attention of everyone in the room shifted

to the dance floor as the DJ announced the father-daughter dance. All eyes swung to the bride, so Diesel managed to navigate his way around the perimeter of the room. Once in the hallway, he found a tufted bench between two potted plants and eased himself down onto it.

He'd forgotten his drink at the bar and right now he could use a swig of Coke to get rid of the hot saliva that had flooded his mouth. Resting his head on the wall, he just concentrated on relaxing his shoulders and breathing deep. It was fine.

But when Tuesday came out of the ballroom carrying two glasses of champagne, he had to admit he was tempted to take one from her, meds or not. "Is that for me?" he asked her, forcing a nonchalant smile.

"Hell to the no," she said, bringing both glasses to her chest covetously. "These are both for me. It saves time if I just get two at once."

Part of him wanted to laugh, but the party girl persona, that devil-may-care attitude wasn't ringing true. There was something far too bright and shiny in her eyes, and an air of desperate bravado clung to her.

"Have a seat." He patted the bench next to him. "I promise not to steal your bubbly."

"Thanks." She sat down and stretched her long, graceful legs out in front of her.

"So why aren't you inside?" he asked.

There was a pause. "It was hot in there. How about you?"

Diesel thought about giving her the same pat response in return, but if he wanted the truth from her, he needed to give her the truth. Since he strongly suspected she needed someone to talk to, he was willing to be honest. "Some little kid ran into me and my bad knee twisted. I needed a breather."

She winced, glancing down at his leg. "Does it hurt really bad?"

"Like a motherfucker."

"I'm sorry. You should have one of these drinks." She tried to hand him the glass but he shook his head.

"Pain meds, remember? Not that they're working much at the moment."

Tuesday set both glasses down on the floor and said, "That sucks."

"It is what it is. I am lucky to be alive, you know." It was true. The doctors had told him the impact he'd sustained should have killed him. So if that meant he had some aches and pains, hell, he'd take it. It was better than pushing daisies for damn sure.

"I'm glad you're not dead," she said vehemently.

Diesel wasn't sure what to say to that, exactly, but Tuesday wasn't finished.

"Death sucks. It really, really sucks. Do you know why I left that ballroom?"

He shook his head.

"Because they're playing the father-daughter dance, and you know what? I'll never get to dance with my father at my wedding, and that really bites the big one." Her face scrunched up and the tears came. "It's not fair."

Oh, damn. Diesel felt his own heart squeeze at the sheer agony in her voice. She looked so miserable, so shocked, so vulnerable, and drunk. "No, it's definitely not fair. Not even close. Come here."

Diesel put his arm around her shoulders and drew her into his chest. She came willingly, burying her face in his dress shirt.

"I'm happy for Kendall, obviously. I mean, I'm thrilled for her." Her voice was trembling, her words punctuated by sobs. "But it just hurts."

"I'm sorry, Tuesday. I can't tell you how much. But I think what you're doing, planning a cancer benefit in your father's honor, is awesome. I'll be happy to make a donation."

Stroking her back, Diesel tried to think of additional words of comfort, but he wasn't sure what else he could say. Grief was hell and you just had to work it through it, step by step.

"As long as it isn't coconut," she said, her sobs settling down into sniffles.

"Hell, yeah, it's going to be coconut. It's going to be coconut cream pie with coconut shavings on top. Coconut cream pie for a year, that's what it will be." It was a stupid thing to say, but he was looking for anything to distract her.

"I'll toss it in your face then."

"Love to see you try."

Tuesday pulled back and stared at him, her eyes searching his. Sniffling, her nose red, she said, "You're a nice guy, aren't you?"

Bemused, he told her, "We do exist. Hard to believe, I know."

She nodded. "An endangered species. I don't think I've ever seen one in the wild."

"Just so you know, I can be badass, too." He wanted to make sure he didn't come off as a total pansy.

Tuesday laughed, wiping her cheeks free of tears. "Well,

that just proves you're clearly all male. I give you a compliment and you want to make sure you're not appearing too sensitive. Typical."

Feeling slightly sheepish, he just shrugged. "Hey, I'm not perfect. Just very nice and extra manly."

"Well, are you man enough to go back into that ballroom and dance with me?"

The thought made his nuts draw up into his body. He did not want to dance, under any circumstances. "It's more manly not to dance. I'll just stand on the edge of the dance floor and grunt while I watch you."

She cocked her head like she was about to argue, but then she nodded. "Alright, I'll take it. But you can skip the grunting."

Tuesday stood up, but not before retrieving her champagne glasses, which she drained, one right after the other, in a move that reminded Diesel of movies about fraternity parties. Impressive.

"I'll grunt if I want to."

She burped, a no-holds-barred belch that seemed at complete odds with her slender body, elegant hairstyle, and bridesmaid dress. Diesel laughed.

Tuesday held her finger out to him. "And there's more where that came from."

"I can't wait." Diesel stood up.

She hadn't backed up, so when he stood, they were close, his thighs brushing against her dress. From this vantage point, Diesel could see how plump and moist her lips were, how smooth her skin was, and he could smell the sweetness of her perfume. Thoughts of kissing her flooded his mind, his fingers itching to dive into her dark hair and mess up that perfect knot twisted on her head. He liked that she was tall, that she could look him in the eye without having to totally strain her neck like most women did. He liked that he could reach right out and rest his hands on her waist if he wanted to.

Those eyes were watching him now, darkening with what he hoped like hell was desire.

All he would have to do would be to lean down and drop his mouth onto hers and take a taste of those sexy red lips.

But then she jerked back, grabbing his hand. "Oh, my God! The chicken dance. You have to dance with me!"

Diesel gritted his teeth as she dragged him to the ballroom. The chicken dance didn't excite him nearly as much as a hot make-out session did.

He who hesitates has to make an ass out of himself on the dance floor.

CHAPTER
TWO

TUESDAY knew she should slow down given that Diesel had just said his knee was bothering him, but she needed to get back into the crowded ballroom. First she had needed to escape, then she needed to dive back in. Go figure. But she had been standing there, staring up at Diesel, and she had suddenly been overwhelmed by the urge to shove him down onto the bench and climb into his lap and ride him.

Not appropriate.

One, this was a wedding, and it might shock Kendall's grandmother if the maid of honor was having sex in the hallway. Two, she wasn't supposed to be thinking about down-and-dirty sex when her dad had just died.

So the chicken dance it was.

She was surprised that Diesel had actually followed her onto the dance floor. Then again, she hadn't really given him much choice, given the death grip she had on his hand.

The ballroom was getting warm from the lighting and all the bodies moving around, and Tuesday found a spot dead center on the dance floor that no one else was brave enough to claim.

As the kitschy music flowed around them and all of Kendall's and Evan's friends and relatives flapped their arms, Tuesday turned to Diesel. She was well aware that she was getting drunk quickly because she felt flushed, her vision a little too sharp, and she was having a hard time controlling what came out of her mouth. Which would explain why she said, "God, I just want to run my fingers through your hair."

His eyes widened, but he just lifted one corner of his mouth. "Go for it."

But she knew that was a bad idea. "No, no, we have to do the chicken dance before the music ends." Jumping in, she started clapping and flapping along with all the other guests.

Diesel just stood there, his arms loosely at his sides, his blue tie a perfect match for the color of his mysterious eyes. She couldn't tell what he was thinking, if he was having fun, or if he just wanted her to go away and leave him the hell alone.

"All you have to do is clap," she told him, yelling over the music.

"I'm good."

"You look like a tree trunk." A very, very cute tree trunk. Tuesday needed to stop staring at him. His cuteness was starting to hurt. It was just painful how freaking adorable he was, from that shaggy hair to that scruffy beard to that steady expression he always wore. Plus he was always free with a shoulder for her to cry on.

Cute. Hot.

She glanced down at his crotch.

Hung.

Oh, my. He had an erection.

As the music swung into the sashay section, she tried to hook her arm in his but Diesel shook his head. "It ain't going to happen."

She would assume that was because of his knee, not because he was morally opposed to dancing like some minister in an '80s movie, so she just sashayed around him solo. It felt a little like she was doing a maypole dance, but she was drunk and having fun, so she was going to roll with it. Diesel seemed amused by it himself, because he was struggling to contain a smile when she rounded his front side and glanced up at him.

"You gotta go the other way now," he told her, pointing back the way she came.

"Oh, right. That is how the dance goes." She reversed, her heel giving her a little bit of trouble on the turn. She almost lost her footing but Diesel grabbed her arm and steadied her.

Huh. That felt kinda nice. Having someone catch her when she was going to fall. Tuesday banished that thought as quickly as it came. She was independent. A grown woman. A sports reporter and famed stock car blogger. She didn't need someone to catch her. She wasn't falling. Ever.

All she was doing was noticing that Diesel had quite an amazing butt in those dress pants. He wasn't wearing a jacket, which afforded her a fabulous view. She couldn't help it. Trailing her fingers across his back as she modified the sashay significantly, she let her hand wander a little lower than was strictly appropriate.

"I don't think that's in the dance," he told her when she rounded the front.

"No? Then I just changed it." She moved in closer to him, her hands on his chest. She wanted to kiss him. She wanted to grind her body against his and forget about everything and everyone except for him and her and the pleasure she was sure they could create together.

But before she could do anything, he took a step back. "The dance is over."

Tuesday blinked. He was right, everyone was abandoning the floor as the DJ switched over from the fast paced chicken dance to some melancholic slow song.

But why did that mean he couldn't kiss her? He had to have seen the look she was giving him, had to have picked up on her cues. Or maybe he just didn't want to kiss her.

Well. That was a sobering thought.

"Are you hungry? They put out some finger food. Maybe you should eat something."

So he thought she was drunk. Well, she was drunk, what of it? That didn't mean she didn't know what she was doing.

"I don't need to eat. I need to dance. And if you're not going to dance with me, I'll find someone who will." A distant relative of Evan's had been hitting on her earlier, and she saw he was eyeing her from the edge of the dance floor. "I'll see you later, Diesel."

She would not be stupidly hurt for no apparent reason.

She would not be offended by Diesel's lack of sexual interest in her. She would not cry—again—at this wedding.

She would dance and flirt with a man she didn't find remotely attractive for an ego boost and a distraction.

See how mature and not drunk she was?

Take that, Diesel Lange.

DIESEL watched Tuesday stomp off, a little unsteady on her feet. He clenched his hands at his sides involuntarily when she strode straight up to some douche bag wearing his necktie like a belt. He tried not to grit his teeth when Tuesday started dancing with him and the guy used that necktie to wrap around her waist and draw her closer to him.

He should have slow danced with her. He could have managed that. Maybe.

He should have kissed her. He could have handled that without taking it to far on the dance floor. Possibly.

At the very least, he should not have suggested she eat some finger food. How lame was that? He'd been thinking it would help slow down her speeding train to trashed town, but all it had done was piss her off. Rightly so. Offering finger food was stupid and grandmotherly. He didn't want to seem like an ancient relative.

So the question was what did he do now? Did he stand there like a loser watching her grind—yes, grind—with some pretty boy, or did he do something about it? He could walk away and abandon the whole idea of Tuesday, which really, what exactly was his idea? Hell if he knew. Or he could save her from what was clearly a bad choice.

Then again, how did he know what was a good choice or

a bad choice for Tuesday? Maybe this dude was someone she would really dig, and they'd get married or something and if he interrupted, he'd destroy her future.

God, his head hurt, and he felt like the longer he stood there, the more his testosterone was draining away. Another five minutes and he'd have to turn in his man card.

The point was, did he want Tuesday or not?

His dick hardened in his dress pants.

That was a yes.

The follow-up question was could he do anything about it tonight?

No. Not when she was as loaded as she was.

But he could certainly protect her from making a drunken mistake she'd probably regret.

Because from the looks of that guy, he had one thing and one thing only in mind. And while Tuesday was laughing as she danced with him, she also kept repeatedly moving his hand off her ass.

Diesel forced his shoulders to relax and he moved to the edge of the dance floor. "Excuse me, I'm cutting in."

The douche king stopped grinning at Tuesday and glared at Diesel. "You can't do that."

"Why not?"

"Because I'm not done with her."

Diesel saw red at the possessive and patronizing tone in the guy's voice. "Oh, you're done. Step away from the lady."

Tuesday was eyeing him, a smile on her face. "You're going to dance with me? Really?"

She was about three beats behind the current conversation, but Diesel felt no small amount of satisfaction at how pleased she sounded. "Yes, sweetheart, I'm going to dance with you."

Hopefully the song would be over in the next ten seconds. But he would dance if it meant getting her away from this guy.

"That's super awesome." Tuesday extracted herself from the other guy's octopus arms and said, "I'm sorry, he's cutting in. Maybe we can dance again later."

"Are you serious?" the guy asked, clearly irritated.

"Yes."

"Bitch," was his final thought before he turned to leave, his tie trailing on the floor.

Diesel reached out and grabbed the guy's arm. He didn't want to make a scene, but that was unacceptable. "Hey. Show a little respect. I think you owe her an apology."

He glanced down at Diesel's hand wrapped around his arm. "Sorry. But maybe you should tell your girlfriend to stop flirting with guys. Or I don't know, maybe this is a game the two of you play."

"I don't play games." The whole idea that any couple would do that actually offended Diesel on a lot of levels, but he was done with this conversation. "Come on, Tuesday, let's go."

"But you're going to dance with me!"

Right. Fighting the urge to sigh, Diesel moved her a few feet away from the idiot. But then he took her in his arms and he no longer regretted his rash promise.

Oh, shit. Tuesday was so damn beautiful. It felt good, it felt right, it felt scary as freaking hell to hold her lightly in his arms. Somewhere in the back of his mind, he was aware of his knee aching, but he ignored it. He had no rhythm whatsoever, but he could sway. So that's what he did, his hands on her waist, her arms wrapped around his neck.

"Happy?" he asked her. "I'm making an ass out of myself for you."

"Oh, whatever." She tossed her head like she wasn't used to her hair being pulled so tautly. "You were dying to dance with me and you know it. You were just playing hard to get."

"Yeah, that's totally me. I'm probably going to bat my eyelashes at you next."

He expected her to say something snarky, but she studied his eyes so long he started to feel uncomfortable. What the hell did she see? Maybe she was staring at the scar he had under his eye from where he'd gotten sliced by an icy snowball in a childhood accident. It had never bothered him before, but what the hell?

"You have beautiful eyes," she told him, her voice a little dreamy.

And slurred.

Diesel still felt flattered, even if her statement was fueled by alcohol. A little embarrassed, too. What guy wants his eyes pointed out as his best feature first? He'd be feeling a bit more manly if she had mentioned his biceps.

"Thanks."

"But you're right, you can't dance."

Diesel laughed. "You have the truth of it there, Tuesday." He tried to loosen up, be less stiff, but his body just didn't cooperate. "By the way, you have beautiful eyes, too, you know."

She did. They were a deep, rich brown with flecks of gold. They were mysterious and sassy and vulnerable, and he was heading into some damn dangerous territory. Tuesday Jones was not in any position tonight—or probably at all—to be getting involved with someone. He wasn't a one-night stand kind of guy either.

But it had been a long time since he'd tasted a woman's skin, felt the slide of her legs over his, buried himself deep inside her hot, moist body . . .

"Thanks," she murmured, wetting her lips.

Diesel followed the progress of her tongue as it dragged slowly across her bottom lip, leaving it shiny and kissable. Damn. Damn. Damn.

He could not take advantage of a drunk woman.

Wouldn't.

"How are you getting home?" he asked her.

Her eyes darkened and he realized the implication of what he'd just said.

"Is the limo taking you? Do you need a ride?"

"No, I have my car."

She was clearly in no position to be driving.

"I should actually call a cab," she said.

It was good to know she was aware of how far into the champagne she was. "I can give you a ride."

The corner of her mouth turned up. "Are you going to take advantage of me if I say yes?"

"Of course not."

"Damn. I was hoping you'd say yes."

Diesel almost groaned. Her hands had slid into his hair and he was enjoying the light touch as she stroked through to the roots. "You don't know what you're saying," he murmured to her.

"Oh, yes, I do." Tuesday's lips fell open and she stood

up on her toes, her body moving closer to his, her mouth heading towards his.

He refused to be the loser who let a woman kiss him first. It didn't work that way.

But before he could take her mouth with his, Tuesday suddenly lost her footing and went down in a heap of orange fabric. He was so stunned that it took him a second to react, and by the time he did, Tuesday was on the floor.

"Oh, shit, are you okay? What happened?" Diesel squatted down, his knee screaming in protest. He scanned her body for obvious injuries, and there was no sign of anything other than shapely calves and firm thighs. A lot of thigh. Like more thigh than should ever be seen short of a woman wearing a bathing suit. Diesel yanked his eyes off her lower half and settled on her face.

She was laughing, legs sprawled out in front of her, dress hiked up to dangerous territory. "I have no idea what just happened."

Then she just laid back completely on the dance floor, her midsection rising up and down from her giggles. A few other dancers were glancing their way, so Diesel fixed the hem of her dress because he couldn't stand the temptation of all that skin, nor did he want any other man checking her out. He couldn't help but grin as she shook with laughter.

Taking her hand he pulled her back to a sitting position. "Come on, you lush. Let's get you home."

"I'm not drunk. Well, okay, I may be slightly drunk, but I'm no lush." This pronouncement was made with her legs spread in a V on the dance floor, and her fingers digging into the top of her dress to adjust her bra.

"Uh-huh."

It wasn't easy, but using the strength in his arms and not his legs, Diesel managed to haul her off the ground without causing himself too much pain. Tuesday immediately tottered again in her spiky heels. "Maybe you should take your shoes off, sweetheart."

"Why are you calling me sweetheart? You're freaking me out." But holding firmly onto his arm, she did lean over and pry off her shoes. There was a precarious moment where she almost went down again, but she held it together.

He had no idea why he was calling her sweetheart. To tell the truth, he hadn't even been aware he was doing it until she'd pointed it out. Heat crawled up his neck and it wasn't from the crowded ballroom. "I can stop if it bothers you."

"Nah." She stood straight up and looked him in the eye boldly. "I don't want you to stop."

Diesel almost groaned. She wasn't going to make this easy. Sometimes being a decent human being sucked.

Fortunately, Evan and Kendall approached them. "You okay, Tuesday?" Evan asked.

"I'm fine."

Kendall took Tuesday's hand and said, "Excuse us, I need to talk to Tuesday for a second."

They moved a few feet away, Diesel and Evan both watching them. "Hey, congrats again, man. Your wife is quite a catch."

"Thanks. I am a lucky man, that's for damn sure." Evan cleared his throat. "Look, I have to be straight with you. Tuesday is Kendall's best friend and I like you, you know that. I respect you and we've known each other a long time.

But she's shitfaced tonight and just needs a ride home, you get what I'm saying?"

Diesel tried not to be offended. Evan was just looking out for Tuesday. "That's all I was planning to do. Unless you'd prefer I call her a cab."

Evan clapped him on the shoulder. "No, that's cool. I trust you. Just glad we're on the same page. She's had a rough couple of weeks, you know?"

"Yeah. I know." Diesel knew that pain. Knew that desire to escape into alcohol or anything that would make you forget. He had fought that battle after he'd lost his mother, and his brother, and his cousin. Then again when he'd had his own accident and realized he'd never be able to drive again. "So she doesn't have a boyfriend or anything, does she?"

It had occurred to him that maybe he should ask that before he thought too much about kissing those sexy lips of hers.

Evan grinned. "So that's how the wind blows, huh? No, she doesn't have a boyfriend. She was doing an online dating thing for a while, but from what Kendall told me, she had a lot of bad first dates and nothing more."

"Yeah?" Diesel tried to sound noncommittal. He wasn't really sure what he was thinking or what he wanted. He just knew he wanted the opportunity, if he chose to take it, of seeing Tuesday again sometime. Possibly.

"I'm sure you can take her out on a bad first date, too."

Was that what he wanted?

Diesel studied the tall brunette in the pumpkin dress and thought he suddenly wanted that more than anything else right now.

* * *

"*YOU* need to drink some water," Kendall said.

"I'm fine," Tuesday insisted. God, she was just drunk. It wasn't like that had never happened before. "Will you go off and bang your husband and not worry about me? I'm a big girl, I can take care of myself." Glancing around the floor, she said, "Shit, what did I do with my shoes?"

"I think Diesel has them."

Tuesday sighed. "He's so fucking cute, Kendall. Would it be bad if I had sex with him tonight?"

"Yes."

She frowned. That was not the answer she wanted. "Why? I bet he rocks the sheets."

"I have no idea if he does or not, but you'll be too drunk to appreciate it."

It wasn't possible to be too drunk to appreciate that hunk of man flesh. "Oh, please. So I've had a little too much champagne. That just means I won't be trying to hide my dimply thighs from his view."

It might also mean that she'd be slurring her words, because her tongue seemed a little larger than normal, but that could be worked around, she was sure.

Kendall put her hands on her shoulders. "Tuesday. Look at me. This is not a good idea. If you want to have sex with Diesel next Saturday after a date, you go for it. But tonight is not the night. You're more likely to vomit on him than have an orgasm."

Just the word "vomit" made Tuesday's stomach slosh around a little. "I don't know . . ."

"Picture his erection coming at you for oral sex. Do you want that in your mouth right now?"

Yikes. That was telling it a little too much like it is. Tuesday clapped her hand over her mouth, her gag reflex firing up. She shook her head. "No."

"There's a time and a place for everything. Tonight you need to sleep alone."

Kendall might have a point. "Can I cuddle with him though?" She had this idea that those strong arms would feel really nice wrapped around her in bed, her head resting on his chest. It seemed like a super solid chest.

"Of course you can if he's cool with cuddling only. Make sure you're clear on that. But in my experience, most men don't want to cuddle unless they're guaranteed to get some."

"This is complicated," Tuesday complained. Getting naked would be so much easier. "I'm leaving." Before her brain started to hurt. "Love you." She leaned over and kissed Kendall loudly on the cheek. "Congratulations again. You know you're a beautiful bride."

"Thanks, you nuttyhead. I'll see you tomorrow for brunch."

Brunch. Eew. Tuesday did not want to sit around a round table with all the women in Kendall's family, making small talk. The only bright spot would be the mimosas. "Right. See you then."

With a wave, she walked over to Diesel, wishing that she could manage a slightly sexier walk. Instead, she just felt like she was working really hard to maintain a forward motion in something of a straight line, because her body wanted to pitch and weave in a zigzag pattern.

"I'm leaving," she told Diesel. Something about her sentence didn't seem quite right, but she wasn't going to worry about it. She suddenly wanted out of the dwindling crowd, out of her orange dress, and out of consciousness.

But he seemed to take it in stride. "I guess we're leaving." He shook Evan's hand and said good night.

"Where are my shoes?" she asked as she headed toward the door, managing a cursory wave in Evan's direction, but feeling like anything more than that was too much effort. If she leaned in for a hug, she just might keep going and knock him down onto the floor.

"They're in my hand."

That seemed weird. She was having a hard time even processing why she'd taken them off in the first place. "Maybe I should put them back on. There's probably like broken glass and shit in the parking lot. I don't want to slice my tender feet."

"If you put these shoes back on you're going to break your ankle. I think I'll just carry you to the car."

That sent a thrill zinging through her. How hot was that? "Really? You're going to carry me? But I'm too heavy," she said, because that's what you were supposed to say. It was a compliment-seeking ploy that all women knew.

Unfortunately, Diesel didn't know the conditioned response, which should have been something like "Are you kidding? You're light as a feather."

What he really said was, "Don't be stupid."

They were hovering in the doorway of the reception hall, the muggy night air hitting Tuesday in the face and making her instantly feel sweaty. The parking lot was an island of blacktop stretching out for a thousand miles, her car somewhere at a distance that felt frankly insurmountable. It would be nice to be carried, even if Diesel didn't how he was supposed to tell her she was teeny tiny, barely weighing anything.

Then she remembered his knee. His bad, bum, sucky knee, which he tried to pretend didn't really bother him. There was no way he could carry her. So grabbing onto his sleeve with one hand and yanking one of her shoes out of his hand with the other, Tuesday leaned over and crammed it on to her foot. Her little toe wound up on the wrong side of the strap, but she didn't give a shit. It was on. She wasn't going to buckle the strap. She was just going to walk carefully.

"You're the one being stupid. I'm perfectly capable of walking."

"Don't get attitude," he told her. "I said I'd carry you. Or smarter still, I can just go get the car and pull it around."

She paused. "Now that, my friend, is freaking brilliant." She grinned at Diesel. "Two heads are better than one, eh?"

"Especially when one is soaked in liquor." He handed her the other shoe. "Don't impale yourself with this. I'll be right back with my car."

"What about my car?" Tuesday hopped as she struggled to cram her foot into her shoe. The motion made the parking lot sway a little and she swallowed hard.

"Two cars are not better than one. We have to leave yours here."

There was probably a reason that should bother her, like the potential for vandalism, and the issue of retrieving it the next day, but she found she just didn't care. Her feet hurt stuffed back into her shoes, there was sweat accumulating between her breasts, and she was so thirsty she would drink from a rain puddle if she could find one.

As she watched him walk away, Tuesday tried to remember why it would be a bad idea to have sex with him. He was super cute. Tall. Lanky. Muscular arms. Scruffy, even dressed up for the reception. A man's man. Which had never been her particular type. She'd always gone for the metrosexuals with good fashion sense and an extensive knowledge of wine. But there was something about Diesel . . . it started with his name and ended with his butt.

When he pulled up in a black sports car, he got out and came around to open the door for her. "What? Why are you looking at me like that?"

"Like what?" she asked, a sudden image of him over top of her flashing through her head.

"Like you don't know what the hell you're looking at."

"Don't be stupid." She repeated his words and climbed into the car. Or fell in, if you wanted to get technical about it. "Do you have a grocery bag in here? Or a box maybe?"

"No. Why?"

In case she felt the sudden need to puke. "No reason."

He popped his head into the passenger side to study her. "Do you want to lie down in the backseat?"

Lolling against the seat with a sigh, grateful to finally be off her feet, Tuesday said, "Are you going to lay in the backseat with me?"

"No."

"Then why would I want to be back there?" Duh.

Diesel pressed his lips together, like he was holding back a laugh. "Of course. Why don't you just close your eyes, sweetheart?"

That sounded like a good idea. But when she rested her head back, eyes closed to stop the spinning that had started up, the heavily hairsprayed bun prevented her from relaxing. It was like she was jutting three feet out from the seat, pins jabbing her scalp. "Damn it." Sitting forward again, she reached up and started yanking at the pins.

Diesel had slid into the driver's seat. "Do you really need to do that right now?"

"Yes. They're bugging me." But she wasn't having much luck. For some weird reason, her fingers didn't seem to be working correctly. All she was doing was pulling on her hair, causing her tear ducts to fire up.

"Here." Diesel reached over and efficiently extracted five or six pins from her hair. He unwound her bun. "Better?"

Using her hands to massage the hair free and relieve her scalp, she sighed. "Much. You'd better quit being so nice to me or I might fall in love with you."

Somewhere, in the part of her brain that had sense, an alarm bell went off that maybe that hadn't been an appropriate thing to say, joke or not. But she barely noticed it, deciding instead to take his advice and lay down. Across his lap.

"Uh . . . how am I supposed to drive like this?"

Tuesday looked up at him, his thighs beneath her head and shoulders. From this vantage point, his hair looked even longer, his chin strong and sharp. She reached up and scratched his beard. Very soft. "Oh, come on. You're a professional. This is no big deal. And don't tell me you've never gotten a blow job while driving."

"Not while professionally driving."

That struck her as hilarious. Tuesday snorted. "No, dork. I mean, just while driving around town. Every guy has had that at least once, right?"

"I don't think I have."

"Really?" Tuesday thought about rolling over and showing him how much fun it could be, but that seemed like a lot of work. Plus her mouth was dry and she was really sleepy. It would be a poor show and that would defeat the point.

She wasn't really sure what the point was, but she knew it was a good one.

"Really. And no, I don't want you to fix that for me right now."

Well. Fine. "Pfft. Who the hell says I was offering?" But if she was, she was damn sure he'd take it. So there.

"You're right. You weren't. I apologize."

That was nice. She settled better into the seat, curling up a little on her side as he shifted gears and pulled out of the parking lot. "But you kinda want me to, don't you?"

"In theory, yes. But in reality, it wouldn't be a good idea."

"Why, because you don't have an erection?"

There was a beat of silence, and Tuesday's eyes started to drift closed. But they flew open when Diesel moved her head just slightly to the left, and she felt an obstruction that was not his wallet.

"Not exactly," he told her, his voice tight.

"Oh." Tuesday wiggled around, getting a sense of its length—long. And its width—thick. Wow. She started to rethink her decision to not go there. Or had she really made that decision? Maybe this was just really doing what she'd wanted to do all night. Her mouth was very close to penis. It was very hard. Big.

She stroked the length of him lightly through his pants. Up and down, feeling it swell even more. It was a really nice erection.

Diesel was similarly stroking her hair, his masculine fingers surprisingly gentle as he worked his way from her roots down to the tips of her hair, petting softly. Arousal stirred to life, her panties dampening, breathing going languid and heavy. She stroked. He stroked. A slow, easy, steady rhythm that felt normal and intimate and safe.

So slow and steady that before she was even aware it was happening, Tuesday fell asleep.

CHAPTER
THREE

"*GET* your head out of my crotch. How many times have I told you that's rude?" Diesel nudged his dog, Wilma, out of the way and went back to the engine he was working on.

This car was his pride and joy. A 1963 Chevy driven by that year's champion driver. It had taken a beating racing, and had fallen into disrepair as it had been passed from hand to hand, and ultimately left to rust in a garage, but Diesel was giving it life back. When he was done, it would be running, dressed in the colors and number of its original driver.

He'd been working on it for two months and he figured another month and it would be good to go. He had a mind to donate it to Tuesday Jones's cancer benefit. It was worth a hell of a lot and there would be plenty of people in attendance who would want a classic piece of stock car racing history.

Diesel wondered how Tuesday was doing this morning. He was tempted to send her a text but realized he didn't have her number. It wouldn't be cool to contact Evan for it since technically this was the morning after his wedding, even if they'd been married for four months already. But he was worried about Tuesday. She was going to have a pounding headache, no doubt about it.

"Hey, kid, how's it going?"

Diesel glanced up from under the hood to see his uncle, Johnny Briggs, strolling into his garage. "Hey, Uncle Johnny, what's up?"

"Not much. Just thought I'd stop by on my way to the cardiologist and see what you're up to."

Looking down the driveway, Diesel didn't see anyone else, but he asked, "Aunt Beth with you?"

"Nope. She's volunteering up at the grandkids' school this morning."

"Everything okay with your appointment?" He had to admit, he worried about his uncle. He had been like a father figure to Diesel growing up, the closest he'd had to a positive male influence after his father had run out on his mother when he was four years old.

"Yep. Just a routine check on the old ticker after the angioplasty. So how's the car coming along?"

Johnny stuck his head under the hood and they stared in companionable silence for a few minutes. His uncle offered a suggestion or two, which Diesel valued. But there was something his uncle wanted to say and Diesel knew it. He was just waiting for the reveal when Johnny was ready.

"So your aunt wanted me to ask you if you're busy Saturday night."

Diesel stood up, eyeing his uncle suspiciously. "Why?" If his uncle invited him to a boat show or something of that ilk it was one thing, but his aunt inquiring over his schedule made him nervous.

"You didn't answer the question, son. Are you busy or not?"

Damn it. "No." Rarely was he busy these days. His Saturday night usually involved a beer and his remote control. Living the dream, that's what he was doing.

"There's this thing up at the church that's like a night at the races and Beth's friend Jean is bringing her daughter, Ellie. There's an extra seat at our table and Beth wants you there."

Diesel fought the urge to groan. Ellie was the kind of marriage-hungry woman on the hunt who made his nuts shrivel up and his bank account squeal. "Johnny, I don't want to sit with Beth's friend Jean's daughter, Ellie. There is nothing more awkward than an obvious set-up date with all of your parents around."

His uncle lifted his ball cap and scratched his forehead. "That's what I told her, but your aunt has her ideas. She means well."

"I can find my own dates." He just chose not to.

"Yeah? When was the last time you had a date? And hanging with Wilma here don't count." Johnny reached down and scratched behind the dog's ears. "Even if she is a pretty dog, aren't you, Wilma?"

"If I wanted a date, I could have one." He was aware that sounded childish, but how the hell did he explain to his uncle that he was afraid to date? The last sexual encounter he'd had with a woman had ended in total deflation of his man parts when his knee had given out in the middle of banging her. He'd had to abort the mission and finish her off manually. It had been one of the single most humiliating experiences of his life and not one he was itching to repeat. "I just don't particularly want one."

Which was something of a lie. He had met a woman he would like to date. He wanted to see Tuesday Jones again and there was no denying he had wanted to have sex with her the night before. But he was fairly certain he wasn't going to do anything about it.

"Why don't you want to date?"

"I have my reasons."

"Look, son, if you're gay you know we'll love you and support you no matter what. You don't have to hide from your family."

Diesel looked at his uncle, who was tomato red and shuffling uncomfortably, and burst out laughing. "I'm not gay. But I do appreciate that you'd accept it if I was."

The red receded and Johnny openly exhaled before throwing up his hand. "Then what the hell is the problem? You're young, you've got money and time, and you've got my genetics in you so you're good-looking. You should be working your way through a steady stream of blondes."

"I like brunettes."

"Don't get smart with me. You're thirty years old. When I was your age I'd been married for almost a decade."

"That's your problem, not mine," Diesel told him mildly. He grinned when his uncle blustered. "I'm kidding. Don't worry about me. Tell Aunt Beth not to worry. I'm fine."

"There's fine, and then there's happy. Which one are you?"

It hit a little too close to home and Diesel found he didn't really have an answer. He was fine. But he wasn't sure he was particularly happy. "Content" was a better word for it.

"Look, your dad was an idiot jackass for leaving like he did. You're my sister's son and I always thought of you and Josh as my boys, too. Now that your mama and your brother and Pete are all gone, it's just you and me and Beth and Petey and Hunter. And we aren't going to be around forever, and Pete's kids have a stepfather now. We want you settled and happy and having kids of your own."

Trying to ignore the lump that had suddenly risen in his throat, Diesel stared hard at his uncle. "Are you sure everything's okay with your heart? If you start gifting me your boat and your cars, I'm going to get worried."

Diesel knew the reality. It was just him and Johnny and Beth. Yeah, Pete's kids were in the picture, and his widow, Tammy, did a fine job of keeping the lines of communication open with Johnny and Beth, but she was remarried. She'd probably be having more kids of her own soon with Elec Monroe, and Diesel couldn't remember the last time he had actually seen those kids. Knowing their family was so small and so finite was scary as hell. He didn't want to lose the two most important people in his life.

"There's nothing wrong with me. I told you that. We just want you to go to the goddamn night at the races at church and sit with Ellie. Is that so goddamn hard?"

Apparently the tender moment had passed and his uncle was getting as impatient with the whole conversation as he was. "Alright, alright, I'll go to the damn night at the races. Jesus, lay off me." He realized they were both swearing in conjunction with talking about church, but a date with tenacious Ellie warranted some mild cursing.

His uncle clapped him on the shoulder and grinned in triumph. "You'll be glad you did it. Ellie is a supersweet girl, very passive."

"Really?" He eyed Johnny skeptically. "Are we talking about Ellie Babcock? Because I'll have you know that she grabbed my junk at the church's walk for hunger."

"She did not," his uncle scoffed. "You must have misunderstood."

Yeah, right. Diesel knew what he knew. "How do you misunderstood a hand on your crotch cupping a squeeze? Or her saying we could go behind the baptismal font for a little slap and tickle?"

"You're making that up."

Diesel felt indignant. "Why the hell would I make that up? It was weird. Ellie is weird and I don't want to sit next to her. She'll molest me under the table."

"Now that's just dumb. Why would she do that in the church hall?"

Was his uncle not listening? "She offered to do me behind the baptismal font! Of course she'll try to cop a feel."

"Well, so? That will probably be the most play you've gotten in months."

Diesel was not enjoying this conversation. His uncle might have a point, but he was not to a level of desperation that the tiger on the prowl was appealing to him. If he let her out of the cage, she'd tear him limb to limb in bed, and he bet he wouldn't even like it.

Fortunately he was saved from having to answer by his phone buzzing in his pocket. Pulling it out, he saw it was a text from Evan Monroe.

Did Tuesday get home ok?

He typed back, *Yes. Hoping she's feeling alright today*.

"Who are you texting?" Johnny asked. "Feel free to text when you're alone with Wilma but when I'm standing here that's rude."

"Sorry. It was Evan Monroe. I gave one of the brides-maids a ride home last night and Evan was checking on her."

"Yeah? Did a little post-wedding horizontal shuffle, huh? No wonder you don't want to meet Ellie."

Really? The horizontal shuffle? Diesel wished. "Of course not. She was completely loaded and passed out the second I got her into her apartment. Actually, she passed out in the car first. I was just being a nice guy."

"Well, good for you. But it would have been a better story if you'd spent the night knocking boots."

"Horizontal shuffle? Knocking boots? Are you afraid to say 'sex,' Uncle Johnny?" he said, deflecting from the fact that he agreed. It would have been much better to have woken up this morning with Tuesday wrapped around him than his dog curled at his feet.

"I can say sex. And that's not the point. The point is if you're thirty and you're not married, you should at least be boinking everything in reach."

"*Boink?*" Diesel laughed. "What am I, an '80s frat boy? Seriously, don't worry about my sex life."

He was worrying enough about it for the both of them.

His phone buzzed again. *Tuesday's not answering her phone*.

Hmm. "Evan says she's not answering her phone. What do you think that means?"

"It means she's hungover and wishing everyone would leave her the hell alone so she can die in peace."

Probably that was true. But what if she'd had blood alcohol poisoning? Passed out in the bathroom and hit her head on the toilet and was unconscious? Diesel started to think maybe he shouldn't have left her alone. He could have stayed and slept on her couch, but he hadn't wanted to invade her privacy. "Maybe I should check on her."

"I'm sure she's fine."

Another text came in. *She's late for the wedding brunch.*

"Shit." Her car was still at the reception hall. "She is supposed to be at some brunch and she's not there and I realized we left her car at the hall last night when I drove her home. She's probably hungover and stranded. I should go over there." Patting his pockets, Diesel found his keys in the left side and pulled them out.

"Alright. That's probably the right thing to do. Who is this girl, by the way?"

"Tuesday Jones."

"Bob's daughter?"

"Yeah. She's having a rough time of it since he passed away."

"I imagine so." His uncle eyeballed him. "Probably not someone you want to get involved with right now."

"No?" he said mildly. He knew his uncle spoke out of concern and he was probably more right than wrong, but Diesel couldn't get Tuesday out of his head. That much he knew.

"No. Now Ellie on the other hand, is totally date-worthy."

Diesel laughed. "You don't even know that. You're just saying it because now you want to win."

"That's probably true." Johnny slapped him on the back. "But you'll see. Hot tamale, that one is."

No doubt about it. "I'm not interested," he repeated, images of a girl in a pepper suit dancing toward him popping into his head.

Funny that a pile of chewed-up coconut in his hand seemed way more appealing.

TUESDAY turned her head in bed and instantly regretted it. The room spun and her stomach heaved.

Damn. She was hungover. Big-time.

Why did the fun of a good escapist buzz always come at the price of a pounding head and a sour stomach? It wasn't fair.

Prying an eye open, she saw that her phone was on the nightstand, but couldn't muster the strength to pick it up and see what time it was. Then she saw the big glass of water sitting there beckoning like nirvana, and two aspirin resting beside it.

Diesel must have done that. Tuesday was equal parts thrilled and mortified. She really wanted the water and she tentatively stretched her arm and shaky hand out for it. What a guy. What a seriously thoughtful guy. But it was also a little more than humiliating to think what a hot mess she must have been by the time he had dumped her into bed.

Not her best foot forward.

Oh, well. Nothing she could do about it, and she hadn't done anything truly inappropriate. She had flirted with him, but big deal. She was just as likely to do that sober. Lying on his lap had been a bit much, but it wasn't like he'd hated it. She was more worried about the fact that she seemed to be wearing nothing but a bra and panties and couldn't remember taking her bridesmaid dress off. Hopefully she had peeled it off after he'd left instead of before.

She sucked down half the glass of water and dragged herself to a semi sitting position. Grabbing the aspirin, she crammed them into her mouth and downed the rest of the water. When she picked up her phone and saw she had six texts from Evan and Kendall and that it was already eight minutes after twelve, she groaned, falling back against the pillows.

"Crap. Crap, crap, crap." She was late for the damn brunch and even if she managed to get her sorry butt in the shower and dressed, she didn't have a ride. Her car was still at the reception hall.

Not the best planning ever.

Not the best bridesmaid ever.

Swallowing back the nausea, Tuesday flung back the covers and stood up. She smelled like sweet-and-sour pork, and a glance in the mirror as she passed the dresser proved that Halloween had come early to her house. Her hair was straight out of a horror film, teased and lumpy and snarled, while her makeup had migrated from her eyes down her face to cluster in black puddles on her chin. Her skin was pale, her under-eyes bruised, lids swollen, eyes bloodshot and beady.

Fright Night.

No doubt about it.

Walking carefully, she rolled her shoulders. It felt like she'd worked out for twelve hours straight. Every inch of her was stiff and sore and she seemed to have a mysterious bruise on her hip. She hated sleeping in a bra and she had the indentation in the skin on her back to prove that she had.

Heading into the hallway, she tripped over her shoes,

which she had obviously just dumped outside the door. She wanted to go back to bed. She wanted coffee. She wanted a new head.

The doorbell rang.

Great. That was probably someone coming to collect her for the brunch. If it was an elderly aunt, she was not answering it. She didn't need that kind of judgment. Glancing through the peephole, she realized it was way worse than some ancient relative in a floral sundress.

It was Diesel.

"Shit," she whispered, lifting a hand to her hair. Not that anything her fingers did could fix that hornet's nest. She couldn't possibly open the door to him.

Then again, he was holding two grande-sized coffee cups in his hand.

It was tempting.

Vanity versus caffeine.

He knocked again. "Tuesday, it's Diesel. I wanted to give you a ride to your car. I brought you some coffee."

She liked that he didn't inquire how she was feeling. There was nothing more annoying than that question when you were hungover.

"Hey," she said through the door. "Thanks. I'm not exactly ready though."

That was an understatement to say the least, given she was in her underwear and looked like she'd spent the night in the woods running from a murderer.

"No problem. I can wait a few minutes."

Tuesday looked through the peephole again. He raised one of the coffee cups and drank from it. She could practically taste it sliding down her throat, easing her suffering.

She had to get to that brunch and Diesel was her best hope for both a ride and a caffeine recovery. To hell with her appearance. If he thought she looked like shit, well, he would be right.

Grabbing a throw off the couch and wrapping it around herself, Tuesday opened her door.

He did blink when he saw her, but made no comment on her appearance. "Good morning. Sorry I didn't call first but I don't have your number."

"That's okay." Her hand was already reaching out, polite or not, for the cup in his hand. "Thanks for the coffee." She took it from him, took a big long swallow, and sighed as the liquid eased the rawness of her throat and the extreme cotton-mouth.

When she took a second sip, she realized she was both hungover and rude. "Sorry, come on in." She shuffled backward a few steps in her makeshift blanket toga and stepped out of the way so he could enter. "I really appreciate you coming over. I'm supposed to be at this brunch and I just woke up and I realized I don't have a car. I suck."

Now that her head was pounding a little less, the guilt was increasing. What kind of person gets bombed at her best friend's wedding, then is too hungover to get to a wedding brunch on time? One that sucked, that's who.

Diesel shrugged. "It happens. You had a good reason to tie one on last night. You were both celebrating and grieving."

She swallowed, gripping her coffee and her blanket, appreciating his matter-of-fact attitude. "You're right. I don't think I was too embarrassing last night." She remembered everything. She'd danced a lot but that was about it for the general crowd. She'd saved most of her outrageousness for

Diesel. Lolling across his lap in the car was not something she normally did with men she barely knew. "Sorry I hit on you."

He grinned. "Are you taking it back? You were just beer-goggling with me?" He put his hand on his heart. "You're shattering my ego, you know."

"That's your heart, not your ego, and I sincerely doubt I'm shattering either one." Tuesday set her coffee down. "I'm just saying thank you for being decent and not taking advantage of the drunk girl and having sex with me."

Though as she eyed those biceps peeking out from his T-shirt and remembered his erection pressed against her, she wasn't sure she would have regretted it.

His eyebrow shot up. "You're welcome." He moved farther into her apartment, setting his own coffee down on the end table. Diesel moved past her, his arm brushing hers, and as he went for the couch, he met her stare head-on. "If I have sex with you, I want you fully aware of everything you're doing. And everything *I'm* doing."

Despite her aching muscles and her pounding head and her stuffed up nose, Tuesday felt that proclamation shoot straight into her vagina. She had not been expecting him to say that. "Is that a hypothetical?" she said, her voice a little breathier than she would have liked.

He flopped on her couch. "That's up to you."

She wasn't sure how to answer that. Her brain wasn't working at full capacity at the moment and she couldn't think of a single clever thing to say. "Well, right now is out of the question."

He laughed. "Probably. Since you have that brunch to go to."

"Yeah, and the fact that I look like ass and smell like someone's grandpa. Which I have to say I appreciate you not mentioning."

"You don't smell like old man, don't be ridiculous." Diesel put his feet on her coffee table and settled back into the couch.

Tuesday waited, but he didn't add anything else. Feeling annoyed, even though she knew it was irrational, she said, "But I do look like ass?" She knew she did. She looked beyond bad. She looked like sewage, like the witches in *Macbeth*, like she'd been in a battle with a monkey and lost. But he could at least lie about it.

"You don't look like ass. You'll always be a beautiful woman. But I have to say I prefer your hair the way it was last night over this look."

It was sweet. Fair. Truthful. But she was still put out. She wanted him to think she was hot. She gave a grudging, "Thank you." Then she dropped the blanket she'd been clutching. "I'm taking a five-minute shower."

His mouth fell open.

Which served him right.

Tuesday figured a bra and panties were no different than a bathing suit, and she was happy with her body. Maybe that view would wipe out the hot mess her hair was. She was playing with fire, but hell, you never got anything if you didn't ask for it. She figured this was the visual equivalent of requesting his erection.

If she wasn't feeling like shit, she wasn't sure she would have taken such a brazen approach, but the alcohol seeping out her pores and wafting around her in a noxious cloud made her self-conscious. This leveled the playing field in some strange way.

Turning on her heel, she headed for the bathroom, swiping her coffee off the table on her way.

Diesel was well aware of the fact that he was speechless, but he couldn't force anything out of his mouth. All of his blood and concentration had rushed south to his cock. Tuesday was . . . naked. Virtually. He had figured there wasn't a whole lot on her body under that blanket, but he had never expected that he'd be given the privilege of seeing it. Today, anyway.

It was a hell of a view. She was a hell of a woman.

With very long legs. A tight backside. And a flat stomach that made him want to lick from her breasts to her navel and right on down to the promised land.

Her skin was creamy and fair, her breasts small but perky, her arms long and elegant.

Yes, her hair looked like she'd jammed her finger into an electrical socket, and it looked like a five-year-old had made free with her makeup, but that was to be expected after a night of overconsumption of alcohol. There had been a lot of hair spray in that twist thing she'd had going on with her hair, so he could imagine this would be the end result even if she had been sober.

She was beautiful; he had been telling the straight-up God's honest truth. And now he knew for certain she had a banging body, and he had the hard-on to prove it. Damn. He hadn't seen that one coming—the dropping the blanket, not the hard-on. He was starting to think that was going to be a perpetual problem around Tuesday.

When he stopped choking on his own drool he managed to call out, "Am I driving you to your car, is that what we're doing here? Or am I just hanging out on your couch for no reason?"

"Yes, you're driving me to my car," she said, her voice grumpy. "How else am I supposed to get to the brunch?"

"Float there with your angel wings?" he asked, a little heavy on the sarcasm.

She popped her head back out of the bathroom. "Don't be a hater. I'm not at my best this morning. I'm hungover. I'm embarrassed. I'm late. I appreciate a ride, seriously. And I appreciate you bringing me home last night."

Wow. That was a refreshing display of honesty. "You're welcome. And you have no reason to be embarrassed. It was a wedding. Everyone was getting their drink on."

Her answer was the shower turning on. Her head had disappeared but she hadn't closed the bathroom door. Which meant she was probably stripping off her bra and panties and stepping into that shower totally naked. Where hot water would bounce off her bare body and trickle down over every inch of her.

Diesel shifted on her couch. He was starting to get more than a little uncomfortable. For a guy who was leery of having sex, he was starting to think that given the option, he'd dive in face-first with Tuesday, bum knee or not.

To distract himself from thoughts of helping her wash her body, he glanced around her apartment. It somehow reminded him of her. Tailored. Clean. Classy. Everything looked like it belonged where it was. Even the nubby blanket she had been wearing was elegant, not your granny's afghan. He hadn't seen much the night before when he'd been struggling to drag her into her apartment. They'd stumbled down the hall together, then she'd taken a facer onto her bed. He'd removed her shoes and turned her onto her back. He'd thought about taking her dress off, but that was crossing a boundary, considering they'd only met twice, so he'd just pulled up her covers and left her with some aspirin and water.

He was feeling a little guilty though for not just crashing on the couch. He'd been tempted, but hadn't wanted her to wake up and think he was some creepy douche bag lingering around going through her underwear drawer.

The shower turned off almost immediately. He was impressed with her speed. A minute later she appeared in the doorway, a towel around her body, a second one on her head.

"Three more minutes," she told him.

"Where is this brunch?" he asked her.

"Statesville. Some bed-and-breakfast."

"That's in the opposite direction of your car. What time were you supposed to be there?"

"Fifteen minutes ago," she called from the recesses of her bedroom.

"Then why don't I just drive you to the brunch? Someone can give you a ride to your car after." It was the least he could do. He was feeling a little responsible for her predicament. He should have thought the whole thing through a little better the night before, given that he'd been the sober one.

She came out wearing a short dress and black high heels, shoving her arm into several bracelets, a pink bag in her hand. "Really? That's awesome of you. Okay, I'm ready."

Given that her hair was still wet, she didn't look ready to

him, but he knew better than to argue with a woman about her hair. "Okay." He stood up. "Want me to grab your coffee?"

"Oh, my God, yes. Thanks, Diesel."

He went and fetched the cup out of the bathroom, trying to ignore the sight of her panties and bra strewn across the tile floor. No time for that. None whatsoever.

Tuesday was grabbing a little black purse and her keys and in a minute they were outside, her slamming the door with such violence that she actually winced.

"Oh, God, my head."

"You look a lot better. Cute dress." Which sounded so lame the minute it came out of his mouth he almost groaned out loud. He was turning into a fourteen-year-old boy around her.

"Thanks. I'm glad you're driving so I can slap on some makeup and pull my hair back. We'll pretend its hair gel giving it a slicked-back look."

A certain scene from a movie involving something that was decidedly not hair gel popped into his head. He needed to get a goddamn grip and fast.

"Why are you so quiet all of a sudden?" she said as she closed the passenger door of his car and flipped down the visor to reveal the mirror.

Because he was struggling with horniness.

"No particular reason."

"God, I don't want to go to this. Everyone is going to be there with their husbands and boyfriends and there will be me, the morning-after girl."

"But you didn't have sex last night so it's all good." Neither had he. Damn. Diesel put his car in reverse and stomped harder on the gas than was necessary.

"That's not the point. I get tired of being the single girl everyone feels sorry for. Don't they know I'm perfectly fine?"

The words his uncle had spoken to him earlier popped into his head. Fine, yes. But happy? Diesel wasn't sure about himself, and he suspected if pressed, Tuesday would be even less sure.

"I hear ya on that one. My uncle is trying to convince me to go to something at his church where a certain single woman will just happen to be. I do think we're all a little old to be fixed up by our families."

"No shit." She smeared something on her face and worked it around with her fingers. "I'll give you twenty bucks if you go to this brunch with me."

The hell he would. "You've mistaken me for someone stupid."

"Oh, come on. You'll get a good meal out of it."

"I'm wearing jeans." Not that he was even considering it. He didn't want a bunch of women grilling him on how he knew Tuesday.

"So what? Come on . . . please?" Her voice took on a wheedling quality that set off alarms in Diesel.

He was helpless against women when they did that, got all soft and needy and pleading. He chanced a glance over at her and her eyes were big and beautiful, the dark circles under them still evident. Damn it.

He was going to give in. He could feel it. But he was getting something out of this himself. "I'll go to the brunch if you go to night at the races at church with me."

Her eyes narrowed. "You drive a hard bargain, Lange."

"Saturday night. You in or out?"

Tuesday looked away, checking her reflection in the mirror again. "Fine. I'll go."

It wasn't the most normal way to go about getting a date, but Diesel had to admit, he was strangely thrilled at the thought of spending more time with Tuesday, even at a wedding brunch and a church fund-raiser.

Which meant he was one hundred percent certifiably insane.

CHAPTER
FOUR

TUESDAY was feeling a little smug about securing Diesel as her date, aka old lady deflector. Her plan was to leave him at the mercy of the elderly aunts while she plowed her way through six plates of food and a gallon of coffee to rid herself of the final hangover remnants. Which was probably more than a little selfish of her, given that Diesel was being supersweet. How many guys would have shown up with coffee the morning after they'd turned down your drunk offer of sex?

She had to admit, she didn't even know what to make of it. Was he just not attracted to her? Was he a supergood Samaritan? She wasn't sure.

But she was really grateful for his sexy ass standing next to her when she walked into the room later than could possibly be socially acceptable, all eyes turning and scrutinizing her. Her hair was still wet in a ponytail and her makeup was half-assed at best. But it was the best she'd been able to do in ten minutes or less.

"I feel really self-conscious," she murmured to him.

"Just smile. You look great."

A glance up at Diesel showed her he didn't look even remotely nervous. But then again, he wasn't a bridesmaid who had let her best friend down. Tuesday knew that she hadn't done anything horrible. She hadn't puked at the reception or blown a groomsmen in the bathroom, but she still felt bad.

That seemed to be the story of her life lately. She managed to forget or escape briefly, then she crashed back down to reality, feeling worse than she had before. Her stomach churned and she found herself edging closer to Diesel. She didn't want to be judged and found lacking. She had always prided herself on her strength, on her ability to keep her emotions private, and since her dad had gotten sick, that had been nearly impossible to do.

Now, standing here in front of all these put-together women, both young and old, her hair wet and her makeup jacked up, totally late and hungover, she suddenly felt raw and exposed. Vulnerable. And Tuesday hated that feeling.

"You're a liar," she told Diesel. "But I appreciate the effort."

She really couldn't figure his deal out. No guy was this nice without some ulterior motive. It just didn't happen.

Or did it? Her dad had been that kind of guy. So when had she started assuming no one would ever measure up to him?

Diesel said, "Do we have assigned seats or what?"

She shook her head no, but the truth was, she wasn't really sure. About anything.

When she would have stood in the doorway indefinitely,

struggling to get her shit together, Diesel took the lead. He took her by the hand, literally, and drew her into the room, choosing a table that had two empty chairs side by side.

Her hand in his felt wonderful, big and strong, like him, and for once she was grateful to have a man taking charge because she wasn't sure she could have walked into that room by herself.

"Are these seats taken?" he asked an ancient relative in a blush pink pantsuit.

"No. Have a seat, sweetie," she told him, patting the chair next to her.

Tuesday swallowed hard as she sat down in the other available chair, smiling to the ladies at the table and struggling to remember any of their names. Her head was pounding again and she felt the inexplicable need to cry. What the hell was wrong with her? Why was she so weepy all the damn time?

"I need to go say hello to Kendall," she told him, dropping her purse on the floor. "And I'll get you a drink. What would you like?"

"Coffee is fine." He smiled at her. "Thanks, babe." Then he reached out and touched the tip of her nose with his finger.

That stopped her urge to blubber. Really? Did she look like a woman who wanted her nose tweaked? She was too tall, too independent, too . . . uptight.

She'd never thought of herself as uptight, but the truth was she was a control freak. And wasn't the one just a synonym for the other?

But she should be grateful he didn't know her well enough to recognize that nose tweaking was a mistake, because his action had prevented her from embarrassing herself any further by crying. She couldn't help but make a face at him as she stood up. Diesel just grinned, like he knew full well that wasn't her style.

Kendall was surrounded by well-wishers, but she extracted herself and said, "Let's get a drink, Tuesday."

Tuesday found herself whisked away to the bar, which was being used to serve juices, coffee, and mimosas. "Sorry I'm late," she told Kendall. "I didn't hear my alarm."

"Did you sleep with Diesel?" Kendall asked, leaning in to whisper conspiratorially. "What's he look like naked?"

"Kendall Holbrook Monroe," Tuesday said with a grin, suddenly feeling better. "Why do you care what he looks like naked? You're an old married woman."

"Doesn't mean I'm not curious. He's really tall for a driver, well over six foot." She paused, glancing around the room, and dropped her voice even lower. "Is he, you know, proportionate? Because I'd hate to think that all that height doesn't translate. It's not fair that we can't judge men's penis size by looking at them. I mean, they can see what our bodies look like, how big our breasts are, but we have no clue until we're confronted with it, and by then it's too late."

Tuesday eyeballed a mimosa and debated whether hair of the dog made sense or not, totally amused by Kendall's speech. "I completely agree with you. We need those scanners they have at the airport so we can gauge his size before we go home with him. But if I didn't know better, I'd think you were lamenting Evan's lack of stature."

Kendall hit her in the arm. "Of course not! Evan has a perfect . . . one. But that doesn't mean I didn't encounter a tiny one or two along the way."

Unfortunately, Tuesday knew about that all too well.

"Yeah, no kidding. For awhile there, I felt like I was strolling through the Munchkinland of penises. Not good. No matter what they want to claim, size matters." She went for the mimosa. One wouldn't hurt. In fact, it might help.

After taking a sip, which tasted like a little bit of orange juice heaven, she then lifted a mug and pulled the spigot to fill it with coffee for Diesel. "But sadly, I can't tell you if he's hung or not, because I never saw it."

"You never looked?" Kendall's mouth dropped open in astonishment. "You must have been drunker than I thought."

"Oh, I was plenty drunk, trust me." Trashed. Bombed. Shit-faced. Whatever you wanted to call it. "But Diesel turned me down. Apparently sloppy drunk women don't do it for him."

Glancing over, she saw he was politely chatting with Pink Pantsuit. Hungover women probably didn't do it for him either, yet here he was, forced to make painful conversation simply because she'd asked him to. "I can't figure him out. If he wasn't interested in getting laid, why is he here with me? Why did he drive me home?"

Kendall shook her head. "It's amazing how blind we can be about our own relationships. Sweetheart, he is interested, he's just too nice of a guy to take advantage of you loaded. And I'm sure he wants you fully conscious, not flopping around like a rag doll."

"How do you know he's interested?" She snuck another glance at him. Damn, he was cute, with his shaggy hair and chin scruff.

"Because he's at a freaking wedding brunch where he only knows about five people and almost everyone in the room is a woman over the age of fifty. Hello. Of course he's interested."

Tuesday wanted to believe that was true, but she wasn't convinced. "I think he just felt sorry for me."

"And I think you're nuts. If you felt sorry for a guy, would you go to his family's Thanksgiving dinner?"

Tuesday made a face. "No, of course not! Ew. Those are totally awkward and then everyone would think we're dating . . . *ooohh*." The light went off in her head. She got where Kendall was going with this. "You're right, people are totally going to assume he and I are a couple. Hell, if he was here with anyone else, I'd be writing about it in my gossip blog."

"Exactly. So I say check it out. Go out with him and see what happens."

"You just want to know about his penis."

Kendall grinned. "Maybe. But really, I think you might actually enjoy yourself. He's a good guy, a good fit for you."

Tuesday didn't know enough about Diesel Lange to make that kind of conclusion. She wasn't even sure *she* knew what was a good fit for her. Her last three relationships had ended with the guys all concluding she was too successful, too independent, too driven. Apparently the modern man wanted a woman up in his shit all the time, as best she could figure. That wasn't her. She had no interest in texting someone eight hundred times a day and spending every free second she had with him. She wanted a partner, an equal, someone whose company she sought because she enjoyed it, not because she was desperately trying to cleave to him so he didn't leave her.

It didn't seem that complicated, but maybe it was. And while she had no clue what Diesel would look for in a relationship, she did know that thus far he'd treated her with kindness and respect, and that was no small thing.

In fact, it meant the man deserved the cup of coffee she was holding for him. "Well, whatever he is, I should get back to him, and you back to your guests."

"Good point. Call me later. You know, after Diesel drives you home." Kendall grinned.

"I feel like ass. I'm definitely not sleeping with him today. If I'm going for it, you can be damn sure I'm going to be in top form."

"Oh, so it matters to you what he thinks?"

With that comment, Kendall flounced away before Tuesday could nail her with a retort. It mattered, just not for the reasons Kendall was implying. It always mattered how people perceived her and she always wanted to do her best, no matter what it was.

Uptight. Control freak. Yeah. That was her.

Taking her seat at the table, she placed the coffee in front of Diesel. "I forgot to ask how you take it. Do you need cream and sugar?"

He smiled at her. "Black is fine."

They just looked at each other for a second, her feeling scrutinized, him giving her a secret small smile. "What?" she finally asked him.

"You just look pretty, that's all."

Tuesday rolled her eyes, knowing she looked like hell, but she had to admit, she was pleased. "Thank you. Note to self: Diesel likes pasty white skin and dark under-eye circles."

"Yep," he said, and took a sip of his coffee. Actually, it was more of a gulp, a man-sized sip that drained half the cup.

Tuesday studied his hands. They were callused and rough, with long fingers, a working man's hands. He might have a sizable bank account, but he was still the guy in the work boots, and she found that inexplicably hot. She found a lot of things about him hot, actually. Like his hair. His pale blue eyes. His jaw. His height. His hands.

Mostly though, she liked his kindness. The way he sat relaxed, laid back, never stressing. She was like a continuous ball of energy—good or bad. She bounced between highs and lows, having a blast and stressing over *everything*, and Diesel didn't seem to do that. He took life in stride, and when he looked at her, she felt like he was truly listening to what she was saying.

Nor would he rise to the bait when she tried to provoke him.

The woman in the pink suit leaned across Diesel to talk to Tuesday. "Your husband is a real sweetheart, dear. He's been letting me show him pictures of my Lottie. She's my Pomeranian."

"Oh, he's not my husband." Tuesday could have let it go, but then what if Diesel thought she was getting off on the concept? She was no marriage-minded gold digger.

Diesel frowned at her. "Well, don't look so relieved."

Tuesday rolled her eyes. Men were such delicate creatures.

"This one's a good catch," the lady told her. "You need to snap him up. What are you waiting for?"

A first date would be helpful. Tuesday reversed her opinion on denying they had a relationship. This was the perfect opportunity to give him a hard time, and she was going to take it. "For him to ask me."

Diesel's eyebrows rose.

Pinky made a clucking sound. "Oh, dear." She touched Diesel's arm. "Are you one of those men who can't commit?"

"Of course I can commit." Diesel looked indignant. "The truth is, I didn't know she wanted me to ask her."

Tuesday almost laughed.

"Well, all women want you to ask. Why else would she be dating you?"

For companionship and hopefully great sex, but Tuesday realized that was a viewpoint foreign to anyone over sixty. Hell, it was foreign to a lot of men her own age. That was all she wanted, really. Just someone to spend time with, was that so hard? But it was amusing to watch Diesel wiggle on the hook.

"Well, you've certainly given me something to think about, Mrs. Crandall."

"Hmpf," was Mrs. Crandall's opinion. She caught Tuesday's eye. "If you don't have a ring by Christmas, dump him."

"Do you really think so?"

"Absolutely. You can't allow these men to be lazy and take you for granted. Are you sleeping with him?"

Diesel made a choking sound next to her. Tuesday fought a grin. "No." She could say that in all honesty.

"Good girl. Never give away the milk for free."

Diesel shoved his chair back and stood up. "Excuse us, Mrs. Crandall, I would like to take a stroll outside with my girlfriend before lunch is served."

"Oh, of course." Mrs. Crandall looked smug. She even shot Tuesday a wink.

"Are you going to ask me to marry you?" Tuesday asked him as Diesel took her arm and led her across the room. "It will make Mrs. Crandall superhappy."

Diesel felt like he should be stern with her, but truthfully, he was amused. As uncomfortable as if someone had dumped itching powder in his shorts, but nonetheless, amused. "I was thinking of asking you to zip your lip, but then I figured that was pointless. I bet you talk even in your sleep."

She stuck her tongue out at him. "What was I supposed to tell her? That we barely know each other but you took my drunk ass home last night? That would shock her and her Pomeranian."

"I'm just giving you a hard time, you know." Diesel thought she looked better. The color was back in her face and her shoulders weren't quite so slumped. Before she'd looked like standing straight had hurt her brain.

"Are we really going for a walk?"

"Sure, why not? Fresh air will do you good."

"Another mimosa would do me more good."

Diesel couldn't tell if she was serious or not. For the first time, he wondered if maybe Tuesday hadn't just drunk too much at the wedding. Maybe she actually had a drinking problem. He might as well call her out on it and find out. "I think drinking before noon is a sign of a problem."

"It's already one. And everyone knows that the best way to recover from a hangover is to have a drink. Weird, but true. Don't worry, I'm not a lush. Last night was an open-bar exception."

He was actually relieved to hear that. He liked Tuesday. Liked her quick wit and her confidence. He found himself looking forward to their pseudo date and he'd hate to think that she had real problems. Dealing with grief was one thing; that was normal and temporary. But if it went deeper than that, Diesel wasn't sure he was the right guy for her.

Not that he was the guy for her. In any way. Right or wrong. He didn't think. It was just hanging out. Once.

"Alright." He let go of her hand and opened the door for her. A blast of summer heat threatened to knock him over. Come to think of it, he could use a beer himself. "We'll get you a drink as soon as we get back."

"My hero." She batted her eyes at him.

There was a bench in the shade a few feet away and she headed toward it. "Can they see us out the windows?"

Diesel checked the banquet room. "No. Why?"

She yanked the band out of her hair and sighed. "Aah. That thing was too tight." Digging in her purse she pulled out a hairbrush. Flipping her head upside down so her hair cascaded forward, she brushed it.

He sat down next to her, feeling oddly comfortable with her. She had done more grooming in front of him than women he'd dated for months and yet she never seemed to think twice about it. He liked that about her; it was refreshing.

"It's disgusting out here," she said, from under her curtain of hair. "It's so hot, it's like being inside my microwave."

"Don't you mean like being inside your oven?" That seemed a more likely metaphor.

She flipped her hair back over her head and looked at him like he was insane. "No. I never use my oven, so why would it be hot in there?"

Diesel laughed. Why did that not surprise him? "So you don't cook?"

"No. That's what restaurants are for. Though I do bake from time to time."

"You going to make me some cookies?" He wasn't sure why he said that, except maybe curiosity as to what her response would be. Tuesday was hard to predict, but always entertaining.

"If you rub my shoulders right now, I'll bake you cookies and let you eat the dough off my naked body."

Yep. Hard to predict. He was torn between wanting to laugh and groan. The image of her with bits of batter in strategic places was hard to shake once it took hold. Diesel cleared his throat. "Well, now, what man would refuse that kind of offer?"

Her mouth opened to give a response.

Diesel stuck his hand up. He wasn't sure he wanted to know what she would say. "Never mind. Turn sideways, I'll rub your shoulders. And I won't even hold you to the naked part."

She sighed in pleasure the minute his hands touched her bare skin. He shoved the thin straps of her dress to the side and dug in to her flesh and the muscle beneath. She was knotted up and tense, probably a result of restless, alcohol-interrupted sleep.

"You're a good man, Charlie Brown," she told him, her sigh morphing into a moan as he worked out a knot.

At the moment, Diesel was feeling more bad than good. He was sorely tempted to follow his fingers with his lips and taste her soft skin. He wanted to push her dress straps off entirely, and take the rest of the dress with it. He wanted to peel her bra and panties off and have her straddle him.

Mrs. Crandall would not approve. The Pomeranian might though. There had been a twinkle in that dog's eye in the pictures.

"Does my hair still look wet?" she asked.

It was cascading over her one shoulder, the dark strands damp in the sunlight. "Yes."

"Damn." She rolled her neck as he massaged her shoulders. "So what do you do with your time, Diesel? Now that you're not driving."

It was an expected and legitimate question, but one that always made him stiffen defensively. He wasn't sure why—it was just idle curiosity, but it always bothered him. Probably because a lot of days since the accident he felt like once his career had been taken away, he'd lost his sense of purpose, and that was frustrating.

"I restore old stock cars. I have a client waiting list at the moment." It gave him pleasure, he was financially independent, and he was alive. What more did he want, right? He was content.

"Oh, really? That's cool. It's great that you managed to stay involved in the sport."

He wouldn't say that, exactly. Diesel didn't float in the same circles anymore. His turn as a superstar driver was over, passed to a new generation the day he'd hit that wall. "It's a living," he told her.

"Hold back there on the enthusiasm."

"You want me to do a cartwheel? I can't with my knee." Okay, that sounded surly, but what was he supposed to say? He liked his job well enough. It satisfied him, kept his hands busy. But it wasn't particularly exciting to talk about.

"Bitterness doesn't really suit you."

Diesel paused in rubbing her shoulders. "Who says I'm bitter?" He didn't really think he was. There were days he was disappointed that he hadn't had more drive time on the track, but for the most part, he had adjusted. It was what it was, and he was damn glad to be alive with all his limbs working, even if his knee sometimes gave him hell. "I am really fortunate that working at all is a choice for me, not a requirement. I've had a good life so far, no doubt about it."

"Well, it's all going to go downhill now that you've met me." She smiled up at him over her shoulder, her eyes bright and glassy in the sunlight.

She looked beautiful. Ethereal, yet strong. Vulnerable, yet scrappy. The overwhelming desire to kiss her rose up inside him. He was shocked at how base and desperate the feeling was and he was already moving closer to her, wanting, needing, to touch her.

But Tuesday stood up, obviously not feeling the same vibe he was. "We need to go back in before they think we're having sex behind a potted plant."

At the moment, Diesel wasn't sure that would be such a bad idea.

TUESDAY walked quickly, not even sure if Diesel was off the bench yet or not. She needed to get out of the sun and away from him. God, there was something about the way he looked at her . . . like she was beautiful and important. The intensity of his expressions unnerved her.

So she had run, dodged the looks that said things she didn't understand. She was used to men who joked around, who went for charming, who talked as much as she did and hovered on the verge of pretentious. Diesel was none of those things. His words were chosen with economy and thus far, she'd never seen him put out or worked up or impatient about anything. Including being left alone with an old lady and her dog pictures.

Why that scared the pee out of her, she wasn't sure, but it did. Diesel's personality, that is, not the lady or the dog.

He was following her. She could sense him moving behind her, and when she got to the door, his hand snaked around her and pulled it open, ever the gentleman. Why did he have to do that? Why couldn't he suck like every other man she met? Because while she was sure she'd love a little between-the-sheets action with Diesel, she wasn't at all sure she was capable of getting emotionally involved with anyone right now. Yet he made her want that. Dirty bastard.

"You seem to be feeling better since you're practically jogging," he commented as they reentered the party room.

"I'm hungry." And panicking.

She just needed sleep, that was all. She was hungover and behind on her sleep. No big deal.

"Me, too. I'm starving."

Something about the tone in his voice made her turn her head and look at him. Oh, damn. He wasn't talking about quiche. That was obvious. He was talking about sex, it was written all over his face. And she liked it, given the way her nipples went hard and warmth flooded her inner thighs.

Her body was betraying her.

She actually felt heat rise into her cheeks. Which she was going to blame on dehydration from last night's champagne.

"Well, the salads are on the table, so we're all good to go." Tuesday mentally winced at how phony her cheerful voice sounded.

He pulled out her chair for her. She was tempted to yank it away from him, but instead forced herself to sit and put her napkin in her lap. She dug into the salad and, between the food and Mrs. Crandall's monopolization of Diesel's attention, she didn't have to talk to him for the entire rest of the brunch.

Which was exactly what she wanted yet had her feeling grumpy by the time everyone started saying their good-byes and heading out.

On the upside, her hair was dry and the food had helped her headache and vertigo.

"Are you ready to go?" Diesel asked her, giving her a complacent smile.

"Yes." Why couldn't he complain like most men? It was really frustrating. "Thanks again for coming with me. I appreciate it—and the ride, of course."

"No problem. And you're not going to worm out of night at the races, are you?"

"Nope. I'll be there." She was both looking forward to it and dreading it. "Just tell me where and what time to meet you."

He shot her a look. "Are you kidding me? I'll pick you up at your place at seven."

"I can drive myself." If he drove her, it would make it a real date. And it wasn't really a *real* date; it was Tuesday repaying the favor. She definitely owed him.

"I'm picking you up. Don't argue with me."

Was she arguing? Tuesday had to say, even though he was hot and she found herself wanting to get to know him better—both with clothes and without—sometimes he was annoying.

Or maybe, if she were honest, she found him refreshing.

He just said it straight out, laid it down. No man had ever done that with her before.

"Alright, fine, waste your time driving all over town to pick me up. That works for me."

Instead of getting irritated with her and her petulant tone, he just shook his hair out of his eyes. "I'll do that. Now if you're ready, let's head out so I can waste more time today driving you to your car."

She was way ahead of him. "Mrs. Holbrook is taking me to my car, so you're off the hook." The truth was, she wasn't sure she could spend any more time with him until she'd gotten about twenty hours of sleep, so she had begged a ride from Kendall's mother.

"Okay, then. Guess I'll see you on Saturday. Seven o'clock." Diesel leaned over and brushed a kiss on her forehead and left the brunch.

Really? He wasn't even going to argue? He wasn't going to insist on giving her a ride? Not that she wanted him to. But it seemed like he would have tried a little harder. Which was completely unreasonable of her.

She watched him walk out the door.

Suddenly her head really hurt again.

A ROYAL STOCK CAR WEDDING IN BRIEF BY TUESDAY TALLADEGA

Cup series drivers Evan Monroe and Kendall Holbrook Monroe made their history-making marriage more than official with a reception Tuesday night. Over two hundred guests were in attendance, including all drivers currently

in contention for the championship, and former fan favor-
ites such as retired driver Diesel Lange. He's still hot and
still single, ladies, which baffles this blogger. Someone
should snap him up faster than you can say start your engines. Abundant hot men aside, the bridesmaids at the elegant fete, including yours truly, wore Vera Wang dresses
in a stunning shade of pumpkin, which looked particularly
impressive while doing the chicken dance.

The bride wore a sheath dress and looked amazing,
and while I could tell you in great detail about food and
flowers, it's time for this writer to sleep off the damage
done by champagne and high heels. Word to the wise,
people, they never mix well . . .

CHAPTER
FIVE

WHEN Tuesday opened her door to him Saturday night, Diesel blinked. She was wearing riding boots, black leggings, a blazer, and a jaunty little cap.

"Uh . . . is there a particular reason you're dressed like that?"

"You said it's night at the races. I figured I might as well have fun with it."

Okay. Expect the unexpected. That's what he had to remind himself with Tuesday. He wasn't sure whether to be mildly uncomfortable with her quirkiness or to laugh. He took the middle of the road. "You forgot your riding crop."

He was kidding.

She was not.

She went into her apartment and picked up a crop off the coffee table. Smacking it on a sofa pillow, she grinned. "No worries, I have it right here."

Yeah, that was his cock standing up and taking notice. "You look mighty comfortable using that."

"I know. I have to admit I'm enjoying it." She thwacked the pillow again, so hard that it jumped a little.

Diesel should have been wincing, but instead he found his erection swelling. There was something incredibly hot about her swinging that. "Remind me to stay on your good side."

"Oh, come on. You know you want me to discipline you." With that shocking statement, she breezed past him toward the front door.

After a split second frozen in time where all his blood rushed south and his tongue swelled too thick to use for speech, Diesel recovered and moved in front of Tuesday, cutting her off.

"I think you're the one who needs to be shown a firm hand."

Her eyes widened, both with surprise and lust. "Excuse me?"

She had thought he wasn't going to call her on it, that was obvious. She was one of those who said outrageous things and relied on the fact that most men wouldn't cross that boundary with her.

He would. "You heard me. Don't announce a game unless you really want to play it."

Her hat slipped a little on her head as she stared at him. He stared back, his legs spread.

She swallowed audibly, then she recovered and gave him a sly smile. "Who says I don't want to play?"

Then play they would. Diesel didn't pause to reflect on whether or not it was a good idea. He was going with his gut, or more realistically, his cock. Lust had taken hold of him, and every muscle in his body was tight with desire for her. Yanking the crop out of her hand, he told her, "This belongs to me then."

She gave a sharp intake of air, but she wasn't appalled. She was aroused by his move, it was clear in the way she rocked slightly toward him, her eyes dark with desire. "Don't steal my crop."

"You let me take it."

Indignation crossed her face. "I did not—"

But Diesel cut her off. He leaned forward, took her head with his hand, and pulled her until the remaining distance between them was gone. When his lips touched hers, his eyes drifted closed on a silent moan. Damn, she tasted good. Her lips were perfect, warm and receptive and full.

It wasn't a gentle kiss, but he wasn't intending for it to be rough. Until Tuesday bit him, her teeth sinking into his bottom lip—not in protest, but to spur him on.

Then all bets were off. Burying his hands in her hair, Diesel kissed her with all the pent-up frustration he'd been feeling. Her hands dug into his ass, her breasts shoved up against his chest, while her tongue darted inside his mouth, stroking him into lustful mania.

Damn. She was giving as good as she got, and Diesel felt a low growl rising in his throat. He was so fucking turned on by this woman, it was scary. He wanted to shove her down onto the floor, yank down her stupid riding pants, and ram himself into her. In an effort to stop himself from doing just that, Diesel let go of her hair, broke off the kiss, and sucked in a ragged breath.

Her lips were shiny and wet, her eyes huge, her breathing as frantic as his own.

Sliding the riding crop between her legs, he rubbed it against the *V* of her thighs, the tight pants showing him he was precisely where he wanted to be.

Her eyes drifted closed as she enjoyed the slow stroking of the rod against her clitoris.

Her legs drifted apart. When her hips started to move, creating more of an impact of the crop against her body, Diesel pulled it away.

"Let's go before we're late," he told her.

Her jaw dropped. But she didn't protest and say a word. Her eyes narrowed. But she brushed past him, her breasts sliding along his arm, her tongue slipping out to tease along his bottom lip.

Diesel tensed. If she touched his cock or bit him again, he wasn't going to make it to the damn night at the races. He was going to spend the next two hours fucking Tuesday well and good.

But she didn't touch or bite him. She did pull the crop back out of his hands. "I believe this is mine."

With that, she walked out the front door, her ass tight and high in those stretchy pants, her head thrown back, her hair flowing.

Diesel had no choice but to follow, aching with lust, and damn impressed with every inch of both her body and her attitude.

He had to admit he could no longer remember why he'd ever shied away from the thought of having sex with her, other than her drunken state. To hell with his bad knee. She could ride him. He could do her bent over the couch. Whatever it took to get him inside her. That was his goal for the night, because now that she'd finally let him kiss her, he wanted way more. He wanted everything.

"Oh, shoot, hang on." Tuesday turned around and walked past him back into her apartment.

Figuring she had forgotten something, Diesel just idled on the front step, waiting for her to reappear with God only knew what.

What she came back with was a plastic kitchen storage container, which she handed to him. It was filled with cookies.

"What are these?" he asked eyeing the treats as she closed her apartment door.

"I told you I'd bake you cookies if you gave me a shoulder rub at the brunch. You did, so I did. I always keep my promises." She sailed past him.

Diesel was both touched and turned on. She'd made him cookies. He wasn't sure a woman had ever made him cookies before. And he'd been stupid enough to let her off the hook for the second half of her offer, which was to eat raw dough off her naked body. His mouth was watering at the very thought.

It was more than a little hellish sitting in the church basement next to her thirty minutes later with a steady stream of dirty thoughts marching through his head. His aunt and uncle were across from him, their eyes wide with curiosity, and the infamous Ellie was alternating between glaring at Tuesday and smiling flirtatiously at him.

Tuesday was in rare form, charming his aunt and uncle with her friendly smiles and witty banter, her hat tilted forward as she made conversation. Diesel was well aware of the fact that her riding crop was leaning on her chair, on the opposite side from where he was sitting, so he couldn't reach it.

"This is our race, Beth, I'm convinced of it," Tuesday told his aunt. "I'm betting another ten bucks."

The way the event worked was that the church played old races on the giant screen at the front of the room. Guests bought individual horses for a small price and if the horse won, they won. There were also opportunities to bet on the placing of the horses and while you could walk away with some winnings, the point was to donate to the charity of your choice.

His aunt laughed. "I love your confidence. I'm in ten more, too."

They both threw ten-dollar bills into the center of the table.

"Beth, you've gone wild tonight," Johnny told her with a beaming grin.

Apparently everyone had. Diesel was feeling more than a little wild himself, though his intensity had nothing to do with the cash in his wallet. He was having a hard time resisting touching Tuesday, and at random moments, he found himself sliding his hand along her knee and even up into the deep recesses of her thighs. It was the pants. They were just outlining all her goods, he couldn't help himself. It was her attitude, too, the way she flung her money down with zest and never hesitated.

She also never stopped his hand from climbing higher than was strictly appropriate.

There was pizza and beer, and while she packed away three slices of meat lover's, Tuesday had stuck to soda, which Diesel liked to see. He figured that meant he was well and truly seeing Tuesday's personality, not the drunken embellishment of it.

"Oh, damn, our chip bowl is empty." Tuesday held it up for Diesel to see that it contained just a few lonely potato chip crumbs.

She had been steadily packing them away all night, and he was smart enough to know she wasn't just pointing out an empty bowl for no apparent reason. "Would you like me to get some more?"

"Would you do that?" She beamed at him. "Why thank you, that's so sweet."

He should be more irritated at her obvious manipulation, but he was just amused. And horny. So very, very outrageously horny.

"I'll go with you," Johnny said, shoving up out of his own metal folding chair. "Beth, you need anything else, hon? Ellie? Jean?"

"No, I'm fine, thanks, dear."

Diesel knew that Johnny wanted to talk to him, and they were barely three feet from the table before his uncle was leaning in conspiratorially. "I thought you didn't want to date."

"I never said that. I said if I wanted a date, I'd get my own."

"You got yourself a good one, I'll give you that. Tuesday is a pistol. Beautiful, clever, and sweet."

Sweet he wasn't so sure about. He'd definitely give her beautiful and clever. "That she is."

"So you really didn't knock boots with her?" His uncle looked disappointed.

"No, I told you she was loaded."

"She's not loaded tonight," he remarked.

"Why are you so interested in my sex life?" Diesel asked in irritation. He had walked away from Tuesday and the table, yes, to get her more chips, but more to get away from the temptation she presented him. He didn't really want to stand around and talk about the fact that he hadn't had the opportunity to see Tuesday naked yet.

"Don't get defensive." Johnny threw his hands up as they approached the snack buffet table. "I'm just hinting that maybe if you want to finally get some action before your wanker gets moldy, tonight might be a good chance to go for it."

The semi-erection Diesel had been battling all night finally disappeared. Somehow that description didn't sound even remotely hot. "I can't believe you just said wanker in the church basement. I feel like I'm twelve. And I don't imagine Tuesday would be very comfortable around you if she realized you're conspiring to get her in my bed." He didn't imagine any woman wanted to be the subject of that kind of gossip.

"Don't be a prude. She wants you, too, it's as plain as the nose on your face."

"What makes you think that?" Diesel figured Johnny was right—that had been a hell of a kiss—but it didn't hurt to have someone else notice their chemistry.

"Now you are twelve. How can you not notice the look on her face when she looks at you?"

"What, disgust? Irritation?"

"Red-hot lust, son. Nothing more, nothing less." Johnny clapped him on the back. "Take advantage of it."

Part of Diesel wanted to do just that. Hell, he'd been thinking of nothing else all night. But then part of him thought that was wrong. That just red-hot lust wasn't right between him and Tuesday. He liked her, too. And he wasn't sure why one had to be independent of the other, or if she liked him in any way beyond sex.

Which they hadn't even had yet.

He was a mess.

"Race is starting. Grab those chips."

Diesel looked back at the screen and saw that the horses were lined up on the film, ready to go. He grabbed more chips and some water and followed his uncle back to the table. Tuesday was on her feet, jumping up and down and cheering her pick on as the horses tore out of the gate and down the track. The movement did amazing things to her ass in those tight stretchy pants and no surprise, his erection was immediately back.

"Whoo!" she was screaming. "Come on, Jolly Roger! Go, Jolly Roger!"

Of course she picked the horse with the dumbest name ever.

"Give me a Jolly Roger!"

Diesel set the bowl of chips down in front of her. "That doesn't sound right, sweetheart."

She spared him a glance between bouncing up and down. "What? Don't be dirty. What could a Jolly Roger possibly be?"

"I could think of a lot of things." Starting with a blow job and ending with swabbing the deck. "All involving pirates and willing wenches."

Her expression turned curious and slightly aroused. "Oh. Well, hold that thought for later. Right now I have a horse to cheer on."

"You go at it." He was just going to sit down, rest his knee, and watch her. It was an oddly satisfying occupation. Tuesday was always animated, always moving, her sleek dark hair sliding over her shoulders. She was a touchy-feely kind of person. She was always touching someone's arm, or back, or leaning in close. At the moment, it was his aunt and uncle who were on the receiving end of her attentions, and Diesel was pleased that she seemed to like them, and vice versa.

He was feeling perfectly content until Ellie shifted into the chair next to him. "Really?" she said to him, disdain in her voice. "This is who you chose over me?"

Awkward. He had to say he wasn't big on this kind of confrontation. What exactly did Ellie expect him to say?

"It's not a competition."

"Of course it is."

Ellie was a buxom brunette who worked hard to maintain her body and her tan. She was an attractive woman, but too damn aggressive for Diesel's tastes. He glanced around, hoping someone would interrupt them and save him from the conversation.

No such luck. His aunt and uncle were standing behind Tuesday, their heads together, while Tuesday was jumping up and down, a bunch of chips in her hand.

"Life is a competition, Diesel. You should know that, given your prior career."

He wasn't sure what her point was, exactly. "You and I don't have a lot in common, Ellie."

Her eyebrows shot up. "You know, you would think that you would appreciate the fact that I don't care that you have no job. Most women aren't going to want a washed-up driver."

It was a total kick in the nuts he wasn't prepared for. Diesel sat there, stunned, for a second. Hell, he knew there were plenty of women who went after men strictly because they were drivers. But he'd never really translated that to mean women wouldn't be interested in him at all. That he was perceived as unemployed.

There were plenty of days he felt that way himself, but it wasn't at all pleasant to hear someone else say it out loud.

It took him a second, but he forced himself to produce a casual and careless tone of voice. "That's very generous of you. But I'm still not interested."

Ellie shoved her chair back, her breasts bouncing in her low-cut tank top. She glanced over at Tuesday. "You're too boring for her you know. You'll never be able to keep her."

Throw a little goddamn salt right into the wound.

Diesel hadn't even really understood his reservations about Tuesday and now Ellie had managed to point them straight out to him. That was helpful. Not.

He was boring. He was a washed-up driver. He wouldn't be able to keep a woman as vibrant as Tuesday interested in him.

Staring after Ellie, who had taken her purse and walked away from the table, Diesel was too busy brooding to notice the outcome of the race until Tuesday waved her hand in front of his face.

"What are you staring at? Did you see that? Jolly Ranger brought it home, baby!"

Diesel forced himself to shove aside the doubts Ellie had

just planted and fake a smile for Tuesday. "Congrats, that's awesome. Guess you can pick 'em."

Without warning, she dropped into his lap. "You know it. I rule at horse picking. I mean, picking the winning horses."

Her tight backside wiggled a little on his thighs as she settled into a comfortable position. Diesel had no idea what to make of her treating him like her personal folding chair. "These are pre-taped. Maybe you've already seen this race."

He didn't think for one minute that was the case, but he figured he would enjoy her reaction. Indignation from her would also be easier to deal with than her snuggling into him in public. He had to admit, he wasn't one for displays of affection around the masses. Especially given that he never brought women to events like this, and everyone was staring at him curiously. And how would he explain when a week or two from now Tuesday was no longer interested in him?

"How dare you," she told him, her nose lifting. "That's an outrageous accusation. And even if I did happen to see it, it doesn't diminish my confidence in Jolly Ranger's talents, nor my enthusiasm for the race. Besides, this is for charity."

Diesel grinned. "So you did see it?"

"Totally," she admitted. She put her finger to his lips. "Don't tell anyone."

Did she have any idea how much she turned him on? How inherently sexual she was? The way she moved when she walked, the way she shook her hair back, the tilt of her head, and the saucy lift of the corner of her mouth all drove him insane. She was on his lap, her finger touching his lip, her other arm on his shoulder for balance, and her ease in the position both intrigued and excited him. He liked that she was honest, that she always said what she was thinking.

"Never," he reassured her. "Because it's for charity."

"Exactly." She dropped her finger. "Tell me three things about you I don't already know."

There she went again, catching him completely off guard. "Seriously?"

"No, I just said it because I don't want you to do it." She rolled her eyes. "Yes, I'm serious."

"Well." He wasn't sure anyone had ever posed a question to him like that. He wasn't sure what she was looking for exactly. But if she could be random, he could be random. "I'm allergic to cats. The only state I haven't been to is North Dakota. And I was born on the fourth of July."

"Ooh. Fireworks for your birthday. That's pretty cool."

"Actually, it's kind of a rip-off sharing your birthday with any holiday. It could be worse, I could have been born on Christmas, but a kid wants his birthday to be all about him."

"Yeah, I can see that. So why haven't you been to North Dakota? Are you avoiding it?"

Diesel chuckled. "No. Just haven't had the chance yet. Seems like I should before I die. So tell me, where did you get the name Tuesday?"

She wiggled again. "My butt's going numb."

Nothing on him was numb. Diesel was forced to put his hand on the small of her back, concerned she might fall off the chair with all that moving around. He didn't want to touch her any more than was necessary given their location, and the fact that he was well aware that riding crop was propped next to the chair.

"It's not a good story," she told him. "My parents couldn't agree on a name for me. They were fighting about it, both of them being somewhat opinionated. Good thing that passed me over." She gave him a grin. "Anyway, I was born on a Tuesday. The nurse was insisting they fill out the birth certificate, my mom was getting annoyed that my dad wouldn't cave, and vice versa. So he just said 'Christ, we should just name her Tuesday.' And that was the end of that. Lamest, most unloving naming story ever. But like you said . . . it could be worse. I could have wound up Female."

"That is true. And hey, it's a very cool name. It makes you unique, unlike having the name Daniel like I do."

"But no one calls you Daniel." She made a mock quizzical face, stroking her chin. "Or do they?"

No one but his mother ever had. "It might be nice to have someone call me Daniel once in a while." He almost added it would mean they were special, or more important, that he was special to them, but he stopped himself before he really came off like a raging dork. "So what are your three things?"

"Well, Daniel, let's see. My nickname when I was little was Toot. Don't ask me why, I won't tell you. I have never been to Europe, which is just wrong. And I've never met a cookie I didn't like."

He liked the sound of his given name on her lips. Struggling not to laugh, Diesel just said, "If you don't want me to ask, why did you tell me?"

"To frustrate you."

He could believe she was good at that. "So you mean there isn't a single cookie you can resist?"

"Nope."

"You just gave me serious ammunition."

The corner of her mouth went up. "That was the point."

Diesel felt a serious kick of lust. Damn, she was sexy. "So, do you think we can leave soon?"

"It depends on where we're going."

"Either your place or mine. Just tell me where you'd be more comfortable getting naked." He was done with this fake gambling on horse races that weren't live, with Ellie and his aunt and uncle all scrutinizing his interaction with Tuesday.

If she was going to get tired of him, he wanted at least one night with her first.

Her eyes darkened. The tip of her tongue came out and moistened her lip. "Which is closer?"

He really liked the way she thought. "I believe that would be my place. And I have cookies in the car, remember. Your cookies."

Tuesday wished she wasn't wearing these damn tight stretchy pants, because she needed more breathing room between her thighs. Diesel had a way of looking at her that just torched her girl parts. His words were like an electrical jolt to her junk. She didn't remember them ever actually establishing they were going to sleep together but they both clearly wanted to. She knew she had wanted to after the wedding but it had been anybody's guess if he had been at all interested in her or if he'd just felt responsible for the drunk girl.

Between that sexy kiss earlier and his words now, it was no longer in question. He wanted her and she was going to let him have her.

"Let me just get my crop and we can be on our way."

His nostrils flared. "Well, alright then."

Diesel didn't say the most creative things, but it was the way he said it, his voice low, his hair falling in his eyes, that drove Tuesday crazy. Just hearing those words now, trailing over her like his hot, demanding kisses, made her panties wet with desire. They needed to get out of there, fast. Before she knocked the chips off the table and spread her thighs for him.

She stood up, taking care to make sure her backside was right in his view. Might as well whet his appetite in whatever way she could. Tuesday said good-bye to the woman whose name she couldn't remember who had been sitting at their table with her daughter. The daughter, Ellie, who had clearly had designs on Diesel, was nowhere to be found, which Tuesday figured was for the best. She didn't want to get into a girl fight, and that woman had looked like a scrapper.

Tuesday would see how good Diesel was in bed first before she decided if he was worth hair pulling and bitch slapping.

His aunt and uncle she definitely liked. "Thanks so much for such an enjoyable night," she told Beth.

Beth wrapped her in a hug. "Oh, it was so nice to meet you, sweetie. I had a great time with you."

Johnny's turn was next. When he wrapped her in his arms for a light hug, Tuesday smelled his cologne wafting up her nostrils, and had a moment of brief confusion, followed by profound grief. He smelled like her dad, his hand rubbing on her back the way her father would have. She suddenly regretted not drinking any of the beer that had been freely flowing all night.

But she faked a smile, finished her good-byes, then

grabbed her crop and purse and got the hell out of there. She assumed Diesel was following her, but she wasn't going to stop and check for fear she might actually start crying.

There were never going to be any nights hanging out with her dad ever again.

After rushing up the steps, Tuesday shoved open the door and burst out in the parking lot of the church. The evening air hit her in the face and she breathed deeply. It was too hot to be wearing her riding jacket without air-conditioning so she stripped it off, her cheeks burning.

She whirled when the door opened behind her and Diesel emerged. She gave him a glare. "What took you so long?"

"I was trying to piss you off," he told her mildly.

Tuesday sighed. Most men would rise to the bait and snap right back at her. That he didn't diffused her anger. She had been itching for a fight with him and he hadn't even done anything wrong. It wasn't his fault her dad was gone, yet she'd been eager to take it out on him. It was a relief that he wasn't going to let her.

She opened her mouth to apologize when he caught her completely off guard. One second she was feeling guilty and deflated, ready to eat crow and tell him she was sorry, the next she found herself stumbling backward as he shoved her against the wall. Hard. Her shoulders hit the bricks of the building and her backside likewise.

As she recovered her balance, she said, "What the fuck are you doing?" even as she knew full well what his intention was.

"I'm kissing you." He edged his knee in between her legs.

Tuesday wondered briefly if anyone inside the building could see them. "No, you're not. You're just manhandling me."

His hands dug into her hair, yanking her head forward off the wall. "You haven't even seen manhandling yet."

Her nipples were hard, inner thighs damp already. She'd had no idea that she could get so turned on so quickly just from a man's words. But there was something about the way he dominated her space, controlled what they were doing, that she found intensely sexy. "Are you going to show me?"

Instead of answering, he kissed her. It wasn't hard, the way she was expecting. He completely caught her off guard yet again by kissing her softly, worshipfully, a gentle caress of his mouth over hers. Her shoulders sunk, her mouth drifted open, her knees actually crumpled as he kissed her with a gentleness in complete contradiction to his rough prelude.

Then he pulled back, so abruptly and so completely away from her that she swayed forward.

"Yes, I'm going to show you. But not right now. I prefer to spank you in private."

Was he serious? Tuesday scanned his face, but she couldn't really read much more than lust in his expression. And if he was serious, what did he mean exactly? A few swats in the middle of the action, sure, she had done that. Both on the giving and the receiving end. But was he talking hard-core corporal punishment, over-the-knee style? He didn't look the type. But then, who did?

She had to admit, she wasn't as appalled as she was just infinitely curious. And aroused. Don't forget that.

Clutching her crop tighter to her chest, she told him, "Good luck with that. I'm the one holding the crop, remember?"

He just smiled, a sly, knowing smile that had her actual womb quivering in anticipation. "For now."

For the first time since her virginal late teens, Tuesday thought she might be out of her league. But she was always up for a challenge.

"Bring it on."

CHAPTER
SIX

TUESDAY expected him to kiss her again. Slap her backside maybe. Do something sexual to cap off her statement, to show her he was the one in control of this night. But just like earlier, in contrast to the sexy words that had been coming out of his mouth, Diesel took her hand, like they were really on a date and said, "Let's go then, sweetheart. Thanks for being so nice to my aunt and uncle."

How did he shift gears like that? One glance down showed he still had an erection. But now he was back to casual nice boy out on a first date. She didn't know what to do with that. Except that he probably expected she wouldn't know what to do with it and would be passive. She wasn't about to give him control that easily. "It was my pleasure. I had fun, and your aunt and uncle are good people."

There was a brief pause where he glanced over at her,

like he was surprised by her own equally casual response. She wasn't going to ask him to explain his behavior. It just wasn't going to happen.

"You're quite the risk taker when it comes to betting."

"Nah. Not normally. But this was for charity, remember? Though I should have had a beer." Between thinking about her father and high-strung nervous anticipation of having Diesel inside her, she could use a drink.

Diesel opened the car door for her. "I don't want you impaired while I'm giving you an orgasm."

Yes. Just the thought of having an O created by Diesel had her clenching her thighs together as she slid into the car. She rolled her eyes up at him. "Like one beer would impair me. Please."

Instead of answering, he slammed the door shut and came around to the driver's side.

"You know, we've spent most of our time together in the car," she told him. It was just a casual observation. Irrelevant. But it did strike her that for a man she'd only known for a few days, they'd spent a large amount of time driving around. "Maybe we should stop at a bar on the way home."

"I'm not buying you a drink."

Why did he have to be so petulant about it? "Who said you have to buy it? Just sit back and watch me pay."

"No."

"Yes."

"No."

At this point, Tuesday didn't really care that much about actually getting the drink. She just wanted to win. He had no right to deny her liquor. This was a free country. "Stop at the convenience store then."

"No." He gave her an exasperated look. "Do you have to be drunk to have sex with me?"

"No, of course not. I just want one drink." She pointed to a gas station. "Pull in, right there."

Diesel didn't say a word as he indeed pulled off the street. When he put the car in park in front of the door, he shot her a look. "You owe me. And I will be collecting."

"Like this is inconvenient for you? I owe you nothing." What had started out as amusing now had just pissed her off. He had no right to order her around. If she had asked for some goddamn chicken nuggets would he have refused as well? He had no business judging her wants.

Tuesday climbed out of the car and slammed the door shut, hard. Stomping into the store, she wandered the aisles. There wasn't quality alcohol to be had. It was mostly beer and cheap wine, the kind that made her want to die, clutching her head, after three glasses. She didn't really like beer all that much, but she wasn't even going to drink it. She was just going to buy it, on principle, so anything would do.

Pulling a six-pack of bottles out of the cooler, she took it to the counter and paid and stomped back out. Riding boots were good for making noise when she was annoyed. Diesel better have a big dick, that's all she was saying.

"Don't be huffy," he told her.

"Who's huffy?" she huffed. "And if I was huffy—which I'm not—I have the right to be since you're bossing me around and accusing me of being drunk." That was a bit of an exaggeration but she was not known for being the most rational when she was irritated.

"When did I say you're drunk? And how could you be

drunk when you haven't even had a drink?" He pulled the car out of the parking spot. "How did we end up here, Jesus?"

She hadn't a clue. "Here, as in the convenience store, or here, as in the middle of having an incredibly pointless and petty argument?"

He laughed. "The second one."

"I don't know." She picked at the price sticker on the lid of one of the bottles in the six-pack in her lap. "Maybe it's because I had a moment where your uncle reminded me of my dad."

She could own her emotions. It wasn't Diesel's fault that she'd done a one-eighty on him, and he deserved to know where her head was.

"Shit, I'm sorry, Tuesday." His voice was heavy with sympathy. "I'm sure that's incredibly hard."

"Yeah, it is." Her finger was covered in sticky gunk from the sticker she had eradicated and balled up. Rolling it back and forth between her fingers, she squeezed it hard. "Plus I'm nervous about us having sex for the first time."

"You are?"

"Well, aren't you? There's been a hell of a buildup. And while I'm sure it will go well, it's still weird, the first time with anyone."

"Yeah, it is. I'm a little on edge myself."

He didn't admit to nervousness exactly, but it was close enough. So they needed to wrap up this argument and get back to the excitement of getting naked together for the first time. "So don't criticize me for suggesting we stop at a bar, have a drink, chat a little, and ease some of the nerves. That's all I was suggesting and you shut me down hard."

There was a pause, his eyes on the road as he drove. "I'm sorry. I wasn't trying to be an asshole."

"Most people aren't trying to be assholes. They just are. So think before you say something." If even half the world would try that, she would be a happy woman.

"I was just offended that you needed to get drunk to have sex with me. But you're right—there's a big difference between drunk and one drink."

Which meant if he was offended at the thought, he cared about her opinion of him. He wanted to spend time with her. It wasn't just about a quick lay for him. Which was hot.

So she was willing to let the whole thing go, given she had tossed a ton of petulance at him to begin with. "Okay, so we're cool." Time to lighten the mood. "Have you ever thought about how bizarre it is that there are about a hundred slang words for being drunk? What does that say about alcohol and English-speaking people?"

"That we're a culture soaked in ale. Though I think a hundred is an exaggeration."

"Let's count. There's drunk, inebriated, trashed, loaded."

"Smashed, shit-faced, bombed."

"Crunk."

"What the hell is crunk?"

"Crazy drunk. Don't you watch reality TV? Get your GTL on then get crunk."

"GTL?"

"Gym, tan, laundry."

"I have no clue what you're talking about."

"It's the mantra of these guys . . . okay, never mind. Back

to the slang." Tuesday picked up a beer bottle, like it would inspire her. "Crocked. Sauced. Wrecked."

"I think wrecked is pushing it. That can mean more than one thing. Such as emotional or unstable. It's not a word exclusive to alcohol."

"Good point, but I'm still counting it because so far we only have eleven and that's highly disappointing."

"Tipsy."

"I can't believe you just said tipsy. That sounded so cute coming out of your mouth."

"I didn't make the word up." Diesel was amazed at how Tuesday could make him feel both intensely masculine and sexy, no matter what he was saying or doing. For the first time ever, he was starting to clue in as to how men could stand there holding a wife or girlfriend's purse and not feel like a complete loser. They were standing there not caring what anyone else thought because their girl managed to make them feel like the very definition of macho.

"That still only makes it twelve. I'm disappointed. I think we need to go to the urban dictionary and check for more."

"Well, we can if you want. We're at my place." Diesel hit the button to open his garage door. "But I was kind of hoping we could do something else instead."

"Eat cookies?" she asked, her tongue slipping out to moisten her lips.

"Yeah." He nodded. "Eat cookies."

But Tuesday was suddenly distracted as they pulled into his four-car garage. "Holy shit. This is a big garage."

"Car parts take up a lot of room." He'd bought the house before his accident, anticipating parking a boat and a hobby car or two. In the two years since, he'd been glad for it since he used most of it for his restoration projects.

"Yeah, but this is a house. I guess I expected you to live in a luxury apartment or a condo or something."

"Why?" Diesel put his car in park and turned to look at her in the dark. The garage light cast a shadow across her face, hiding her eyes but showing her porcelain cheek.

He stared at her lips as she spoke. "I don't know. Weird, huh? But I think of single guys as determined to be unattached to anything . . . even real estate."

"I've never been determined to be unattached. I just haven't met the woman I want to spend the rest of my life with. But I love this house, even if it is too big for me."

"What style is it?"

"I believe the architect called it French country. To me, its just brick and wood and pretty damn awesome looking." He opened his car door, holding the container of cookies she'd baked him in his hand. "And you can see it if you get out of the car."

She stuck her tongue out at him, but she did open her door as well. Diesel got out and walked around the front of his car. For some reason, he felt the urge to reach for her hand, but that seemed too intimate, too girlfriend-boyfriend. That wasn't what they were doing.

He had no clue what exactly they were doing, given they kept shifting between sexual and friendly and confessional, but holding hands like high school sweethearts wasn't the mood he wanted to strike at the moment. So he swept his arm toward the door and gave a mock carnival voice. "Right this way, step inside, if you dare."

"Is this the house of wonders or the house of freaks?"

she asked, twirling her crop in her fingers as she strolled past him, her hips swaying.

"Both." Damn, he was just amazed at how naturally sexy Tuesday was. The way she took the three stairs to his back door showed she was aware of how every inch of her body moved, and what his reaction to it would be.

Turning to glance back at him, she tossed her hair over her shoulder. "Promise?"

"Guaranteed." Diesel slid his hand over her ass, cupping her cheek before moving between her legs and stroking. "Now open the door before I nail you in the garage."

Her hand reached out for the knob but she didn't turn around. "Someone needs to learn patience."

Moving in behind her, Diesel bumped his erection into her backside. "I'll have plenty of patience once we're naked. But now I want to get you inside so I can see some of that body you flashed at me the other day."

"I didn't flash anything at you."

"What do you call dropping your blanket onto the floor? You were only wearing a very tiny bra and panties." The vision was burned into his memory.

"I was hungover. That doesn't count."

"It counts. You meant to do it."

She stepped into the house and gave him a grin over her shoulder. "You're right. I did mean to do it. You deserved it for not denying I looked like ass. I was trying to prove a point."

"What point was that again, exactly?" Diesel couldn't really follow the logic. Nor was he able to focus on anything other than the fact that she had stopped moving just inside the doorway.

"Oh, hello, there's a dog here." Tuesday bent over and petted Wilma, who had appeared, looking half asleep, her tail wagging lightly.

"That's Wilma."

"Wilma? Do you have an old lady fetish?"

"She's named after Fred Flintstone's wife. And even if I had an old lady fetish, what does that have to do with my dog?"

"Good point. I don't know."

"Speaking of points, what was yours again when you danced the blanket the other day?" He wanted to get back to that topic. Naked woman conversation trumped dog talk.

"I wanted you to see that I look alright."

"Sweetheart, you look way more than alright." He reached out and grabbed the lapel of her riding jacket and yanked her over to him. "In case you doubt it, here's proof." With his free hand he took her and guided her right to his erection, pressing hard.

"That's definitely proof of something." She looked like she was going to make a smart-ass remark but then her eyes fluttered shut briefly and she gave a sigh as she stroked him all on her own. "Damn, that's a lovely penis."

He wasn't sure how he felt about having his dick called lovely, but he'd take it for a compliment. "And you haven't even seen it yet. Or tasted it. Or felt it deep inside your wet pussy."

Her eyes snapped open and her hand stilled. "Who's to say my pussy's wet?"

Diesel liked that she didn't balk at his graphic language. She gave it right back. His cock throbbed, hot desire tensing his muscles from head to toe as he fought for control. "Well, let's find out."

"Suit yourself." Her shrug was nonchalant, but her hips tilted toward him and her legs spread ever so slightly in invitation.

The stretchy pants were a damn fine clothing choice because all he had to do was peel back the waistband and slide on in. What he was met with was smooth, soft skin, a swollen clitoris, and nothing else between him and her very wet, very juicy pussy. He groaned, startled and aroused all at the same time. "No panties?" he asked, his voice gruff as he pressed his thumb into all that sweet moisture.

Her head was tilting to the side, her breathing deepening from his touch. "I didn't want lines. These pants are fitted, you know."

"Oh, I know. I fucking know."

"You don't mind, do you?"

"No panties? Uh, no, not a problem." Nor was it a problem that Tuesday was almost entirely bare down there. From what he could feel, and he was feeling as much as he could, there was nothing but a landing strip of curls on either side. Which was very, very sexy. He was already imagining how easy it would be to move his tongue along that silky hot skin. His fingers were doing just that, teasing up and down, circling around her swollen clitoris, then pressing in slightly before pulling out.

Tuesday gave a soft little moan, her hips following his finger as he pulled back.

"What's the matter?" he asked her, brushing a kiss alongside her temple.

"You're teasing me."

"Hell yeah." He intended to do a lot of that. "You know you like it."

"I don't think I do, actually," she murmured, still wiggling around trying to get him to penetrate her. "I like to just be given what I ask for."

"I'm perfectly willing to do that out of the bedroom." He already had, he thought. He'd let Tuesday call the shots. He was a laid-back guy most of the time and wanted any woman he was with to be happy.

"Except for when I asked you for a drink." Tuesday rubbed up and down on his cock through his denim, before nipping at his earlobe.

He put his hand over hers. "You're right. Sorry about that. Normally the only place I insist on controlling the situation is in bed."

"You insist? So you're saying you're a dom?"

Maybe he shouldn't be talking about it. Maybe he should just be showing her. Diesel took both of her wrists with his hand and moved them up over her head. "Nothing as official as that. It's just a preference, that's all. You don't mind, do you?"

"The funny thing is," she said, her eyes slumberous, her breasts rising up and down with her ragged breathing, "I like to be in control everywhere *except* the bedroom. It's the one time I'm perfectly willing to be told what to do. And if you're good at it . . ."

Diesel moved his left knee in between her thighs and rubbed the spot he'd abandoned with his finger. "Yeah?"

"If you're good at it, you can get me to pretty much do anything."

Now it was his turn to groan. "Anything?"

The corner of her mouth tilted up in a saucy smile. "Almost. Where are the cookies?"

"In my hand. But I'm setting them down." Diesel erased the space between them and kissed her hard, deeply, his tongue thrusting into her partially open mouth. She turned him on like no woman ever had and while in the back of his mind he worried that his knee wouldn't hold out for this kind of extended play, he was willing to take the chance. His fingers tangled in her long hair, his other hand still pinning her arms to the wall. An image of Tuesday tied up, legs spread for him flashed through his head, and he knew he needed to get her to his bed now. He wanted to taste and touch and feel every inch of her.

Breaking off the kiss, Diesel also completely stepped back from her. His heart was racing, erection throbbing. But with slow deliberation, he bent over and retrieved the crop Tuesday had dropped at some point. With it he pointed down the hall. "The stairs are that way. Use them."

She sucked in a breath, her finger rubbing over her bottom swollen lip. Her eyes widened, and Diesel fully expected her to argue, or at the very least make a smart-ass remark. But she didn't. Without a word, she started down the hall in the direction he had indicated. Which was one of the hottest things he had ever seen.

But just because her ass was there in front of him, tight and high, and because he had a crop in his hand, he swatted her with it. Not hard, but enough to get her attention. She jumped a little, obviously startled, and Diesel wasn't sure what was hotter—the actual swat, or the fact that she didn't snark at him about it.

He knew enough about her to suspect she'd want to look around at his house, to comment, but she didn't. She did glance around, but she didn't say a word as she went up the stairs, tossing him a smoldering look over her shoulder. Diesel followed her, flicking the lights on and testing the sting of the crop on his palm. She was going to either regret or really appreciate the fact that she had brought it. Without it, it was possible he would have been able to control himself a little more, keep this first time vanilla and gentle.

But that little prop had changed any of his best intentions. Now he just wanted to take her exactly how he wanted.

"Which way?" she asked. "Or am I supposed to guess?"

There was some of that customary sass he was used to from her. He liked that she wasn't going to be totally submissive. He didn't really want blind obedience. He just wanted to be the director of their little show. He wanted to drive her wild to the point where she was willing to do just about anything, like she had said. That was hot to him. "Why don't you guess? And if you're wrong, I'll punish you."

She hesitated for a brief second, studying him. "You know, I shouldn't trust you, but I do. Or maybe I'm just horny and stupid."

Diesel let the crop lower. He didn't want her to have any doubts at all. "Hey. I would never do anything to hurt you." He reached out and stroked along her cheek, enjoying her soft skin. "I'm a nice guy, remember? If anything makes you uncomfortable, just tell me and I'll stop. And if this is too much for the first time . . ." He waved the crop a little. "Just tell me and we'll take a different approach."

All that mattered to him was that she was enjoying herself. There would be time for more exploratory activities later. He could go traditional if she wanted, and hell, she had a point. How was she really supposed to trust him?

But she shook her head. "I'm not uncomfortable. I'm so

comfortable it's making me feel like I should be uncomfortable. But I'm not."

She turned and studied the doors in his hallway. "So I'm going to guess which room in the *master* bedroom."

The emphasis on master was slight, but Diesel heard it and he swallowed hard. Damn, she was amazing.

Poking her head in the first doorway on her right, she immediately shook her head. "No way. This is an office."

"That one was a giveaway." He was hoping his multiple guest rooms were going to trip her up. He wanted nothing more than to take his hand to her bare backside and give her a nice resounding smack. They would both enjoy it, that was obvious, and now that the idea had taken root, Diesel didn't want to let it go.

"This one isn't the master either. It's too small." Tuesday moved down the hallway, her hips sashaying. "This is easier than I thought."

So she thought. She was approaching his room and the two guest rooms that all were about the same size and had their own bathrooms. They had all been decorated by the woman he had hired, and looked equally elegant and masculine. Given that he wasn't big on clutter, there would be virtually no way to know which room was his without stepping in to the bathroom.

Victory was going to taste very sweet.

Her eyebrows drew together when she glanced in the first room on the right, then the second. "Huh. One door left." She peeked into what was his real bedroom and her frown deepened. "Why the hell do you have so many beds?"

"For people to sleep in."

She rolled her eyes at him. "You tricked me, you know."

"No, I didn't. You agreed to guess." Though he couldn't help but grin just a little. Tuesday hated to lose. He had already figured that out about her already, and while she would enjoy the punishment, it would drive her insane that she had lost.

"I didn't know you had identical bedrooms." Tuesday glanced in the rooms again, longer this time, studying each one carefully. "You set me up to fail."

Maybe. "Never."

"Cheat." She was clearly about to grumble, when she did a double-take into his bedroom again. "Never mind. I pick this room. This is where you sleep." She tossed her thumb in the direction of his bedroom.

Damn. She was right. "What makes you think that?"

"You made your bed but you forgot to put the throw pillows back on. They're laying on the floor."

He hated to admit it, but he couldn't lie to her. "Okay, you're right. Good deduction."

"I'm fucking brilliant, that's what I am."

"Fucking brilliant. And brilliantly fuckable. I totally agree."

"Brilliantly fuckable? I like that. Maybe I'll put that on my business cards."

"The hell you will." Diesel ran his fingers through her long hair, loving the sheen of it in the muted hallway lights. "Now since you guessed correctly I'll let you pick which bedroom I'm going to fuck you in."

"Oh, without a doubt, your bedroom." She turned and entered his room. "I want to roll around naked on your sheets."

Tuesday was feeling turned on and totally in control, despite the game they were playing. She did trust Diesel, and while he was domineering he wasn't rough. Not in any way she didn't like, that is. She wasn't sure she'd ever been this turned on by a man before and they hadn't even really done anything yet. All the talk was exciting, spiking her anticipation.

She was walking toward his bed when he startled her yet again by yanking off her hat. It had been slipping all night and irritating her, but since they'd gotten in the car, she'd basically forgotten about it. Now she was made aware of it again as well as of him when he tore it off her head and tossed in onto his dresser.

"You have an issue with that hat?" she asked him.

"I have an issue with you wearing too many clothes."

"That's not clothing. It's an accessory." And she had thought it might actually be fun to well, ride Diesel, with her riding boots and hat on. "A rather cute one at that."

But he shook his head. "No hat. No boots. Not this time."

Did he freaking read minds? She was starting to think he did, because every time she turned around it seemed like Diesel was anticipating either her thoughts or her actions. It was unnerving. A little hot. But mostly freakish.

It was warm in his room and she wanted to be naked anyway. While wearing a jacket had been cute in concept, on the back end of August it wasn't the wisest of choices, so she peeled it off and let it drop to the floor. Under it she was wearing a black tank top, designed to boost her less-than-ample chest.

Diesel paused in the middle of turning on the bedside lamp. "I'd tell you you're beautiful but you already know it."

She didn't always know that. She was confident, for the most part, in her looks and in her personality, but lately she'd been doubting everything. Who she was. How she carried herself. What the future held for her. A little reassurance and ego stroking wouldn't be a bad thing. "Doesn't hurt to hear it said out loud."

Diesel came toward her and cupped her face with both his hands. "You're beautiful," he whispered, in a tone so soft and sincere that Tuesday felt her breath catch.

There was no control with him, that's what she was learning. He constantly knocked her off-kilter, shifting from arrogant to tender to dominating to gentle.

She liked it.

She liked him.

And she didn't know what that meant.

Except that she was starting to think he was more than just a casual hookup.

He was . . . something more.

Maybe she had known that since the second she had cried on his shirt at her father's funeral.

"Oh, God," she whispered when his tongue swept over her bottom lip. She never knew what to expect from him, but she always knew she was going to enjoy it.

Warmth was flooding between her legs already and she couldn't prevent herself from bumping up against his erection. She wanted to see him naked, touch his hard muscles with her bare fingers. He was wearing a T-shirt and jeans, a typical guy uniform, though the cut and quality said they weren't from the local discount store. From the brief glimpse into his bedrooms, it was clear Diesel liked nice things, and he had the money to purchase them. Which meant he wouldn't be wearing some cheap tightie-whities.

She found the snap of his jeans and she fumbled with it as he dragged his tongue from one corner of her mouth to the other. He was driving her insane with all that teasing and she just suddenly wanted him inside her more than anything else. Screw the foreplay, she wanted cock.

"Hey, Slow down," he told her, knocking her hand off of his button.

Never had she thought of herself as a whimperer but at that moment she was definitely one. What leaped out of her mouth was a whimper and a whine all rolled into one. "Come on, seriously? Just let me have a feel."

He nuzzled her ear, his tongue slipping inside with a damp tickle.

Tuesday shivered and tried for the button again, but he held her hand still against the waist of his jeans. "Now you've become the dude and I'm the chick. I want to take it slow and you're all about the wham-bam."

"What's wrong with the wham-bam?" she asked. "Sometimes there is a time and place for it, and I think now is one of them."

"Well, I disagree. And I'm the one in charge." Diesel stepped back completely.

Tuesday was starting to really hate it when he did that.

But then he reached out and in one swift motion peeled her tank top off. There he was again—totally unpredictable. But this had a positive result. She was out of her already sweaty tank top and standing in front of him in her bra, stretchy pants, and riding boots. If that didn't force the man out of his pants, she was going to be seriously impressed with his control.

It was a push-up bra, after all. The girls were shoved high and tight and a quick glance down showed they were looking mighty fine, if she did say so herself.

"You like what you see?" he asked her with a sly grin. "Because I do."

"They're not bad in a bra," she admitted. "And I've been told my nipples are one of my better features."

"Oh really? And who the fuck told you that?"

Was that some sort of ridiculous jealousy rearing its head? Tuesday grinned. "The dozens and dozens of men I've slept with. Songs have been written about my nipples. Artwork created. Lives changed forever after an encounter with La Nipples."

His head tilted. "You're a smart-ass."

"Always."

"But you're playing with fire."

Actually she was feeling pretty pleased with herself. It was fun to turn the tables on him.

Except she couldn't hold control for long. Diesel took it right back by stripping off his T-shirt and showing her one of the most amazing male chests she'd ever seen outside of a calendar. Flipping his hair out of his eyes, he lifted his arm to finish what the flick of his neck hadn't completed, and the whole motion made Tuesday's mouth go dry. His muscles were rippling, his jeans were slipping, and she was perilously close to coming just looking at him. He had a tattoo down his right side, some kind of tribal symbol.

"Touch your nipples," he told her.

"What?" She had lost the thread of what they were talking about when he'd taken his shirt off.

"Touch your nipples since they're so damn amazing. Show me how good they feel."

She'd much rather touch his but she knew he wasn't going to allow that. "With my bra on or off?"

His nostrils actually flared. "Start with it on, then take it off."

She could do that. "I feel like I need a playlist going." Music would make it feel more natural, but she went for it anyway. Sliding her hands up her thighs and her waist, Tuesday finally reached her breasts, cupping them. It was an astonishing bra. The truth was, she couldn't really feel herself through all that padding and Lycra, or whatever miracle material had created actual cleavage for her. After a few swirls of her thumb over where she thought her nipples should be, Tuesday decided it was time to send the bra on its way.

Diesel was standing with his thumbs hooked loosely in the pockets of his jeans, his hair falling in his eyes, his chest a study in manly perfection. He was clearly enjoying the show, but she wanted a reaction from him. She wanted him to lose control, to close the distance between them and grab her, suck her nipples, and tear her pants off.

So to encourage him to make that happen, Tuesday bent her knee, tossed her hair back over her shoulder, and unhooked her bra. In a move she hoped was seductive, she leaned forward slightly, giving him a clear view of her cleavage, and letting the loose straps fall off her shoulders. Then she reached between her breasts, tugged the bra, and let it drop to the floor. It was actually a very freeing feeling to stand there with him watching her while she felt confident and sexy. She ran her fingers through her hair to move it off her face first before she reached down and rubbed both her nipples with her thumbs.

That small sensation, while he watched with an erection clearly bulging through his jeans, aroused her completely. She was so ready to have an orgasm, so ready to feel him thrusting deep inside her. Starting to work her nipples harder, Tuesday shifted her thighs restlessly. She wanted to ask Diesel what he thought, but at the same time, she just wanted to wait for him to speak first. So she let her eyes drift half closed and she concentrated on her own body, on the feeling each tweak and tug was creating deep between her legs. When she pinched hard, she let out a soft moan.

Her eyes flew back open when Diesel was suddenly in her space. "You're beautiful," he told her again, his hands snaking around her waist. Bending his head, he flicked his tongue over her nipple, catching both her tight bud and her finger, which was still covering it.

Now she gasped, shocked at how such a slight contact could make everything inside her tighten and jolt. He moved her hands down away from her nipples and slowly laved across first one, then the other. He blew on her moist flesh each time he pulled away, heightening her awareness. Tuesday grabbed on to his waist, needing something to hold on to while he sucked her, first going at her gently and seductively, then switching to nipping and sucking hard, drawing her fully into his mouth.

She wanted to say something, to beg him for consistency, to pick a mood and stick with it, yet she didn't because it was the very thing about his sexual approach that got her the hottest. It didn't make sense, but his ability to strip away her control, to direct everything they were doing completely turned her on. So she let him switch at random intervals, sucking and biting and then softly licking, until she was breathing hard, clinging to him, squeezing her legs together and ready to beg.

He suddenly stopped altogether, just taking a step back before giving her left nipple one final pinch. "You're right. These are very impressive nipples. First class."

A breathy laugh escaped her mouth, despite the fact that she wanted to moan at his departure. "Why thank you."

She reached out and tried to go for his zipper but Diesel stopped her yet again. "Stop stopping me," she told him in frustration.

"Anticipation is part of the fun," he said, leaning in and kissing the side of her neck.

An unexpected sharp swat on her backside had her eyes flinging open in shock. He had taken the crop to her again and damn, if it didn't turn her on.

"And you need to learn some patience."

As Tuesday quivered in desire, his lips on her neck, grip tight on her hands above her head, her ass receiving yet another quick smack, she knew she was about to be taught a lesson in that.

CHAPTER
SEVEN

TUESDAY let her head fall back for better access and sighed when her bare breasts made contact with his hard chest. "Oh, that feels good." She bumped her inner thighs against his erection, both wanting to give in to his domination, and wanting to resist. "And for the record, anticipation is overrated."

"So you like instant gratification?"

"Yes." She liked to think of it more as knowing what she wanted and getting it right away.

He dropped his hand, releasing her wrists. "Then I'm going to give it to you."

Before she even realized what he was about to do, Diesel had stripped her pants down to her knees and his mouth was buried between her thighs.

"Oh, shit," was all she could manage before she dug her

fingers into his hair and held on as he licked from one end of her slit to the other.

His hands gripped her ass tightly as he worked her hard and tight with his tongue. Tuesday threw her head back and gasped, instinctively trying to move away from the intensity of his touch.

He just held her tighter, his fingers digging into her flesh, nose pressing against her belly as he pulled her swollen clit into his mouth and sucked. Tuesday knew she was going to come and she knotted her fingers in his hair. When he slid back down inside her moist, hot center, she bit her bottom lip and let the orgasm rip through her. She didn't make any sound, just let it rock through her as they gripped each other tightly. It was one of the hardest orgasms she'd ever had, and when the waves of pleasure subsided slightly, she still didn't speak, just sucked in some air and tried to comprehend what the hell he had just done to her.

Diesel stepped back and stood straight, tossing his hair out of his eyes. "Instant gratification. But now you'll anticipate the second time you come. So in the end, we'll still do it my way."

She shivered, no doubt in her mind that he could make her come again in another ninety seconds if he chose.

About to make a comment, hell, give him a compliment, she stopped when she realized that he had winced then tried to hide it. He had been down on his knees eating her out, and it was obvious that had been a bad idea. Instantly flooded with both guilt and compassion, Tuesday reached for his hand.

"Are you okay?"

But his eyebrows shot up and she knew it was the wrong thing to say. He avoided her touch, and with his foot came down on her pants, still hovering around her ankles. "Don't do that. Don't feel sorry for me."

That irritated her. She wasn't feeling sorry for him. She was expressing concern. There was a big difference and she didn't like his attitude. "Maybe you should appreciate that I give a shit how you feel."

"If you give a shit how I feel you would step out of your pants and get on my bed."

While she had to admit she liked the way he dominated in the bedroom, this was different. Even as she did kick her pants entirely off, she told him, "Only after you tell me you're okay."

It was a face-off. He stared at her, jaw set. She stared back, chin up, ready to do battle. She wasn't going to be responsible for him spending the next day in swollen agony from straining his knee.

For a second, she thought they were going to wind up ending the evening right there. But then his shoulders eased up a little and he shook his head.

"I'm fine. Thank you, sweetheart."

It absolutely one hundred percent melted her heart. Tuesday felt her breath catch, felt her chest squeeze, felt something really shocking rise up in her. He was one of the most amazing men she'd ever encountered, able to flip between alpha and beta, strong and sensitive all at once.

"You're welcome," she said, and was about to say something about her appreciation when he took her by the arms and shoved her backward down onto his bed. Stunned, she lay there for a second, trying to focus on the ceiling and process her changed perspective when it was altered again. Gripping her by the calves, he yanked her down to the edge of the bed so that her legs dangled toward the floor.

She thought he was going to use his tongue on her again, but he surprised her by simply placing a gentle kiss on her sex then standing up. Her arms were up behind her head, and Tuesday felt completely at ease and aroused. She had won a round with Diesel and now she was perfectly content to let him do whatever he wanted in whatever time frame he liked.

What he wanted to do was thrust into her.

Tuesday hadn't even realized he had undone his jeans so when she felt the first push of his penis into her, she gasped in pure ecstasy. But he was barely in her before he was out again, just teasing at her with the very tip of his erection.

"What are you doing?" she asked, her eyes rolling back in her head, fingers digging at the comforter on his bed for purchase, something to ground her as she fought the urge to squirm.

Diesel bent over and flicked his tongue over her nipple. "I'm torturing you."

He wasn't lying. She was definitely feeling like she was in pain. "Please. Please give it to me. Please?"

Hearing that soft pleading coming off of Tuesday's lips nearly undid Diesel. She was a sassy, feisty woman, despite her earlier assertion that she would be submissive in bed. Already she had butted heads with him a couple of times, and Diesel liked that. He liked that she said whatever she was thinking. But he also liked that he had reduced her to the point of begging him softly, little mews punctuating each word, her eyes squeezed shut, and her nails digging into the bed.

He wasn't just torturing Tuesday, he was definitely on the verge of doing himself in at the same time. The taste of her was still on his mouth, the feel of her coming, her thighs pressed against him, embedded in his memory, and he wanted to just pound away at her until he exploded all inside her. He prided himself on control during sex and she was on the verge of making him lose it. So he was gritting his teeth and pulling back, teasing them both by just touching her silky opening before retreating, over and over.

It was exciting as hell that she was so clean shaven down there, allowing him to see every inch of her dewy pink sex, allowing him to reach down and lap at a trail of moisture that had trickled down her thigh. She was so sexy, her legs long and beautiful, her breasts high and tight. He knew he needed to get a condom, but the warm tightness of her body opening for him was just too good of a feeling. He fought back a groan when she wrapped her legs around his ass and pulled him in closer with her heels.

He would have held off except she actually kicked him, a little encouraging giddy-up. Then he couldn't wait any longer, especially when she said in a tight anxious voice, "I'm on the pill. Unless you have some gross disease, you need to fuck me right now."

That was all the information he needed. He knew he was clean and he trusted she was, too.

Holding on to her thighs, Diesel thrust into her with one hard push. She groaned. He groaned. Pausing to let the ecstasy roll over him, his cock throbbing inside her, Diesel savored the sensation of her wrapped around him, hot and wet.

"My God, you feel so good," he told her.

Her answer was both a soft moan and a tightening of her inner muscles on him. It felt so amazing that Diesel jerked in response, his hands digging into her flesh, a sweat breaking out on his forehead, his legs twitching as he fought the urge to orgasm immediately. He wanted to make this last, but she wasn't going to make it easy on him.

So he gave in and just started pounding away on her, thrusting in and out as her moans got louder and his desire spiraled out of control. She was so tight and hot, her legs spread so willingly for him, her head turning back and forth as she voiced her pleasure, louder and louder with each thrust. When her hand came up onto his chest, pushing into him like she couldn't take it anymore, Diesel knew it was time to finish this. Taking her even harder, he reached down and flicked his finger over her clitoris. Tuesday rewarded him by immediately coming, her muscles milking his cock as she moaned through her orgasm.

It was all he needed to pull back and give one last push, then he exploded inside her, teeth gritted, eyes clamped shut.

Good God.

The pleasure was so intense Diesel forgot to breathe for a second. When the final waves quieted, he pried his eyes open and sucked in some much-needed air. Looking down at Tuesday, he just panted and gazed at her in amazement. What the hell was that? He hadn't felt anything like that . . . ever. Damn, she was incredible.

She looked like she had enjoyed herself equally. Her hands were still above her head, but she dragged one over to rake her hair out of her face. She was dewy with sweat, her cheeks flushed a deep pink. With a little laugh, she kicked him in the ass again with her heel.

"You need to quit kicking me, sweetheart," he told her.

"No," she said, a satisfied smile on her beautiful face.

How could he resist that? With a grin of his own, Diesel leaned down and gave her a nice smacking kiss before easing himself out of her.

She complained, trying to hold him inside.

"Give me ten minutes then you can have it back."

"Promise?"

Her voice was actually a little dreamy and Diesel swallowed hard, his throat suddenly tight. She looked absolutely beautiful lying there like that and he had unexpected alien feelings rising up in him. The fact that he was experiencing anything other than ball-draining satisfaction sent him into a minor panic, so he worked his bad knee a few times and backed away from the bed. "Let me get you a towel," he told her.

"Don't worry about it. It's already all on your sheets." She shrugged, that lazy smile still on her face. "Come snuggle with me."

He wasn't sure that he had ever actually had a woman ask him to snuggle. Presumably women wanted to, but they were never bold enough to ask for it. Nor did he think he would have said yes to any woman but Tuesday. She was just such a paradox, strong and yet vulnerable, and he found that he really did want to lay in bed with her and do nothing.

So he surprised the hell out of himself by climbing onto the bed and arranging himself next to her. With an ease that should have scared him, he pulled her partially onto his chest, while her leg entwined with his.

"Mmm," she said, her breathing slow and deep.

Her hair draped across his shoulder, and the V of her legs where they had just been joined in such pleasant friction, was warm against his thigh. Her back was smooth as he stroked it absently with the pad of his thumb.

"You'd better not fall asleep," he told her, nudging her a little. "I have plans for you."

"You said ten minutes. I'm regrouping."

"I think we're down to eight."

"Uh-oh." She yawned then kissed his chest. "Maybe we should just pull a blanket over us and fall asleep."

"You're the one who made me promise I'd give it to you again soon." Diesel smacked her tight backside with his hand, wishing he hadn't dropped the crop. "No sleeping. In fact, get over here." Using his hand to cup her ass, he hauled her over onto him fully. "Time's up."

"Ahhh," she said in protest, her body limp as she landed on him, all limbs and warm skin.

"Be quiet." Diesel squeezed her ass, his body already stirring to life with the feel of her splayed out on top of him. "Now kiss me."

She made a grumbling sound of protest against his chest, but she did prop herself up slightly, and toss her hair back out of her face. "You're bossy."

"I believe we've already established that." Nor was he about to change. Tuesday made him tight with need, determined to take her, direct what they were doing. It was his way of grabbing control when he wasn't feeling it.

So he told her again, "Kiss me."

But instead of being offended at the demanding tone of his voice, she just smiled down at him, tickling the whiskers on his chin. "You're so cute. Why are you so cute?"

Way to make him feel badass. He had to admit though, it pleased him. She thought he was cute. That was kind of hot. Flattering. Sweet.

He didn't want to think about it right at the moment though. He just wanted to feel her lips on his. So he took the back of her head and brought her mouth down onto his.

She sighed right before contact. It was a delicious kiss, the kind that made Diesel want to hang around in that moment for a good long while. Their bodies were warm pressed together, the scent of their earlier arousal still in the air, her hair tickling across him. It was easy to kiss Tuesday. There was no awkwardness, no jockeying for position. They just fit and he kissed her again and again, soft and tender yet purposeful. He was in no hurry to do anything other than tease her tongue with his.

But like he was fast learning, Tuesday had different ideas. She was already starting to bump against him, swiveling her hips to get the highest level of contact. He loved listening to her as she shifted from casual enjoyment to excited and determined. She bit his bottom lip at the same time she settled her legs more carefully on either side of his thighs. All that hot wetness making contact with his cock had him groaning. She was just so damn juicy and so eager, her hand reaching down between them and taking him into her grip.

Diesel gritted his teeth when she took his erection and slid it along her moist inner thighs, then swirled it over her clitoris. He laid back and let her play, repeating the motion over and over, until his cock was slick with her moisture and they were both panting in excitement. He loved that she had the confidence to just take what she wanted, that she could use him to please herself. It made her even sexier to him.

So he let her set the rhythm, let her get herself off until she couldn't take it anymore, and she finally aligned him with herself and sank onto his erection.

"Yeah, baby," he told her. "You feel amazing."

"So do you." Tuesday was leaning forward, propped up by both her hands on the bed, so low her breasts were brushing against his chest.

He was going to force her to sit up but then he realized that Tuesday was already on the verge of an orgasm. In fact, she came right then, her hip undulating slowly, lips pursed together, eyes locked with his. She had taken herself right to the edge with his cock, and that was freaking hot.

"You like that?" he asked her, sliding his hands down over her ass. Damn, she looked good. She felt good. She tasted good.

She nodded, as she shuddered through the end of her orgasm. "Duh."

He laughed. "Smart-ass." He gripped her hips. "Sit up. You'll like this even more." Or at least he would.

"I'm too tired," she said, her body languid, her intention to lay on his chest obvious.

But Diesel forced her to sit up, using the palms of his hands.

She made a noise of complaint, but he just swatted her backside again with enough sting to get a reaction from her.

It was proving to be the most effective way to ensure her obedience.

"Hey," she grumbled, using her hand to rub where he had just spanked. "That hurt." But she did sit up, and she looked like it had renewed a bit of her arousal.

"I'm sorry," he told her even though he knew he hadn't hit her hard enough for it to really hurt. She just liked to grumble. Diesel thrust up into her.

She gave a soft gasp. "No, you're not."

"No, not really." He held her by the hips and starting moving faster, working in tandem, lifting his hips as he brought her down onto him. The collision between them felt fantastic and he closed his eyes.

Then immediately changed his mind and forced them back open. He wanted to watch her on him. Tuesday, despite her complaining, was clearly enjoying herself. She had lifted her arms and was holding her hair back off her face. The position did great things to her breasts, which bounced a little as he moved inside her. There was no reason not to just explode inside her, so he did exactly that, his fingers digging into her thighs, and a deep guttural groan wrenching out of him.

When he finally relaxed, dropping his head back onto the bed, trying to catch his breath, Tuesday collapsed back down onto his chest.

"Yummy," she said, then yawned.

"Indeed."

"You have a good penis," she told him.

Diesel laughed. She said the funniest damn things. "Thanks, sweetheart. I can't take any credit for it, but I appreciate it."

"I like your tattoo." Her finger ran up and down his side, lightly. "Very badass."

"Thanks. I didn't notice any ink on you. Not your thing?"

Her shoulder lifted in a shrug. "I don't know. I just couldn't ever imagine what I would want on my body permanently. I'm not opposed to it."

Laying there was sticky and comfortable. Diesel felt his own yawn building up and he tried to squelch it. "You want a shower before we sleep?"

Her head lifted and she pulled a face. "Sure, a shower would be good, but I can't sleep. I'm hungry."

"You're hungry?" Was she serious? "It's . . ." He glanced at his cell phone on the nightstand. "Two in the morning."

"I want Chinese food."

"Chinese food? Are you kidding me? You ate like three pieces of pizza and a whole bowl of chips."

She peeled herself off his chest and gave him a cold raised eyebrow stare. "You got a problem with a woman who likes to eat? Would you prefer I be like Jonas Strickland's wife Nikki and carry around a bag of lettuce as my go-to snack?"

Shit. He had sounded like an ass, hadn't he? "No, of course not. I'm just impressed, that's all. Most women wouldn't be confident enough to order Chinese food at two in the morning." He wasn't sure that sounded right either, but what the hell was he supposed to say? He started sweating, trying to think of something better to say.

Tuesday wanted to laugh at the look of fear on Diesel's face. This was the first time she'd ever seen him look at all nervous. It was kind of fun, a refreshing change of pace. She didn't really give a shit what he thought of her eating habits. So she wanted fried rice, what of it? Thanks to her parents, she'd been blessed with a very high metabolism. Between that and working out five days a week, weight wasn't an issue for her. So if post-sex she wanted deep-fried crap, she was going to eat it. But seeing him trying to retreat out of his faux pas was really damn amusing.

"I opened the door completely hungover because I wanted the coffee you had for me. My stomach always takes precedence over vanity." Rolling off of him, sighing a little when their bodies separated, she added, "Besides, a lack of confidence is not my issue."

"What is your issue?"

Like she'd tell him. If she knew what it was, that is. She really wasn't sure what was wrong, aside from the obvious—she was grieving desperately for the loss of her father. It wasn't anything more than that. She didn't think.

She wasn't even sure why her head was going in that direction at all. Maybe it was just that being with Diesel was different. It was intense. It loosened the reins of her control, and that had her spinning out in directions she didn't necessarily want to go. Which wasn't acceptable.

"My issue is that I'm not going to be able to sleep until I've had at least another orgasm." Keep it light. Sexual. Not on real stuff. Because she really was having a hell of a good time and she didn't want that to change.

He studied her for a second, but he went along with her. He said, "That's easy enough. Chinese food. Orgasm. In that order?"

"Yes, in that order. I'm sure you can handle it." Tuesday gave him a lingering kiss with plenty of tongue, before peeling herself off the bed. "Is this the bathroom?" she asked, heading toward the door that looked like the most likely candidate.

"Yep. Are you taking a shower? There are towels under the sink."

"I'm just going to pee."

Diesel laughed.

"What?" she asked, padding carefully across the carpet. With just the one lamp on by the bed, it was a little dark in there and she didn't want to stub her toe. Diesel was incredibly neat though, and there was nothing on the floor that would trip her up. "Real women pee and eat pizza, though not usually at the same time. I hate to break this to you, but it's true—women are human." She opened her mouth in mock horror, even though he probably couldn't see her particularly well. "We even burp!"

He didn't look shocked. "I know. You've already burped in front of me."

"Oh. Right." Tuesday refused to feel embarrassed. "Well, good. You clearly need the reality check."

"And you're clearly here to give it to me." Diesel lolled on his bed, very naked, very relaxed. He opened his mouth and let out a gigantic burp.

Really? Tuesday went into the bathroom before she laughed. What a moron. A very cute, very sexy, very incredible moron.

His bathroom was clean. He either had a maid or he was good with a sponge. Impressive. After using the toilet Tuesday checked herself out in the mirror while she washed her hands. Yep. She was looking like she had been in bed for the last two hours. It was about time. Her hair was a disaster and her skin was flushed and dewy. Or sweaty, however you wanted to look at it.

It was definitely satisfying to see the visual of how she felt.

When she walked back into the bedroom, Diesel was sitting up scrolling through his phone. "I found a place that will deliver at this insane hour."

"Awesome."

He patted a pile of clothes on the bed next to him. "And I got you a T-shirt and a pair of shorts to wear. I figured you won't want to lounge around in riding boots."

It was such a small thing. A normal, thoughtful gesture. But for some reason, Tuesday felt the sudden urge to cry. What the hell was the matter with her? She knew she could be too demanding sometimes. Producing Chinese food in the middle of the night wasn't exactly easy and she had kind of obligated him to at least try. So she didn't really expect that he would be inclined to be additionally thoughtful, yet he was. Stupid that she would react at all, but she couldn't help it. She was.

She hadn't been lying to him when she had told him that she wasn't used to men being anything short of selfish. The one man who had consistently treated her well had been her father and now he was gone.

Ducking her head so he wouldn't see her expression, Tuesday flopped onto the bed next to him. "Thanks. And I'll take orange chicken, please."

"Okey doke."

"Okey doke?" Tuesday shook out the neatly folded T-shirt on the bed. It had a beer logo printed on it. Of course. "Are you going old man on me?"

"Maybe. You've probably aged me ten years in a week."

Tuesday rolled her eyes. "Doing what?" She pulled the shirt on over her head.

Diesel rubbed her thigh as she stretched her legs out to pull on the shorts. "You're a lot of work."

Even though he was teasing her, Tuesday couldn't help but bristle just a smidge. "Screw you."

He just laughed, leaning over to give her a loud, smacking kiss. In the position she was in, she half fell on her side as his weight threw her off balance. Her hands wound up tangled in the nylon shorts under her thighs and her hair was poking her in the eyes. But she was pleased instead of annoyed. Being with Diesel was natural and comfortable. She felt totally at ease, saying whatever she was thinking, not worried about his reaction.

"Let's go outside," she told him. "It's kind of cold in here from the a/c and I bet it's beautiful out now."

"Sure." He dialed a number on his phone. "You're dying to nose around my house, aren't you?"

Duh. "Of course. I'm trying to figure out why one heterosexual man has so many throw pillows."

"The decorator bought all of those. She was a Christmas present from my aunt when I got this house." Then he held up his finger as someone obviously answered the phone.

As he ordered their food, Tuesday played with the waistband of her borrowed basketball shorts. Why was it so damn sexy to wear a man's clothes? But she wanted to wrap her arms around herself and just grin. All those lovely orgasms and now she was wearing his oversized gym clothes. It was a good night.

Five minutes later they were out on his back patio with

Wilma accompanying them, and Tuesday felt even more content. The August night was beautiful. There was a multitude of stars twinkling overhead and the crickets were chatting noisily. Diesel had tossed a match down onto the logs in his fire pit and they were crackling, a sweet smoke rising in the air. There was a chaise that Tuesday would have loved to have snuggled in with Diesel, but she had noticed he was limping. He didn't say anything, obviously, but she didn't want to risk putting pressure on his knee or accidentally bumping it. So she had sat down at the dining table.

It was wrought iron and pressing into her butt, but that was a minor inconvenience. Dragging her legs up onto the seat, she pulled the T-shirt over her knees and rested her chin on her elbows. "It feels awesome out here. This is a beautiful yard."

"Thanks. I like it. I like to go fishing in the pond."

"You have a pond?"

"Yep." He gestured into the blackness. "We can walk down there if you like."

Doing that in the total darkness seemed like a recipe for drowning death. But she didn't want to be a buzz kill. "Maybe another time."

"You afraid of the dark?"

"No. I'm not afraid of anything." Just being alone. Dropping her feet so her legs dangled above the brick patio, she added, "I have no phobias. Heights, spiders, small spaces . . . none of those bother me."

"But a pond does?"

"Who said the pond bothers me?"

"You did."

"I did not!" He liked to mess with her and Tuesday couldn't help it, she walked right into it every single time. "God, where's a throw pillow when you need one?"

"Why would you need a throw pillow?"

"To smother you."

Diesel laughed. He glanced down at his phone as it lit up. "Food must be here. Are you going to drink your crappy beer with it that you insisted we stop for? I can grab it out of the car."

"I'm not drinking that swill. I bought that just to prove a point to you." She stood up. "Give it to your decorator."

"Oh, my God." Diesel stood up as well. "You're a nut, you know that?"

"It's part of my unique charm."

They cut through the garage, the lights going on automatically when Diesel opened the back door. His garage was amazing, a man cave of machinery, car parts, and saw dust. It was the only part of his house she'd seen so far that wasn't completely tidy. It seemed like the garage was where he really lived, where he spent a lot of time. There were empty soda cans lying around and a balled-up McDonald's bag. She was happy to note there were no largely naked women posters hanging up on the walls. There was nothing more deflating than to see an airbrushed blonde in a bikini with leg warmers displayed prominently in an otherwise intelligent man's house.

The delivery guy was holding his arm up to his eyes like the light was blinding him. Tuesday figured they were Captain and Lady Obvious here with their bedhead and 2 A.M. food order. But the man holding the food just gave them a dismissive once-over. She was a little disappointed. What was the point of walking around post-sex with no bra on if the delivery guy wasn't going to be jealous?

"He was checking you out," Diesel said, an edge of annoyance in his voice as they walked back through the garage.

"What? He was not." Tuesday gave him an incredulous look. "He didn't even look at me."

"He was totally checking you out."

Was Diesel actually jealous? She wasn't sure how to feel about that. "Now you're the one who's insane."

"Insane enough to be ordering fried rice at three in the morning."

"How did 2 A.M. become 3 A.M.? And you act like you haven't seen either one in a decade."

"It's possible I haven't."

"Now you really are acting like an old man." His response was to swat her backside. "Ow. Will you stop that? You need to stay away from my butt."

He smirked. "You won't be saying that later."

She wasn't touching that one. "Eat your egg roll."

They sat back at the table and started to eat in companionable silence. Egg roll half in his mouth, Diesel tossed his hair back and reached over and stole her fortune cookie.

"Hey. That's mine." She smacked his wrist with her chopsticks.

"I need it for bribery. You said you'd do anything for cookies."

"Fortune cookies don't count."

"I'm not surprised you know how to use chopsticks." He was using a plastic fork. "You're that kind of woman."

"What kind of woman?" Tuesday shoved a piece of chicken in her mouth.

"The kind of woman who *knows* things." He smiled at her.

She wasn't sure how much she really knew about anything but she did know that smile was going to have her naked again if he didn't stop. It was just so sexy and naughty. "You look like you know a thing or two yourself. That garage has machinery from one end to the other. You could build a nuclear weapon in there."

"Just building cars."

"Rocket ships."

"Cars."

"A time machine."

"Or cars."

"Damn." Tuesday shoved her food aside, full already. "I wanted to go back to ancient Egypt."

"Next weekend."

She laughed. He was just so casual and matter of fact. Regardless of what stupid thing she said, he never got annoyed. He just rolled with it.

Tired of the metal chair pressing into her butt, Tuesday got up and eyed the grass. It looked soft. Flopping down onto it, she laid on her back, arm under her head and stared up at the sky.

"What the hell are you doing?"

"I'm resting. The grass is soft."

"You're going to get bitten up by mosquitoes."

"So? What's a little blood loss when the night is this beautiful. See? Wilma likes it, too." Diesel's dog had roused herself from where she'd been laying on the bricks and came over to nudge Tuesday's arm. After a lick on the cheek, the dog collapsed with a sigh on the grass next to her.

"You're probably both laying in dog shit."

For a second, Tuesday panicked but after a quick inspection she was reassured. "Nothing. We're clear. Quit ruining my fun."

She didn't expect him to join her and he didn't. He was still eating, and laying on the grass didn't really seem like his style. But it was comfortable being together, just hanging out. "What do you think is up there?" she asked, gazing at the inky sky.

"Nothing. Everything. Whatever you want."

"What do you think happens to us when we die?" she asked, her hand lifting his T-shirt to idly scratch her stomach. "Where do we go? And why are there so many of us in such a collective vastness?"

"Big questions." Diesel put down his fork and glanced up at the night. "I don't know where we go but I know we don't just stop existing altogether. When you blow out a candle the flame disappears but the smoke still dissipates . . . maybe that's what we're like."

"How did your mom die?" she asked him quietly, knowing that of all her friends, Diesel was probably the most likely to understand how she felt.

"She had breast cancer. She died six months after her diagnosis."

"I'm sorry. That's terrible."

"Thanks. It's not fair, as you well know."

She hesitated, but then asked it anyway. Diesel didn't seem like the type to get annoyed with her questions. "And your brother?"

"He died of an asthma attack on spring break in Florida with his friends. They were young, didn't understand how serious it was, didn't call for help until it was too late."

"Oh, my God." She rolled on her side, trying to see his expression in the dark. "Diesel, I'm so sorry."

"Yeah, me, too. It was a waste of a wonderful life. Josh was a really good kid. My mom died nine months later. I always wondered if Josh hadn't died if she would have fought harder to survive."

"I wish I could do something," she said. She meant it. She wished she had the power to ease his pain, to bring back his family, her father. Where was that time machine when you needed it?

"You know what you could do?"

"What?" Tuesday scratched behind Wilma's ears, enjoying the comfort of the warm doggie body next to her.

"You could call me Daniel from time to time. I miss that."

That touched her. Tremendously. "I could do that." He was the kind of man who, here in the dark, the warm summer breeze drifting over her, she knew she could really fall for. And it didn't even feel particularly scary. "How did you get your nickname anyway?"

"I'm not telling you that, Toot."

Tuesday groaned. "God, don't call me that."

"Then you shouldn't have told me." Diesel stood up, gathering the remnants of their meal. "Come on, Toot, let's go to bed."

She liked the sound of that, even with the dumb childhood nickname tacked onto it.

CHAPTER
EIGHT

DIESEL could have let her just fall asleep. They could have cuddled and left it at that.

But the minute he saw her crawling across his bed on all fours toward the pillow he decided he wasn't quite ready to let her sleep. He hadn't been expecting a week earlier that he would have Tuesday in his bed and he wasn't sure that he ever would again, so he figured he might as well enjoy every second of it.

"Ah, I can't wait to go to sleep." Tuesday pulled back the covers.

Diesel grabbed her thighs to hold her in place before she scooted under and disappeared from his view. His basketball shorts were hanging loosely on her and he liked that she was wearing his clothes. It made him feel territorial, something he had no business feeling, but there it was. And he was going to pull those down and thrust into her from behind, where he could see the curve of her tight ass surrounding him.

"What?" she asked. "Is something wrong?"

His response was to yank those shorts down to her thighs. "I'm not ready to sleep yet."

"No?" Her tone had changed from curious to intrigued.

"No." The minute he saw her bare skin in front of him as she was on all fours he had an idea. "Stay just like that. Don't move."

"Yes, sir," she said, her tone so filled with arousal Diesel almost changed his mind and plunged into her.

But instead he stuck to his original thought and went over to the dresser and retrieved the riding hat she'd been wearing earlier and the crop. Bending over, he grabbed her boots off the floor and brought it all to the bed. Amazingly, she was still exactly as he'd left her, up on all fours, facing front.

He lifted each of her knees and pulled the shorts off of her completely. She sucked in a breath with his first touch, and he enjoyed the sound of it. She didn't know what he was going to do or where he was going to touch, yet she was completely letting him take control. He found that hot as hell.

"Sit up and take your shirt off."

She did, without hesitation, her long arms lifting in the air, her back a smooth expanse of pale skin, her waist dipping in. Diesel slid his hands along her curves, his body tight with anticipation.

He put the hat on her head. "Now back on all fours."

As he pulled his jeans off, she paused, her eyebrows raised as she glanced at him over her shoulder.

"What am I, a horse?" she asked with a sniff of disdain.

"No, not at all." Diesel took the crop and ran the handle across the bare flesh of her backside, watching the goose bumps raise on her skin. "But if you were, you'd be a wild horse. That needs to be broken."

He meant it as playful, as sexy bedroom talk, and he hoped she would take it that way. When he moved the crop between her legs, letting the handle rub against her clitoris as he drew it back and forth, back and forth between her thighs, he felt her tense.

Unsure of what that meant, he paused, giving her the opportunity to yell at him or protest or give him the affirmative that she was willing to play the game.

She tossed her hair over her shoulder as she turned to look at him, her eyes glassy and her lips apart. "Then I guess you'd better put me through my paces."

Tuesday had always liked men who took charge in the bedroom and she had always attributed it to laziness on her part. It was easy to let them steer the ship of sex.

But with Diesel it was totally difference. When he moved that crop between her legs, and gave her commands with a smoldering look, his tone suggesting he expected her obedience, she found it incredibly arousing. Her nipples were tight, her inner thighs humming in anticipation, her shoulders tense. She wasn't always easy to get along with, she knew that, but here, she could forget her natural need to spar and to get in the last word. She could do whatever he wanted and the last word would be an orgasm.

Diesel tweaked her nipple, then pushed her back down onto all fours. The hat slipped on her head and fell onto her forehead, but she didn't bother to fix it. "Boots?" she asked breathlessly, suddenly completely into the idea of wearing nothing but the riding accessories. And what man didn't want to bang a woman wearing boots?

"Roll over and pull them on."

He sounded so urgent that Tuesday was already moving onto her back before his sentence was over. He was stripping his jeans off and she got a nice view of his jutting erection. Grabbing a boot, Tuesday yanked it on, her leg up in front of his chest.

Diesel paused in removing his pants and tilted his head. She knew exactly where he was looking. Right between her thighs.

"Now that is a million-dollar view," he told her.

She bet it was. Switching legs and drawing on the other boot, Tuesday licked her lips. "Why, thank you."

Once the boots were on, Diesel hooked his hands under her knees and hauled them up. He ran the crop over her sex, the tip swirling around her clitoris. Tuesday's mouth went hot with saliva and anticipation. For a second, as he trailed it down lower, she thought he was going to push the end into her, and she tensed, both intrigued and a little nervous at the thought.

But he didn't. He tossed it to the side. "You're being so good, I don't think I need this."

She didn't have time to respond before he was inside her. Tuesday closed her eyes on a moan, the sensation delightful as he filled her. She could get used to this.

"I can't believe how sexy you are," he told her.

She couldn't believe how hot he was. As he moved over her, his biceps taut, hair falling in his eyes, tattoo marching up his side, she came so quickly it took her completely by surprise. She barely had time to grab his arm for support before her back was lifting off the bed as she exploded.

The intensity of his gaze only added to her pleasure and she stared up at him, amazed that she could be so open, so willing with a man. But it felt sensual, natural with Diesel, and when he lifted her ankles in those riding boots onto his shoulders, she refused to close her eyes, no matter how amazing it felt.

She wanted to watch him as he came.

And he did, just a few strokes later, his jaw clenched, fingers digging into her waist, eyes dark with desire, her black boots bouncing on either side of his face.

Yeah, she could definitely get used to this.

IT had been a very long time since Diesel had woken up with a woman in his bed, and he had to admit, he liked it. It was Sunday morning, the sun was streaming in his bedroom window, Wilma was softly snoring at his feet, and Tuesday was snuggled up against his chest.

He certainly didn't mind being alone, but there was something to be said for having the right to touch another person. Just running his fingers along her back felt good. Tuesday woke up the same way she did everything—with lots of words. She was saying something about the hair on his legs and he was only half listening. Normally he did find her interesting and entertaining but it was too early, so he just nodded occasionally and let her do her thing.

"I'm hungry."

Of course she was. "Why does that not surprise me? I

think you have a tapeworm. It's the only explanation for how you can eat so much and be so damn skinny."

"That's the most beautiful thing you've ever said to me."

"You're welcome."

Tuesday yawned and sat up. "But unfortunately I need to go. I have to watch the race. Sundays are not my day off."

Diesel remembered that all too well. "Sucks to be you. I can stay in bed all day long if I want to." Not that doing so by himself sounded all that appealing. Not after having Tuesday draped across him. Tuesday under him. He felt an erection stirring to life.

She was well aware of it, too, because she dropped her hand down onto him and squeezed. "Ooh, don't tempt me. I really do have to go."

"Then quit touching it." Or he was going to make her late. He leaned over to kiss her, wondering if he could talk her into a quickie.

But she squawked and rolled away from him. "No, I'm resisting you and your penis." She stood up and stretched.

Diesel let her go without a fight, not wanting to be responsible for interfering with her work. But she came out of the bathroom, her clothes bundled in her arms, back in his T-shirt and shorts, but now clearly with a bra on, he was tempted to tumble her back onto the bed with him. "Shit. I just realized I have to drive you home."

"Being a gentleman is a pain in the ass, isn't it?" she told him, smirking. "I told you I should have met you at the church last night."

Giving a mighty yawn, he forced himself out of bed. "No."

"No, what?"

"Just no."

He pulled jeans and a T-shirt on and he was ready. "Alright, let's go."

"Can I wear your clothes home?"

"Of course. Though I'd kind of like to see you wear the riding boots with my basketball shorts."

"No, thanks." She headed down the hall. "Can Wilma go with us?"

"Sure. But she'll want to sit on your lap."

"That's fine."

Most women didn't like his dog. Wilma was big and slobbery and on the jealous side. Yet she and Tuesday seemed to really dig each other.

They went through a drive-thru for his coffee and for a breakfast sandwich for Tuesday. He did like that she had an appetite. He wouldn't have to feel guilty if he ever wanted ice cream. Assuming they saw each other again. Which he definitely wanted to happen.

"So you busy next weekend?" he asked her as he pulled into the parking lot of her apartment building.

"No."

"Want to do something?" He wasn't one to beat around the bush.

She smiled, then leaned around Wilma and gave him a kiss. "I'd like that, Daniel. Give me a call."

Then she was out of the car and he was left sitting there with his dog, wanting an aspirin for his knee and for her to be back in his passenger seat.

"Wilma, I may be in trouble here."

His dog licked his face before giving a bark.

"Tell me about it."

Tuesday reached the door to her apartment and turned back. She waved to him with her crop, a grin on her face.

Oh, yeah. He was in trouble.

TUESDAY stared at the three manila folders in front of her, a thumb drive resting on the stack, and tried to force herself to open one of them. Inside was the last article her father had been working on before he'd gotten too sick to use his computer. The sports editor had asked her to finish it as an homage to her father.

She couldn't even bring herself to look at it. She didn't know what it was even about. She just knew she couldn't handle it. So she ignored it. Again. Opening up her word processing program, she stared at the blank screen, at a loss for an idea of what to write for her daily blog. It didn't have to be elaborate, just newsworthy or at least gossip-worthy. But all she could think about was that she had been in Diesel Lange's bed and had the sore vagina to prove it.

It wasn't a productive line of thought.

Yet it was the only one she had. Sipping her now-cold coffee, Tuesday made a face. She needed to troll the Internet and see what was going on in the world of racing. Or she could just continue to stare at the screen and remember what it felt like to come at the hands, or tongue actually, of a very skilled man.

There was a knock on her door. Given that it was Sunday, it couldn't be a deliveryman so she was betting it was either her next-door neighbor, who frequently got bored with his retirement and wanted to chat with her, or Diesel. Which meant it had to be her neighbor, because why in the world would Diesel be at her door twenty minutes after he'd dropped her off?

He wouldn't and she was a lunatic for letting her hopes jump up for even a split second.

Glancing at the manila envelopes again as she headed toward the door to answer it, she had a disturbing thought. What if she were distracted by Diesel as a way to distract herself from her father? That would really make her one messed-up chick, which she refused to believe. Diesel was plenty distracting all on his own.

She opened the door and discovered her mother standing on the other side, a basket in her hand.

"Hi, sweetie, I brought you lunch." Her mother breezed in, fluffing her short gray hair with an elegant hand.

Tuesday's heart sank. Seeing her mother made her feel guilty. Her mother had lost twenty pounds in the months since her husband's diagnosis, and she had been thin to begin with. She'd stopped dyeing her hair and had abandoned her Pilates class. Tuesday thought she looked fragile, tenuous, and that upset her. It upset her even more to realize that she hadn't called her mother in days because she didn't know how to deal with her own grief, let alone her mother's.

"Hi, Mom." She leaned in and kissed her mother on the cheek. "You didn't have to do that."

"Keeping busy is good for me." Her mother gave a brief smile. "Besides, I've baked every other day for the last two weeks. I need someone to give all these desserts to."

Her mother had always been the type who headed to the kitchen when she was stressed or upset. Tuesday preferred her own method of turning to liquor but she did understand where her mom was coming from. "Mom, you know I love dessert, but don't you think eventually all the butter and sugar you ply me with will catch up with me?"

"No. You have my metabolism and it's never caught up with me."

"That's true. In fact, you could stand to gain back about ten pounds." Tuesday opened the basket. There were chicken salad sandwiches, fruit, and brownies inside. Her mouth started to water.

"So I hear you had a date," her mother said, ignoring the weight comment.

Brownie halfway to her mouth, Tuesday paused. "How on earth do you know that?" The woman was a little scary.

"I hear things. So how was night at the races? And more important, how was Diesel Lange?"

She so didn't want to go into this with her mother. "It was fine. He was fine. He's nice and we're friends." Who did wicked naked things to each other in the dark.

"Well, that's good. I heard he was at the wedding brunch with you as well. Does this mean we can finally start planning a wedding of our own?"

Tuesday swallowed the brownie bite she'd been chewing with no small degree of difficulty. "That's a hell of a leap. Don't pull out any bridal magazines just yet. I'm not even sure I'll be seeing him again." He had asked her out again, but men did that all the time. When you would be just fine walking away after a night together they had to ruin it by claiming they wanted to see you again and would call you. Then didn't do either. Now that she thought about it, they hadn't even talked about a day, let alone a time or place.

Suddenly feeling glum, Tuesday took another bite of the brownie.

"You like him, don't you?" Her mother studied her.

"I guess. Who knows?" Yes, she was well aware she sounded petulant but she didn't want to talk about the reality of dating with her mother. She just wanted to lay on the couch and daydream about her and Diesel's sexcapades. What they had done. All the things they could do. Fun stuff like that.

"I worry about you, Tuesday."

Oh, Lord. Like she needed that guilt heaped on her. "You don't need to worry about me. If anyone should be worrying it should be me worrying about you."

"You don't need to worry about me." But even as she spoke, tears welled up in her mother's eyes. "Your father was so proud of you, you know."

Tuesday's throat tightened up. "I know."

"You were the best of both worlds—his beautiful daughter, but also like a son. That's why we only had one child. You were everything we could have asked for."

Her mother was acting like she was the one who had died. Uncomfortable with the conversation, Tuesday picked at the front of Diesel's T-shirt, which she was still wearing. "I tried to be a good daughter."

"Do you remember that time we went to the lake? You must have been about seven years old. Your father took you fishing and he was so proud because you caught one bigger than anyone else on the water that day."

She nodded. She did remember that trip. She'd been thrilled to be spending alone time with her dad. "He was a great father."

"He used to wear his lucky T-shirt fishing. I wonder

what happened to that shirt?" Without warning, her mother's face crumpled.

Tuesday's heart crawled up her throat. "It's okay." She wrapped her mother in a hug. What she was finding harder to deal with than she had expected was that her mother seemed to want to cope with grief by talking about her husband. Whereas Tuesday wasn't ready yet. She just wasn't. She wanted to bury her sacred memories until she could bring them out without bawling and losing control. "I'm sorry, Mom."

Her mother recovered quickly, pulling back and waving her off. "I have the disabled veterans coming to the house tomorrow to pick up all your father's clothes. No sense in them collecting dust. But those T-shirts he wore when he was sick, those I just threw out. No one should have to wear those, no matter how many times they're washed, or how in need a person is."

Tuesday's gut started to churn unpleasantly. She wondered desperately how long her mom planned to stay. She was tired and way too vulnerable to have this conversation. "Do you need me to come over and help you box things up?"

"Oh, no, I already sorted through everything." Her mother turned and finished emptying the basket. "I'll head on out of here."

"Aren't you going to stay and eat with me?"

"No, I'm not hungry."

Tuesday debated arguing, but her mother's hand was shaking slightly and she didn't want to upset her further. "Oh, okay. Well, thanks for lunch, Mom. It looks awesome. Let me know if you need anything."

Her mother turned and then frowned. "Those shorts look terrible on you. Where did you get them?"

Willing her cheeks not to turn pink, Tuesday shrugged. "I was at the gym. They're comfortable." That much was true at least if not the first part.

"Alright. Love you." Her mother waved.

"Love you, too."

"Oh, and I'm having a mass said for your father for the two-month anniversary . . . it was the soonest one I could get. Can you make it?"

Trying not to blanch, Tuesday nodded. "Of course." She'd rather tear out all her eyelashes, but for her mother, she'd force herself to go.

With a smile, like the past ten minutes had been therapeutic for her, her mother waved again and left. Tuesday just felt drained. Avoiding the manila envelopes and her computer, she flopped facedown on the couch. But images just kept assaulting her, first of her father on that fishing trip, then him sick, and on his deathbed. Then even worse, she thought about Diesel and how hot sex with him had been, and what a nice guy he was, and then she felt like an appalling human being. Who is so selfish as to think about getting their rocks off when they had just lost a parent?

She was, clearly.

Forcing herself to the computer, she checked on the live race standings. Neither Kendall nor Evan seemed to be having a particularly good run out there on the track. Elec Monroe was in first place with two hundred laps down. She started to type her blog, making her predictions for finishes when she did it again, found herself just staring at the screen.

She wondered if Diesel missed racing. Wondered if he rethought through his accident, thinking he could have done something different. She suspected she would do just that. But maybe not Diesel. He didn't seem like the type for regrets. Then again, how well did she really know him?

Not as well as she thought she would like to know him.

Banging her head on the keyboard, she wondered exactly how long she would have to wait for him to call her.

Because it had only been two hours and she was exhausted.

DIESEL almost never agreed to go on the golf outings his old friends were constantly inviting him to, but today he'd said yes, even though his knee was acting up. Today, he felt a little lonely. His house suddenly felt empty since Tuesday had spent the night, and he was annoyed by that feeling. So despite the fact that it was about a thousand degrees outside and he'd had to take two pain pills, he was standing on the green next to Ryder Jefferson and Ty McCordle, who managed to look a little bit redneck even on the golf course.

"Where are the Monroe boys?" he asked.

"Evan got a call that the girl he knocked boots with, Nikki's friend Sara, is giving birth right now in Kentucky."

Diesel whistled. "That's a big deal. He sure it's his?" Last Diesel had heard, there was some whispering going on that maybe it wasn't.

"No. Sara admitted she wasn't sure. That's why she went back home, to sort some things out and have her baby with family around. She seemed like a nice enough girl," Ty said.

"She and Evan were both a little bit drunk that night and I think they're handling the situation as best they can. Evan wants to make sure she and the baby are okay then he's sending off his DNA."

"That's a tough spot to be in." One Diesel was glad he had never encountered. Though he had been damn irresponsible the other night, he had to admit. Since when was he stupid enough to just trust a woman who said she was on birth control?

But he did trust Tuesday. Which did make him stupid.

"I feel kinda responsible," Ryder said.

"How the hell do you figure that?" Ty asked. "You didn't stick his dick in her, did you?"

There was an image.

Ryder studied his shot, taking multiple swings. "Don't be disgusting. No, I just mean we were all on that camping trip. Sara was there because Nikki came to check on Jonas. And Suzanne got roped into being there and we went off alone together . . . and you and Imogen went off into your tent. Nikki and Jonas likewise. I mean, what was the poor guy supposed to do?"

"Carry condoms. I always did in my single days. I imagine you do the same, Lange."

Hardly. Before last week, Diesel hadn't been getting any, and when he finally had, he hadn't used a condom any more than Evan Monroe apparently had. Which made him suddenly anxious. What if Tuesday had gotten pregnant? But he just nodded because it was the expected response.

"You know, my wife got pregnant on that same camping trip. How bizarre is that? Something in the air that night. I'm surprised Imogen didn't pop up pregnant, too."

Ty blanched. "We haven't even walked down the aisle yet. I am not ready for a baby."

Neither was Diesel, he had to say. It was a risk, but he decided to run a question past his friends. They might mock him, but he was needing some advice and reassurance. "So hey, say you asked a girl out for the weekend and she said yes. How soon do you call her to make some definite plans?" Because suddenly he was experiencing all kinds of irritating doubts.

"Well, I'll be dipped. Diesel has a girl." Ryder grinned. "Never thought I'd see the day."

"Is she hot?" Ty asked. "I think that factors in to how soon you call her."

"Of course she's hot. You think he'd be getting this worked up if she was butt ugly?"

"I don't know. He could just be desperate."

"This isn't helping." Diesel rolled his eyes.

"Who is it? Anyone we know?"

Shifting in his golf shoes, Diesel debated for a solid sixty seconds whether or not he should tell them the truth.

"Oh, come on." Ryder narrowed his eyes. "Don't you trust us, man?"

Fine. "It's Tuesday Jones."

Ty whistled. "Little Miss Tuesday Talladega? The biggest mouth in stock car reporting? You got bigger cojones than I realized, Lange."

"I don't think she has that big of a mouth." Which even Diesel realized was a load a crap. Tuesday was *the* mouth, at least in her personal life. He couldn't claim to have followed her journalism career all that closely.

Both of his buddies laughed.

"Now that I know we're talking about Tuesday, I say you call her today. If you wait until Friday, she'll tell you to go fuck yourself," was Ryder's opinion.

That was possible. "You don't think she'll think I'm a loser if I call too soon?"

"You *are* a loser."

"Thanks, you guys are a big help."

Ty clapped him on the back. "No problem."

"That was sarcasm."

Ryder pulled out his phone and checked the screen. "Whoa, holy shit. I need to cut this short, boys. My wife thinks she's in labor."

"Tell Suzanne she's got lousy timing." But Ty clapped him on the back. "Good luck, brother."

Diesel took the club Ryder was shoving at him. "Let us know when the baby's born. Congrats, man."

They sent a panicked-looking Ryder back to the country club with the golf cart and Ty and Diesel finished their eighteen holes. When they were walking back, Diesel decided to text Tuesday.

Friday or Saturday. Your choice.

She liked bold. Direct. No playing around.

Are you freaking kidding me?

Not the answer he'd been expecting.

No. Not kidding.

A how are you would be nice.

A little embarrassed, he wasn't sure what to say. He certainly wasn't going to ask Ty for advice. He'd never hear the end of it.

After a second, he wrote, *How are you?*

Her response to that was an emoticon of someone sticking their tongue out. Damn it. He should have just called her. That was bold. Direct. Not a text message. But he had to wait until Ty was gone before he could.

"How are the wedding plans going?" he asked Ty.

Ty shook his head. "I don't understand why it takes so damn long to plan a wedding. It's just totally beyond me. But it's what Imogen wants, so there it is."

Diesel wanted to ask him if he was happy, but the truth was, he could tell Ty was very happy. His face lit up whenever he mentioned his fiancée and it was clear he was incredibly proud of her. Maybe he did want that for himself. Maybe he'd been fooling himself when he kept repeating that he was content being alone.

"You're down to the wire now, huh?"

"Yep. Right before Christmas." Ty grinned. "At the risk of sounding like a girl, I'm excited. Can't wait to call her my wife."

"You're a lucky man." Diesel paused then dropped the dig Ty was expecting. "Even if you are really just a girl."

"Looks who's talking. Your hair looks like Farrah Fawcett's, circa 1978. You need a haircut."

"I've thought about it. Never quite get around to it." Now he didn't see himself pursuing it at all since Tuesday had mentioned how much she liked it on the longer side.

They walked in silence for another minute, the sun warming the back of his neck.

Then Ty said, "Tuesday Jones, huh? Really?"

"Yep." Tuesday Jones. She had definitely gotten under his skin. Diesel had been having trouble concentrating on anything other than how she had felt beneath him, her soft moans of pleasure one of the sweetest sounds he'd ever heard.

"Go figure."

"Yeah. Sort of like you and Imogen. Go figure." The minute the words were out of his mouth, Diesel realized that made it sound like he was as serious about Tuesday as Ty was about his future wife. He opened his mouth to somehow downplay the statement, or distract Ty, but it was too late.

His friend broke into a huge grin. "So that's where it's at, huh?" He clapped Diesel on the back. "Well, enjoy yourself. And wear a condom."

Could he have any more reasons to squirm? They reached the club. "I have to make a phone call. I'll catch you later."

Ty made a kissy face in his direction. "Go call your girl-friend."

Diesel laughed, despite his worry. "You're an ass. What are you, twelve years old?"

"That's not what my bank account says." Ty gave him a wave and went on into the building.

Diesel called Tuesday, hoping she would actually answer. She did.

"Hello?"

"Hey, how are you doing?" Her hello sounded belligerent and he felt like an ass. Maybe the bottom line was she just didn't want to go out with him again.

"I'm fine. Tired. I didn't get much sleep last night."

A little bit of a flirt had crept into her voice and he instantly felt much better. "That's funny. Neither did I. So would you like to not get any sleep on Friday night?" His gut told him to pick a day and give her the right of refusal, not to let her make the initial plans.

"I think I can swing that."

He debated asking her why she had sent him a tongue sticking out but he decided to leave it the hell alone. She was agreeing to see him, that's all that mattered. "Great. Is it Friday yet?"

She laughed, that low throaty sound that was like fingers caressing him. "Pick me up at nine. I'm hanging out with Kendall earlier."

"Where are we going?"

"Does it matter?"

"No." It definitely didn't. Diesel was starting to feel like he would follow Tuesday just about anywhere for that matter. Stopping off at a bed on the way.

BABY BOOM BY TUESDAY TALLADEGA

The world of racing expanded this week with the birth of Ryder Jefferson's first child with his wife, Suzanne. The newest Jefferson made his debut in the wee hours of Tuesday morning, weighing in at an impressive 8.9 pounds. Little Track (no, I'm not kidding, that's what they named him) is doing fine despite being saddled with the ultimate of ironic monikers. Expect him to be kicking ass on the asphalt by the time he's five.

Also giving birth this past Sunday was one Sara Parker, who made headlines back in the spring when she announced the father of her unborn child was Evan Monroe, one whole week after his marriage to rookie driver Kendall Holbrook. Oops on the timing. But it turns out Evan is not the father after all, as DNA test results proved this morning. Double oops. But hey, props to Evan for sticking by her side until the results came back, and not unleashing a pack of lawyers until anyone knew what was what. That's the way to man up and stick by your di— ahem, decisions.

Tuesday didn't know what to say to Kendall, who was tearing up and cuddling with a throw pillow. "I think it's totally normal to have conflicting feelings. This was a really stressful thing to go through. Don't beat yourself up over it."

"But I feel so guilty. I mean, I was hoping all along that this baby wasn't Evan's."

"I think any woman in your position would have felt the same way. I mean come on, you just get married and like two seconds later some chick he slept with announces she's pregnant?" Tuesday was pretty sure she would have been chomping at the bit for paternity testing to be done even before the baby's birth.

"You're the one who told me that I was being stupid for shutting Evan out."

Now who felt guilty? Tuesday folded her feet under her thighs as she sat on the easy chair across from Kendall. They didn't get to spend a whole lot of time hanging out given Kendall's busy schedule, but her best friend was headed to the airport for this weekend's race, and had asked to stop by on her way. Tuesday was happy to be an ear for her, even though she couldn't really do anything to help Kendall. She needed to work through her emotions on her own, unfortunately, but Tuesday could listen and be supportive.

"Kendall, that was two different things, and I was in a bad place. I'd just found out my dad was dying." And she had taken it out on Kendall, yelling at her for breaking things off with her new husband when she'd found out about Sara's baby. At the time, all Tuesday had been able to think was that life was clearly too damn short and no one should give up someone they love so easily. But she hadn't handled it in the best way possible. "I'm sorry for the way I just yelled at you. That wasn't what you needed."

"I think it was exactly what I needed. I needed you to remind me that I had lost Evan once, and did I really want to do that again? So we wound up together, thank God, and it's been amazing. But knowing that he was possibly going to have a child, well, that was hard to deal with, I'm not gonna lie. I think every woman wants to be the first to give her husband a child. I was jealous. And unsure what my role would be in the baby's life."

"All totally understandable."

"But now, I just feel bad that it's not Evan's baby. Like I willed it that way."

"Well, you didn't. It's not Evan's baby because she slept with two guys around the same time. Which happens sometimes. Is he disappointed?" Personally, Tuesday figured he'd just have to get the hell over it. In the long run, this was going to be better for everyone involved.

"Yeah, he is, though he's not saying much. But I think a part of him had gotten really excited about being a father and now it's gone."

"Well, it's not like the two of you can't have kids."

Kendall shrugged. "I know. But not now, not while my career is just taking off. I'm a little disappointed, too, in some small way. I was having baby fantasies, which is so stupid. There would have been nothing simple about that parenting arrangement."

"No. Especially since Sara got married herself in the meantime." Again, probably the best-case scenario for everyone involved. "Her husband isn't the father either, so talk about an emotional and legal mess for all four of you. Not to mention what the kid would have felt like when she got older."

Swiping at her eyes, Kendall nodded vehemently. "You're right. You're absolutely right. This way Sara has no ties with the true biological father, who apparently signed away all rights months ago when she contacted him, and her baby has a stable home life with two parents, no joint custody or anything like that."

"You still have your nieces and nephews if you want to get your mommy fix in." Tuesday personally wasn't ready for motherhood and was pretty sure she would lay an egg if she found out she was expecting a baby. She liked kids, just when they belonged to other people. Which means going without a condom with Diesel had been stupid. She had learned long ago from other people that it was always better to be safe than sorry, which meant doubling up on the birth control. Sperm were tricky, and she planned to have a lot of sex with Diesel.

"Yeah. I know. All's well that ends well, I guess. After four months of emotional ups and downs, it's done." Kendall tossed the pillow back onto the couch. "So how are you?"

"I'm fine." Tuesday thought she actually was, most of the time. She was coping by not really coping. Ignoring would work for the time being and she figured she wasn't the first person to have dealt with a loss that way. Plus she was going out with Diesel again, so she was actually looking forward to that. "Thanks for letting me run that little blurb about the baby. It would have looked odd if I hadn't, but I appreciate you giving me the go-ahead."

Kendall messed with her ponytail, trying to shove some blond strands that had escaped back into it. "That's exactly it. It would have looked weird. And what you wrote was kind, so I should be thanking you. A lot of other journalists would have trashed Evan. And me, for that matter."

"Evan handled it the right way. I was just telling it like it is."

"By the way, I saw you didn't hold back on Ryder and Suzanne's choice of baby names."

Tuesday rolled her eyes. She was not going to feel bad for that one. "Well, come on. I really like both of them as people, you know that, and Suzanne and I had a little chat and came to an understanding after I commented on Ryder's love life way back when. I consider her a friend. But they just left the door wide open."

Kendall made a face. "God, I hate to admit it, but they really did. But knowing Suzanne, it was probably intentional irony. A big middle finger to the world. Truthfully, I think it's a cute name."

"It would be if his father wasn't a stock car driver." She knew what she was talking about here. "Trust me, it sucks to have an odd name. I spent my whole childhood being mocked for being named after a weekday."

"Kids are going to pick on other kids no matter what. You're dating a man named Diesel, which I have to say is worse than Track."

Tuesday bristled, tugging her shorts down from where

they had hiked up into her crotch. It was not worse. Diesel was a cute name. "That's a nickname! His real name is Daniel. And for the record, we're not dating. We're seeing each other."

"Explain the difference in that to me." Kendall grinned. "Especially given how you just leaped to his defense."

"I did not." Maybe she had. "But seriously, a racing nickname is not the same as a given name."

"How did he get that nickname anyway?"

"I don't know. He hasn't told me." Truthfully, Diesel didn't share a whole lot of his thoughts with her. She didn't know anything about the accident from him directly and he had only told her about his mother and brother when she had asked him straight out. That was typical for most men she could stand being around—they were closed off. The ones who verbally vomited all their feelings usually turned out to be whiners. Or they gave her information braggart style so that it came off as a lecture. Neither really did it for her. But she had to admit, she did want to know Diesel better. She had a feeling there were some interesting thoughts rolling around in that head of his.

"You like him, don't you?"

"Well, duh. I guess I wouldn't be sleeping with him if I didn't like him."

"Yeah, but there's a difference between liking him well enough and *liking* him." Kendall was studying her so intently it was unnerving. "I think you like him more than any other guy I've ever seen you with."

It felt like Kendall was accusing her of a crush. Having deeper feelings than she did. Yeah, she enjoyed him, but it wasn't like she was picking out china or naming their children. "Then clearly I haven't liked enough men in my life. Which only goes to show that the pool of interesting men is in reality the size of a partially evaporated puddle."

"So you admit you like him?"

Her friend was starting to annoy her. "I'm not admitting anything." Her cell phone rang on the coffee table and she ignored it, recognizing her mom's ringtone.

"You can answer that."

"It's my mom. I'll call her back later."

"Why can't you just admit that maybe, even though you just met Diesel, this could be different?"

"Because it's not. You know me. I'm very good at dating with a cool head. I can separate my emotions. I can have casual sex. I can walk away from a guy who's not good for me and not regret it. Falling for someone after three days together is flaky. I'm not flaky."

"Maybe for once you should let yourself be flaky. There is something legitimate about instant attractions . . . I'm not talking love at first sight. Nor am I talking about pure lust. I mean when you meet someone and that spark is there. It's both physical and intellectual. It's like every time they smile you feel it in your hoohah, and every time they say something *you* smile because it's funny or insightful or exactly how you feel about it."

Tuesday undid her legs and drew her knees up to her chest so she could hug them. She didn't want to have this conversation at all. Maybe because if she stopped and thought about it, she would have to admit that she might be feeling exactly what Kendall was describing. When Diesel smiled, her inner thighs burned. When he spoke, she smiled. Or maybe more in her case, she rolled her eyes and tried not to laugh, which was the same implicit approval.

Shit. Damn. Hell.

She liked him.

"You suck," she told Kendall.

Her best friend laughed. "What? I just speak the truth and you might as well enjoy it instead of fighting it."

"How am I supposed to enjoy it now that I have to worry that I might fall for him?" Tuesday rubbed her palms on her legs vigorously, frustrated. "Ugh. I don't need this."

"Will you relax?" Kendall stood up. "Go take your shower and get all sexified for Diesel. I'm going to pick up my husband then catch our plane to Atlanta."

"Good luck in the race." Tuesday forced herself to stand up.

"Thanks. And thanks for letting me talk about the baby."

"No problem." For some reason, a lump rose in Tuesday's throat. She was so glad she was friends with Kendall. They had been there for each other through the good and the bad. "I'm always here, you know that."

"I know. Likewise." Kendall gave her a hug then she headed out.

Tuesday sighed, torn between excitement over seeing Diesel and dread. She did not need to fall head over ass for him and then have him turn out to be a douche bag, or worse, be awesome but dump her anyway. That would really screw with her right now, and she couldn't deal with it. But if she kept a little distance, she could enjoy the fabulous sex and his company and not get hurt.

She hoped.

Picking up her phone, she played her mom's voice mail.

"Hi, hon, it's Mom. I just wanted to let you know that I won't be able to see you tomorrow after all. Tom Reynolds and I are seeing each other."

Tuesday made a face, her gut clenching. Tom Reynolds was her mother's high school sweetheart, the one she used to joke around about and say was the one who had gotten away. Of course, she'd been kidding, but it had always bugged Tuesday, even if it hadn't seemed to irritate her father. And what was this "seeing each other" crap? Did her mother mean that they were just physically seeing each other for lunch or something, or did she mean they were dating?

What the fuckity fuck.

Suddenly feeling like she couldn't breathe, Tuesday played the message again. She wasn't sure what to think. Her mother sounded happy, maybe even a little giddy. Definitely not like a grieving widow. Was her mother seriously dating again just four freaking weeks after her husband had died?

She did need to get in the shower before her date with Diesel, but all she could do for a solid minute was stand there with her phone in her shaking hand. Should she listen to the message again? Call her mom and clarify?

No, she couldn't do that. If her mother said no, she would feel like shit for suspecting that and for insulting her mother's feelings for her father. If she said yes, well, Tuesday knew she couldn't handle that at all.

So she couldn't call her mom.

What she could do was have a drink before the shower.

Tuesday headed to the kitchen and her liquor cabinet.

CHAPTER
NINE

RYDER debated whether or not to show his wife what Tuesday had written about their choice in baby names, but he figured Suzanne was going to find out sooner or later and it might as well not be in public.

At the moment, she was nursing their son on the couch in their new house, her hair tousled, but looking amazing. Beautiful. Content. Ryder got an inflated feeling in his chest every time he looked at the two of them together. Track was a tiny little picture perfect blend of the two of them, and yet he had almost never happened. Ryder and Suzanne had been divorced, for all practical if not legal purposes. Now here they were, less than a year later, married all over again, with a new house and a baby boy. There wasn't a goddamn thing left in the world he could ask for.

But Suzanne was going to be pissed when she saw Tuesday's blog, no doubt about it.

"Hey beautiful," he told her, kissing her on the top of the head. Leaning over, he smoothed a finger over Track's cheek and smiled when his mouth moved in a sucking motion. His son glanced up at him, and Ryder felt his gut clench. He didn't want to leave, even though he had to.

"You all set for your flight?" his wife asked him, giving him a smile.

"Yeah, I guess so. I wish I didn't have to go. Are you sure you're going to be okay?" Suzanne had taken to motherhood with ease and she looked confident and very happy.

"I'll be fine. I have all my girlfriends around if I need to call for advice, and your mom said she'll be here tomorrow by two." She glanced up at him as he hovered in front of her. "Something bothering you?"

"I just don't want to leave both of you." Ryder had known it was going to be difficult to travel every weekend once the baby was born, but he hadn't realized just how hard it would be to tear himself away, especially when his son was only four days old. "And just so you know, Tuesday Jones announced Track's birth. And she poked fun at his name."

Ryder expected Suzanne to bristle but she just laughed. "I figured she would. No big deal, it's her job to call 'em like she sees 'em. And people are going to think his name is dumb." She looked down at Track. "But your mama will just tell them to go suck it, yes, she will. They can suck it hard. We don't give a fat rat's ass what they think."

It was odd to hear his wife sounding just like his wife, but in a singsong mommy voice. Ryder laughed. "You're something else, you know that?"

"That something better be a good thing."

"It is. Trust me, it is."

She lifted the baby off her breast to burp him. "So did you hear about Evan not being a baby daddy after all?"

"Yeah. I think he's pretty torn up about it. While the whole damn situation was awkward, I think he'd started to like the idea of being a father."

"I can see that. But Kendall must be relieved. She was the one getting the real shaft."

"I guess in the end, it's best for all involved."

"All kinds of drama going on this week. Tammy says Elec brought up that maybe they should look into adopting a baby. Just clear out of the blue."

Ryder sat down on the couch, running his hand across the diaper butt of his son. It still amazed him how he was just a miniature version of a person, every body part a tiny little piece of perfection. "Is that something Tammy wants?"

"She says she's only thought about having more children in passing. But she's feeling like how can she deny Elec the opportunity to parent a baby from day one. He's a great step-daddy but those kids were half grown when he stepped in."

"I don't think Hunter could qualify as half grown despite her sass, but I see what you mean. I also think that Elec knew Tammy might not want more kids and he married her anyway. You need to think long and hard before you bring a child into your life."

Suzanne snorted. "Oh, like we did? I got knocked up in my car!"

Ryder felt a rush of lust just thinking about that night. "Yeah, but we were meant to be. We always wanted kids. We just took the roundabout way getting there."

"God, we were dirty that night." She grinned at him.

"How long until we can do it again?"

"Keep it in your pants, Jefferson. We have five more weeks."

"That's a hell of a long time." Maybe he could talk her into giving him a little mouth action.

"And no, I'm not blowing you."

Damn.

Track ripped off a loud burp, the rumbling setting his head to bobbling. "You take after your mother," he told him.

"Shush." As she brought the baby back to her other breast, Suz asked, "Hey, so what do you think about Tuesday and Diesel? Doesn't that seem like an odd pairing to you?"

"Definitely. He's so laid-back and she's so . . . verbal."

"Well, I like it. I know her blog ticks me off from time to time but I do appreciate that she's honest. And in person, she's a hoot. But you're right, they're all sorts of different from each other. But hell, maybe that works."

"Maybe. Diesel is a good guy, I hope it works out for him. He hasn't had an easy time of it."

"Speaking of hard times, I forgot to tell you that Nikki Strickland was told she won't be able to get pregnant until she gains some weight. Turns out she's so underweight she's anemic and doesn't get her periods. Crazy, huh?"

That was crazy, but really not at all surprising. "Do you think she'll be able to do it? Gain weight, I mean?"

"I guess if she wants a child badly enough. Maybe at the very least she'll lay off her husband and let Jonas eat a chip now and again."

"You're right, there is a ton of drama going on." Suddenly he wasn't feeling so bad about having to go off to work.

"I think we should have a dinner party."

Leave it to Suz. "You just had a baby! You're not throwing a party."

"I just think that everyone could use a social night together."

"So you can pull people aside and try and interfere in their private lives."

"Of course not." Then she gave in. "Okay, maybe. But what can I say? I care about my friends, and if we hadn't interfered, Elec and Tammy would have never gotten together."

That was subject to debate, but he'd just let her have that one. "No one needs to be fixed up."

"Diesel and Tuesday need to be observed to determine if they're right for each other or not."

Oh, Lord. "No." Ryder brushed her hair off her face. "Now give me a big old good-bye kiss."

"You can't just tell me no, you know."

"We can talk about it when I get home." And he would tell her no all over again.

"Alright."

She puckered up and he gave her a nice, long kiss, wanting to pour all of his heart and soul into it, so she would know what she meant to him. What she had given back to him. "I love you."

"I love you, too. Now kick some ass out there."

With one last kiss for both his wife and newborn son, Ryder went to do just that.

* * *

EVAN Monroe laid on the couch in his RV, Kendall tucked up next to him. They were in Atlanta for the week's race, and they were having a rare quiet moment together. He rubbed her arm, loving the feel of her so close to him. She was his wife, his lover, his best friend.

"How are you doing?" she asked him. "Are you okay?"

He knew exactly what she was asking him. He had found out earlier in the day that the baby Sara Parker had given birth to wasn't his. After four months of worry, fear, excitement, now he had the answer. He wasn't going to be a father, and damn if he wasn't disappointed.

"I don't know. I guess. I know it would have been really difficult to be a quality part of that baby's life, given my schedule and Sara's new husband and life in Kentucky, and that it was asking a hell of a lot of you, but I liked the idea of being a father. That's selfish, isn't it?" He'd been struggling with that all day. He knew how much Kendall had suffered when she had found out about this baby, and he was worried that it didn't say good things about his character if he had secretly wanted the baby to be his.

"How does that make you selfish?" She looked up at him, pulling an errant blond hair out of her mouth. Her forehead wrinkled. "You never criticized Sara, you offered her money and any help she needed, you left lawyers out it . . . and you wanted to have a little girl call you daddy. I think that's amazing. And hell, I was having a fantasy or two about being a stepmommy."

"You were?" Evan stared down at the woman he loved

more than anything in the world and he wondered if it were possible she was thinking what he was thinking. "Do you . . . do you think . . . do you want to start our own family? Sooner than later?"

"It's insane," she whispered, her eyes wide and glassy. "It will set my career back. But I don't care. I want to have a baby with you, Evan. Maybe that was what we were supposed to learn from this. That our marriage, creating a family, is more important than anything else."

Evan thought for a second that he was actually going to cry. He managed to hold the tears at bay, but he did squeeze Kendall close against his body, leaning his forehead down onto hers. "I want a family with you more than anything. I love you, God, so much."

"I love you, too." She gave him a grin. "Want to try right now?"

He wasn't stupid enough to turn that down. "First one naked gets to name our first child."

As they scrambled out of denim and cotton, Evan was damn grateful that he really felt like he had his life all together.

THE minute Tuesday opened the door, Diesel knew she had been drinking. There was a glassy look in her eye and a sloppy grin on her face.

"Hey," she drawled, tossing her hair back. "What's up?"

Disappointed, Diesel stepped into her apartment. It wasn't even nine yet and she was drunk. Not only did he not want to spend the night being her designated driver, he had been looking forward to spending time with the real Tuesday, not the one under the influence.

"Hey," he replied. "Been hitting the cocktails already, have you?" It was probably the wrong tactic to take with Tuesday if he wanted her to stop drinking, but he was annoyed. Did she have to get loaded to see him?

The look she gave him could have cut glass. "So what if I have? A lot of people have a drink after work."

"I think you've had more than one."

"What are you, my mom?" Then her expression suddenly changed from belligerent to shocked, like she had remembered something. She quickly ducked her head down so he couldn't see her expression anymore. "So, what, are you saying you don't want to go out with me tonight because I've had three glasses of wine? Or four."

She had regained her composure and had raised her head to him defiantly. Diesel didn't understand Tuesday. She lashed out when he wasn't expecting it, showing a vulnerability that was raw and tender, yet other times she was so tough. "I'm not saying anything, other than it's clear you've been drinking."

"Maybe you should, too. It would certainly loosen you up."

"Oh, I'm uptight?"

"That's the understatement of the year. It's boring."

Diesel felt the slow burn of anger rising up from his gut. Why was she tearing into him? He'd just shown up to take her to dinner. And that was his fear . . . that she would lose interest in him because he was boring. He didn't want it pointed out to him so baldly. "I don't think drinking a bottle of wine is the smartest way to relax. Nor do I think I'm that uptight. I many not be the most exciting guy on the planet, but I'm not wound tight either."

"No, you're just loosened up from Vicodin."

Now that was a low blow. Diesel pulled his keys back out of his pocket. She was clearly itching for a fight and he wasn't about to oblige her. "Maybe we should go to dinner another night. I've suddenly lost my appetite."

Her eyes narrowed. "You're canceling on me?"

"Deferring. I think it's probably for the best, don't you?"

"If you walk out that door and leave me hungry when I was counting on dinner and sex, don't bother to call me again."

Despite her swaying a little, Tuesday looked beautiful and fierce. She was wearing dark jeans, sandals with heels, and a bright blue stretchy shirt that made the most of her smaller cleavage. She had on very little makeup except for her lips, which were an enticing coral color.

Did he want to have sex with her?

Hell, yeah. He'd been looking forward to it all day. All week.

But he also wanted to have a decent conversation with her. And he had no desire to be fending off barbs all night.

Leaving was the only thing that made sense.

"I'll call you tomorrow," he told her. "Though you'll probably have a hangover."

"At least I'm an honest drunk. You're hiding your problems behind a prescription bottle."

That was it. Diesel took a deep breath before he said something he would truly regret. "Good night, Tuesday."

Her response was a very vehement, "Fuck you."

Yep. It was time to leave.

Diesel walked out, catching a draft as she slammed the door shut behind him, nearly clipping his heels.

He did not have a prescription drug problem. He only took his pain pills one or two days a week when it was too much to handle with working. He wasn't hiding behind anything and he didn't have any problems. Tuesday, on the other hand, was clearly having some issues.

Feeling frustrated and furious and disappointed, Diesel got into his car and started home. Only with each mile he ate up, his anger turned to worry. What if Tuesday decided to get in her own car and drive somewhere? She probably was hungry and she was the type who would go for chicken tenders at the drive-thru when she'd been drinking. He knew that sober she would be appalled at the idea of anyone driving under the influence of alcohol, but that was the whole problem with it. Most people didn't get behind the wheel knowing they were trashed—their judgment was so impaired they thought they were fine.

Diesel drummed his fingers on the steering wheel, thinking about how her *s*'s had slurred and just how glassy her eyes had been. She was also wearing shoes and was ready to go out. He would never be able to live with himself if something happened to her of if she injured someone else on the road.

"Shit." Pulling into the next driveway, he turned around and headed back to Tuesday's apartment, realizing he didn't even know what kind of car she drove so he couldn't scan the road for her.

Maybe he should call her. Pulling his phone out of his pocket, he dialed her number, keeping one eye on the road. She didn't pick up.

Fortunately, he hadn't gone far, so two minutes later he was in her parking lot and moving to her door as fast as possible.

Diesel pounded on it, impatiently shifting back and forth from foot to foot. When she didn't answer, he knocked again and dialed her phone simultaneously.

After five rings, she answered the phone. "What?"

"Where are you?"

"I'm standing in my living room trying to ignore you calling me and knocking on my door."

He let out a sigh of relief. "Good."

"Where did you think I was?"

"Never mind. Can I come in?"

"Why? So you can insult me some more?" The anger seemed to have gone out of her voice and she sounded petulant, but tired.

"No. No, I have no intention of insulting you." His anger had disappeared too, buried under the worry he had felt when he'd thought of her crashing into a ditch. "Please. I wanted to say I'm sorry."

He was sorry. It wasn't his right to criticize her. He could express concern but there were better ways to do it than the way he had, thirty seconds after walking in her door.

She hung up on him.

Diesel stared at his phone for a second, dumbfounded. Seriously? He had just apologized, not an easy thing to do he had to say.

But then she opened the door, her phone in her hand. "I'm sorry, too. I shouldn't have told you to fuck off."

He smiled, relieved all over again. "I actually think you told me 'fuck you.' But who's keeping track?"

"Not me."

She sniffled, and Diesel realized that her eyes were red, her cheeks damp.

Holy shit, had he made her cry? "Hey, hey, what's wrong?" Diesel moved into the apartment without an invitation and wrapped his arms around her.

For half a second, he thought she was going to shove him away, but she just took a deep breath and shuddered.

"I'm sorry, Tuesday. That wasn't fair of me."

"It's fine. I overreacted. Bringing up your medication was a low blow, too. I really didn't mean to suggest you have an addiction to pain pills." She wasn't hugging him in return, but she was letting him hold her. "And just for the record, I'm totally drunk."

He loved that she was so honest. Drunk or sober, she usually told it just like it was. "Maybe you're just tipsy."

"I hate it when you use that word. You sound like my grandmother. And I don't want to get it on with my grandmother."

"I don't really want you to get it on with your grandmother either. Okay, so you're shit-faced. How did that happen?"

"One glass at a time." Tuesday peeled back from him and moved to the left. She tripped over two big bags of dog food and stumbled before dropping down onto her couch.

"Why do you have dog food?" He'd never seen a dog in her apartment.

"Because I like dogs, but this complex is no dogs, so I buy food for the shelter. Makes me feel better."

That didn't surprise him. He could see her wanting to help out. Tuesday wasn't a traditional do-gooder, she was sharp-tongued and somewhat bossy, but she had a big heart. He truly believed that. If she didn't, she wouldn't be suffering her father's loss so deeply.

"Damn, the room is spinning."

Diesel knew that was a fairly awful feeling. Nothing but time and some water could make it go away. "So you cracked open a bottle of wine and didn't realize how much you were drinking?"

"I think I was fully aware of how much I was drinking."

Diesel wasn't sure what to say without her telling him off again, this time actually hitting him with the door on his way out. But she had to realize that her explanation was sketchy. "So, was there any particular reason you reached for the first glass?"

Obviously a ton of people didn't have any particular reason for drinking a glass of wine other than the fact that they enjoyed it. But they stopped before they drank—Diesel checked out her coffee table—almost two entire bottles.

Tuesday pointed her finger at him like she was about to give a lengthy explanation, but then the only thing she actually said was, "Yes."

He sat down next to her, waiting for the follow-up, debating taking his shoes off. He was spending the night until her buzz wore off, whether she liked it or not. But he probably should take her out for food and some coffee. "Yeah?" he prompted, hoping she'd continue.

Instead she picked up her phone and started fiddling with it. "Listen to this." She shoved it at him. Diesel put it up to his ear.

A voice mail started to play. "Hi, hon, it's Mom. I just

wanted to let you know that I won't be able to meet you tomorrow after all. Tom Reynolds and I are seeing each other."

Okay. He wasn't sure why he was supposed to be hearing that, so he just made a noncommittal sound.

"So what the hell do you think that means?" she asked, studying her phone really intently, having obvious focus issues, before pushing a button to resave the message.

He had no idea. "Can you give me some context here? Who is Tom Reynolds? And what do *you* think it means?"

"Tom Reynolds is my mother's high school boyfriend. She always joked around that he was the one who got away. So does that sound like a date to you, or what?"

So that's what this was about. Tuesday was worried her mother was dating already, moving on from her father. With a high school boyfriend, maybe it even had her concerned her parent's marriage hadn't been quite what she'd thought it was. Diesel rubbed her knee. "No, it does not sound like a date to me. It sounds like two old friends getting together."

"How do you know?" She bit her fingernail anxiously.

"Well, what time were you supposed to meet your mom?"

"Noon. For lunch."

"That doesn't sound like a date to me." It didn't. It sounded exactly like what he had said it was.

"Yeah, but, how do you know?"

"You could ask your mother."

"Hell no!" She looked horrified at the prospect. "What if . . ."

She left the sentence unfinished, but he knew what she meant. What if it were true? "Well, was he friends with your father, too?"

"Not really. Tom and my mom didn't even really talk all that often. That I was aware of anyway."

"Was he at the funeral?"

She gave him a look. "I couldn't even tell you who was at that funeral. It's a blur. Just a big black blur." Glancing down at his hand on her knee she added, "Except for you. You letting me cry on you. And why would it matter if he was there or not?"

"It would show that he respected your father, respected your mother's feelings. He wouldn't be swooping in this soon."

"You respected my father and you weren't there. At least, I think you respected my father."

Diesel stared at her for a second, not sure what to say. She was even drunker than he'd thought. "Of course I was there. You just said so two seconds ago."

"You weren't *there* there. You were there to visit your family."

Had she really thought for the last month that he hadn't attended her father's funeral? That it was a coincidence?

"No, I was there for your father's funeral. I just stopped by my family's grave sites on my way out. I knew your dad for years, Tuesday. I wanted to show my respect."

"Oh," she said, looking as stunned as he felt. "Duh. That would have been quite a coincidence I guess, huh? And now that I think about it, you were wearing a suit. Yikes, I'm such a moron."

He was getting pretty damn sick of her cutting herself down all the time, no matter how it was masked behind sarcasm. "Shush. You're not a moron. Cut yourself some slack. The last six months have been rough for you."

"No shit," she said with fire.

She laid herself across his lap. It seemed to be a favorite position of hers when she was drunk. "Thank you for attending the funeral. You were my dad's favorite driver you know. He thought you were old school and hardworking. Honest. A true sportsman."

Diesel felt a rush of satisfaction, and no small amount of embarrassment. That was exactly how he would like to be remembered in his career and it pleased the hell out of him at the same time he felt a little like squirming. "I appreciate that." He stroked her hair. "Do you want to go get something to eat still?"

"Mm."

Her eyes were closed. Diesel leaned forward and fished around for the remote control. He turned the TV on and relaxed back, figuring sleeping off the wine was the best thing for her. Channel surfing, he found a baseball game on.

"I hate baseball," she muttered two minutes later.

Diesel grinned, rubbing her backside before giving it a little swat. She was a pain in the ass, and it was clear he really liked her or he'd never put up with her.

"Deal with it," he told her.

He was expecting a tongue being shoved out at him, but all he got was a light snore. Putting his feet on the coffee table, he settled in for the long haul.

TUESDAY woke up with a jolt, sitting half up, then instantly regretting that action. Her head throbbed. Where the hell was she?

Her bed. Reaching down, she patted herself. She was in

her shirt and bra, but had no pants on. Panties were intact. She had no memory whatsoever of going to bed, which was scary. The last thing she remembered was blubbering on Diesel and coming to the realization that he had in fact attended her father's funeral. Then . . . nothing.

Glancing over, she saw he was in bed with her, sleeping. It looked like he didn't have a shirt on. Swallowing hard, her mouth as dry as the Sahara, Tuesday concentrated on her inner thighs. Did it feel like she'd had sex? She wasn't sure, and damn, it would be so disappointing if they had and she didn't remember it. Curious, she snaked her hand to his side under the blanket and touched his leg. It was bare thigh. She went just a little bit higher and encountered the fabric of his boxer shorts.

Hmm. That didn't rule out sex though. He could have pulled those back on afterward, though she was starting to think nothing had happened. She'd been so drunk she wouldn't have bothered to put her panties on afterward. Another two inches of creeping up his leg and she found herself hitting a solid wall of erection. Hello. Despite feeling like ass, she couldn't help but stroke it just a little. It was such a damn fine penis.

"I'd prefer you do that when I'm awake," Diesel mumbled, his hand covering hers and stilling her movements.

"You sound awake to me."

He turned to look at her, tossing his hair out of his eyes. "How are you feeling, sweetheart?"

"Like crap," she admitted. "Which I guess is to be expected. I drank a whole bottle of wine, didn't I?"

He studied her in the early morning light peeking through

her blinds. "Actually it was almost two bottles. But who's counting?"

"Oh, God." Tuesday shoved her hair off her face. "I'm sorry."

"It happens." He shrugged and pulled her over onto his chest.

Her stomach roiled a little and her head spun, but once settled on him, his hot skin felt strangely good on her clammy cheek. She relaxed with a sigh. "If we had sex, I'm disappointed to say I don't remember it."

"You blacked out?"

"Yeah, after we were talking in the living room, I don't remember anything. I don't have any clue how I got to the bedroom."

His hand stroking her back felt good, through she could do without her bra. The underwire was jabbing her.

"No? So then you don't remember us having anal sex."

Tuesday forgot all about her underwire. Anal sex. She'd let him in the back door and she didn't remember it? "You can't be serious." He couldn't be. She would know if his you-know-what went you-know-where.

He swatted her butt, something he seemed to really love to do, given the rate with which he did it. "No, I'm not serious. We didn't do anything at all. You passed out on me on the couch and I brought you in here. There's water on the nightstand if you need it."

"Does a chicken have a pecker? Yes, I need water." Relieved that she hadn't missed some potentially erotic encounter, Tuesday rolled very, very carefully onto her side and reached for the glass. "Thank you."

She drank the entire glass in three gulps then lay back down with a sigh. "Why do I do this to myself?"

"I'm assuming that's a rhetorical question?"

"Yeah, I guess it is." She had been upset about her mother, that's why she had reached for the wine. The problem was, which she could admit, was that she had no shut-off valve. Once she started drinking, she lost track of how much she'd had, and then suddenly it was all ugly. She was glad Diesel had been there with her because the idea that she had blacked out and could have done anything was scary. Granted, she'd just been in her own place and probably would have just passed out on the couch, but it was still unnerving. "So you really don't think my mother is dating her high school sweetheart?"

"No. It's just a couple of old friends getting together."

She was glad he didn't say something like she needed to accept at some point that her mother might date and re-marry, because while somewhere in the back of her mind she knew that, she sure in the hell didn't want it to happen anytime soon.

"I'm holding you to that," she told him.

He gave a low, grumbling laugh. "Come here and give me a kiss."

The look he was giving her, one of lust, but something else, something like genuine affection, made her heart squeeze. Feeling a wave of tenderness for him, Tuesday scooted over toward him again. "I guess I could do that."

It was a nice, slow, sensual kiss. They moved easily together. Tuesday was amazed by that, by how natural it was with Diesel. And by how with just a single touch, a look, a word, he could utterly and completely turn her on.

She broke off the kiss and looked down at him, propped up on his chest with her elbows. "By the way, thank you for putting me to bed."

"You're welcome." He pulled her on top of him in one smooth move, his erection connecting with her sweet spot.

The move left her both breathless and highly aroused.

"Now, unless you have any objections, I'm going to keep you in bed."

Shaking her head, she also verbalized the gesture, just in case he had any doubt as to her answer. "No, no objections."

She still felt a little rough, but she figured that was nothing an orgasm couldn't fix.

"Good." He pulled her head down for a kiss.

Tuesday felt a pang of self-consciousness. She probably didn't have the freshest breath ever.

"Kiss me," he demanded.

"I need to brush my teeth." She flicked her hair out of her eyes.

"I don't want to kiss a mint, I want to kiss you."

Okay, then, that was hot. This time when he put his hand on the back of her neck to guide her toward him, she didn't resist. If he didn't care, she sure wasn't going to. Kissing Diesel like this, her body splayed across his from her breasts down to her toes was dangerous. It was intense, intimate, arousing, yes, but something more than that. Here she was, slightly hungover and feeling like she wasn't capable of putting effort into anything whatsoever at the moment, yet she knew she would with Diesel. There was something incredibly sexy about knowing he saw her less-than-perfect side and didn't give a shit.

She kissed him hard, enjoying the more powerful position

of being on top. Digging her hands into his hair, she bit his bottom lip. Something about the sweep of his tongue inside her mouth, his hands sliding across her back, the way he was clearly going to take it gentle with her, made her want it rough.

He sucked in a breath when she nipped him. "Oh, someone's feeling frisky."

Looking down into his brown eyes, she forgot her headache, forgot her sore muscles, and was only aware of him and the deep, needy ache he created between her legs. Rocking her hips onto his erection, she just gave him a wicked smile. "I'm sopping wet," she told him. "You know what that means."

His finger snaked down between their bodies and slipped inside her panties and into her without preamble. Tuesday gasped, rolling her head back.

"Well, well, so you are . . . tell me what that means, sweetheart." He hooked his index finger inside her, hitting all her pleasure spots perfectly.

She forgot to answer him for a second, just enjoying the contact, moving her hips slowly and sensually so that her body moved with his finger. It was a slow tease . . . it seemed satisfying at first, then it wasn't enough to fill her, even when she started rocking faster, pumping with a quick, hard rhythm.

"It means you need to fuck me," she said, breathless, hair a wild tangle around her face, her body heating up from pleasure, her face resting on his shoulder.

Diesel tugged her hair hard enough that it both aroused her and forced her back off of him. That little sting wasn't painful so much as it was exciting and she said, "What?"

His eyes were dark with desire, his hand still fisted into the back of her hair. "I think in this position *you* need to fuck *me*. So get to it."

It should have pissed her off, his roughness, his dominating words in bed. It just turned her on even more. She was so wet that when he pulled his finger out of her, she felt the trail of her own arousal across her thigh. When another tug of her hair had her up in a sitting position, Tuesday yanked her T-shirt off with frantic pulls. She just wanted to be naked and be on him, slamming their bodies together.

"That's it," he told her. He wasn't wearing a shirt, and he lifted them both up slightly off the bed so he could dispense with his boxers.

There was no time to worry about her panties. They were shoved to the side from his attentions and that was good enough for her. Tuesday took his erection into her hand, gave it a few greedy strokes, then aligned herself with the tip of his penis. When she sank down onto him, they both moaned.

He felt so right inside her, just the perfect fit. Tuesday started moving her hips, loving the way he looked right at her, eyes locked with hers, his hands on her waist, gripping hard. Putting her hands in her hair to get it back off her face, she closed her eyes briefly just to concentrate on that amazing connection, that slide of her over him, his erection stretching her deliciously. She was definitely going to come.

Most men she'd known would have taken over control by this point, forcing the rhythm themselves, but Diesel moved with her, let her set the pace, let her be the one driving down onto him. Ironic that the most alpha male in bed was enjoying letting her ride him like a cowgirl. But maybe he knew that ultimately he was still in control because she was so aroused, she wouldn't argue with anything he wanted to do.

Her movements were getting frantic, her moans louder, and she felt the orgasm rush over her in an explosive wave, a hot, desperate all consuming pleasure. Not changing her pace at all, she drew it out, refusing to close her eyes. Instead she watched Diesel, loving the way his moans had joined hers, the way he was clearly as hot for her as she was for him. She knew the moment he was going to have his own orgasm. She could feel it inside her body, the tensing of his cock, could see it in his expression, hear it in his voice, as everything paused just for a split second before he exploded inside her.

Damn, there was nothing better than being on top and knowing she had made her man come. Her. She had done that, to both of them.

When the last shudders subsided, Diesel relaxed back onto the pillow. "Damn, sweetheart. Just damn."

Tuesday gave a little laugh and leaned down and gave him a smacking kiss, their bodies still pleasantly and warmly joined.

CHAPTER
TEN

TUESDAY collapsed next to Diesel, sighing. "That's the best cure for a hangover I've ever tried."

Diesel hadn't had a drop to drink the night before and he was feeling pretty damn cured himself. "I'm glad it worked for you."

He had to admit, he'd spent a lot of the night tossing and turning, wondering what exactly his feelings for Tuesday were. Wondering if he should be concerned about her drinking. Wondering how willing he was to put himself out there. He'd spent the last two years basically alone because he didn't want anyone's pity. It was difficult to be known as the face of tragedy instead of just a man.

But lying on her bed, the sun warming the room up already, Tuesday's cheeks pink from the exertion of riding him, his body spent and satisfied, he didn't care. None of it mattered. He wanted to see where this was going. If it crashed and burned, then so be it.

Hell, it probably would. Didn't everything eventually?

In the meantime, though, he could enjoy it. He was going to enjoy the hell out of it, if the last twenty minutes had been any indication.

She grinned at him, her leg still sprawled over his, looking completely relaxed. "Oh, I think it worked for you, too."

"I never said it didn't."

"Hold back on the enthusiasm there, buddy."

The good thing was, she didn't look annoyed. Diesel knew he was too emotionally reserved for some women—hell, most women—but Tuesday was confident enough that it never seemed to raise insecurities in her the way it did other women. He didn't mean to be remote, it just didn't feel natural to him to gush about his feelings. It made him feel stupid and vulnerable. He said things in his own way, on his own terms, and he stood by the concept of actions speaking louder than words.

"I think I showed you just how enthusiastic I can be."

She sighed, a satisfied smile on her face. "Indeed."

He loved her smile, that smirk that frequently crossed her lips. It stunned him a little to look at her and realize just how beautiful he thought she was . . . when she had been moving over him, her head thrown back, he had been in awe of how stunning she had looked.

It was starting to occur to him that he was really falling for her. The question was, how did she really feel about him?

He guessed there was only one way to figure it out. "So do you have plans for today?"

She yawned. "I should work a little but other than that, no."

"You want to do something?"

There was no hesitation. "Sure. Like what?"

That was a good question. "I should go home and get Wilma and let her out. Do you want to go to the dog park? Or we could take her down the trails by the lake."

"I vote dog park. I'm feeling okay, but I'm not sure I'm up for tromping around the woods today. Let's save that for a day when I haven't consumed my weight in wine the night before."

Good point. He didn't want to put her through the paces when he knew how lousy the day after drinking could be. "No problem."

"Do you want to shower at your place so we don't have poor Wilma crossing her legs any longer than she has to?"

There it was again, that tug on his heart. Damn, she killed him when she showed care for his dog. "That would be great." Diesel sat up and stretched. "The mutt will appreciate it."

Having pulled her panties into some semblance of order, Tuesday came around his side of the bed and started rooting around in her dresser. He was momentarily distracted from his purpose of pulling his jeans back on. Her butt was perilously close to his face and he wanted to suck the spot where her waist dipped in.

"I need to give you your clothes back that I borrowed."

"Huh?" Diesel had a hard time focusing on her words, mesmerized by the lengthy expanse of ivory skin on her back, her shoulder blades moving gracefully as she dug through a drawer. He felt an erection stirring to life.

"Are you even listening to me?" Tuesday turned around. Her exasperation disappeared when she saw his dick, sail fully raised. "Oh, my." Tuesday licked her lips, her mouth sliding open.

For a split second he thought she was going to lean over and take him into her mouth. The thought made him throb. But she backed up against her dresser, like she needed distance from temptation.

"No, we need to let Wilma out."

He knew she was right, but he was tempted to risk a puddle on the floor for five more minutes. Not that he would actually let her suck him. Why waste time on that when he could be deep inside her? Just thinking about the way it felt to have her hot, moist body snug around him had him reaching for her.

But then the mood was ruined when she put a hand to her chest and said, "Look at your knee, oh, my God."

Nothing like pity to kill an erection. Fighting the urge to wince, he said, "Pretty, huh?"

The wreck had shattered his kneecap. The part he had now was plastic, and he'd been fighting the resulting scar tissue around it. So he'd had both an initial surgery and two subsequent ones, leaving him a network of red, angry scars, and a significant dip in one spot where the tissue had been removed.

Tuesday seemed to recover from her initial shock and tempered her expression. "I'm sorry, I didn't mean it like that. It just looks . . . angry."

That was a very accurate description of it. "I imagine it is a little pissed about being crushed. I've apologized to it, but it still seems inclined to be annoyed."

"Want me to tell it to calm down?" She looked ready to beat the crap out of his knee. Considering she was standing there in just a pair of panties and there was nothing she could do about his injury, her indignation was funny as hell.

Diesel laughed. "Uh, sweetheart, no offense, but I don't think you're the best person to calm anyone or anything down."

"Should I be insulted?"

"No. But what you should be doing is forgetting about my knee and putting a freaking shirt on before I bite your nipple." Really, how much was he expected to resist? Her back was bad enough, but her breasts, nipples jutting out at him, was really damn challenging.

"You don't want to do that."

Hah. "Oh, yes, I do."

With a speed that defied her hangover she moved away from him, a bra dangling in her hand. "You can bite me later."

"I'm holding you to that."

"As long as you buy me some coffee in the next ten minutes, you can do whatever you want."

Diesel grinned. "Oh, yeah? Anything?"

"Within reason," she amended, hooking her bra.

"That's subject to interpretation." Something he was going to have a lot of fun with later. But he let her off the hook for now and got dressed. "Alright, let's roll, sexy."

She was wearing shorts and a tank top. Whereas most women would have been content to leave it at that, Tuesday took the time to add bracelets and a necklace, then find matching sandals. There was something very finished and polished about her all the time, even when she was coming off a night of sucking down wine. He wondered if it was a little bit like armor, like her way of showing she was in control.

Or hell, maybe she just liked jewelry.

Diesel did a mental eye roll. He needed to lay off the talk shows.

She caught him off guard when she was ready to leave the bedroom and she turned to him and said, "Do you want to talk about it?"

He stared at her blankly, distracted by thoughts of wanting to kiss the back of her long, smooth neck. "Talk about what?"

"Your accident. Your injuries. I know I can be the queen of snark, but I am actually a really good listener." Her expression was full of compassion.

He appreciated it at the same time he resented it. "Thank you, but no, I don't want to talk about it." He had no intention of laying all out his failures and weaknesses in front of her. She already knew he was a gimp, he didn't need to talk about it.

She said, "Okay, I understand. But I'm here if you want a friend."

On impulse, Diesel reached out and took her hand as they walked through her apartment.

It felt good, damn good.

They went through the drive-thru and ordered Tuesday a giant coffee and a six-pack of doughnuts. "You really going to eat all those?" he asked her with a dubious glance at the box sitting in her lap after they pulled away.

"Not at one time. But yes, I'm going to eat all of them. And if you have a problem with that, you can suck it."

He laughed. That was his girl.

His girl?

The thought should have made him freeze in terror, his nuts drawing up into his body in shock and horror.

But instead, he thought he kinda liked the sound of it.

Him and Tuesday.

Who'd have thought?

"I don't have a problem with it. I was just debating how badly you'd hurt me if I stole one."

"I told you to pick one for yourself."

"You did. I didn't think I'd want one."

Tuesday had opened the box and was plunging her tongue into the hole on the side of a jelly-filled doughnut. Holy crap, did she have any idea how hot she was?

"But suddenly I want one."

She retracted her tongue and dragged it across her bottom lip. "Oh, yeah? Maybe I'll let you have a bite."

No doubt about it. She knew exactly how sexy she was.

"That's two bites you've offered me now today and I haven't actually gotten to enjoy either."

Her response was to shove her doughnut in his face. Diesel kept an eye on the road while he took an enormous bite, powdered sugar floating up his nose. "Mm. Thanks, babe."

"You ate half of it in one bite," she complained.

Idling at a red light, he turned and gave her a smile. "Don't be bitter. You have five left."

"You're lucky you're cute."

"Am I?" He was stupidly pleased to hear her say that.

Was he kidding? Diesel was so cute Tuesday wanted to eat him with a spoon. After she squeezed him and licked him from head to toe. He owned cute.

Which was why it was damn near impossible to feel like anything other than a teenage girl around him. She had a crush. For the first time in a decade she had a bona fide giggle-inducing, dot-your-I's-with-a-heart crush. It was embarrassing.

So she rolled her eyes and told him, "Not really. I just said that to make you feel better about yourself."

"Liar."

"It's called sarcasm."

"It's called we're here." He pulled into his garage. "Close your doughnut box before we open the door or Wilma will have you on the ground."

Tuesday wandered in behind Diesel, greeting Wilma after he did. The dog bounded around and jumped on her leg, obviously glad to have some company. Diesel whistled for the dog and she ran past him to the back door. Setting the doughnut box on his kitchen counter, Tuesday followed him. His backyard was beautiful in the daylight, a mass expanse of green ending in a bucolic pond that shimmered in the summer sunlight.

It suited him. It was relaxed, laid-back.

Tuesday settled into a deck chair and watched as he stood in the grass and tossed a tennis ball to Wilma. They weren't wimpy throws, he was hurling the ball fifty feet and Wilma was tearing after it each time, bringing it back faster than Tuesday would have thought possible.

Glancing down at her feet, she checked her pedicure peeking out from behind her gold sandals. It was still intact. She wished she could say the same for the rest of her.

The timing of this—whatever it was—with Diesel was

terrible. She knew she didn't entirely have it together. She knew she was vulnerable. She had always been good at being rational in relationships and she wasn't sure she was completely capable of that right now.

It would be easy to get hurt.

Yet she didn't seem to be standing up and leaving.

She was either a masochist or maybe, just maybe, on the verge of something wonderful.

Wilma came running up to her, dropping the soggy ball in her lap.

"Hey, mutt, bring it to me. Tuesday doesn't want your nasty ball."

"I don't mind." After giving the dog a scratch on the head, she threw the ball. It didn't have the velocity of Diesel's throws, but it made it to the grass at least. Wilma bounded off after it.

"This is my life," Diesel told her. "Entertaining a dog."

But he didn't look like he minded. "In return she gives you unconditional love. You can't beat that."

"True." Diesel had sat down next to her and he rubbed Wilma when she inserted her head between his legs. "So Ty McCordle tells me you're planning a cancer benefit in your father's name."

"Yes. It's in two weeks." She had thought it would ease her pain a little, but the truth was, she was having the opposite reaction. It made her feel even more raw, and she waffled between bouts of aggressive planning and the desire to run and hide from everything. It was on target mainly because Kendall had lent her her PR person for the event. Otherwise Tuesday wasn't sure she would have been able to pull it together. "The drivers have all been great. They've donated personal meet-and-greets, memorabilia, driver's experiences. Everyone has been really generous."

It had meant a lot to her as she had been soliciting donations to hear so many of the drivers speak highly of her father. They had all stepped up to the plate to help out and then some. "I think we can really bring in some money. Kendall's assistant has done the advertising and we have several hundred people attending."

She was proud of what she had managed to pull together. "I'm hoping for several hundred thousand dollars at the end of the night. That would be a great boon to cancer research."

It wouldn't do anything for her father, but if anything she did could prevent someone else from losing a loved one, she wanted to make that happen.

"I could donate something."

Tuesday glanced at him. He looked sincere. She had thought about asking Diesel, but then hadn't wanted it to seem like she was twisting his arm. She hadn't wanted him to feel obligated since they were sleeping with each other.

"That's awesome. I would appreciate it."

"How about a car?"

She had been reaching for the coffee cup she'd set down on the table next to her and she froze mid-reach at his words. "Excuse me?" A car? Did he mean like a dye-cast car? Because surely he couldn't mean a whole freaking car.

"The one I've been working on. It's a vintage stock car, raced in the '63 season, won the championship. It's worth about a hundred grand I'd guess, after my restoration. Should help meet your goal."

Her heart started to race a lot faster than was strictly normal. "Are you kidding me? You would do that?"

He shrugged. "Of course I would. My mom died of cancer, too. If I can help, I'm happy to."

"But how much did that car cost you? And you've been working on it for months." It both baffled and touched her that he would be willing to do something so huge.

"So? I'm fortunate enough to not have to pinch every penny. I want to do this."

Would he think she was stupid if she reached over and squeezed his hand? She decided she didn't care. She did just that, running her thumb over the calluses of his work-roughened hands. "Thank you. That's amazing, Daniel."

It felt right to use his given name right then and the sharp intake of breath he took told her he felt the same way. She was looking into his pale eyes, thinking that this was a very worthy man. One that she could easily fall in love with. One she wasn't sure she actually deserved.

"It's my pleasure."

An idea popped into her head as she leaned into him, holding his hand, and gazing into his eyes. "You should offer to take the highest bidder on a drive."

She thought it was a fabulous idea, him taking someone for a spin around the track in the vintage car. Collectors and enthusiasts would love that kind of opportunity.

What she didn't expect was for him to pull his hand out of hers and look down at his dog. "No, sorry, that I'm not doing."

Bewildered, she was upset her words had broken the mood, but unsure why they had exactly. "Why not?" She knew he could drive a car. He'd been hauling her ass all over town for the past ten days. He wasn't that injured.

"Because I don't want to."

There was an answer designed to irritate her. "Well, that clears that right up."

The look he gave her was not a smile, that was for sure. "Just leave it alone."

"So you're not going to give me a reason?"

"Nope."

"You're infuriating."

"You don't look that infuriated. I've seen you a lot more worked up."

Bastard had a point. She was irritated though, because he clearly was refusing to drive the car because of his accident. She just wasn't sure why exactly, and she wished he would trust her enough to confide in her. It wasn't like she hadn't verbally vomited her emotions on him multiple times. He couldn't possibly think she would judge him.

But she wasn't going to push him. If he didn't want to talk to her, she couldn't make him. Not right now anyway. She was a reporter, after all. She knew how to pry information out of someone when they weren't expecting it. Right how his guard was up and probing would only result in him digging his heels in and her getting as worked up as he'd suggested she'd been in the past.

Time to retreat for the time being.

"That's true." Tuesday leaned back in the chair and closed her eyes, enjoying the sun on her face. "And I'm too tired today to get worked up, so you're off the hook."

"Want to skip the dog park? We can grill some steaks here and take Wilma down to the pond for a swim."

"Sounds perfect to me." It did. It was a great way to spend a lazy Saturday. "So can you send me the information on the car you're donating? I'll have the PR person get the word out on that right away."

"Sure. Just remember I'm not driving it."

Point taken. Geez. Tuesday lightly kicked his shin. "I know. I heard you loud and clear."

"Ow, you just nailed my knee." Diesel reached down and grabbed it.

Tuesday sat up in alarm, instant guilt flooding her. "Oh, my God, I'm sorry! Are you—"

The jerk grinned. "Just kidding."

She smacked his arm, way harder than the paltry kick had been. "That is not funny. I was feeling sorry for you, jackass."

He just continued to laugh like it was the funniest thing he'd ever seen. Tuesday wanted to fight it, but she couldn't. She ended up laughing with him.

"Are you going to cook me a steak or what?" she asked him.

Diesel leaned over and kissed her temple, still grinning. "Yes. I am."

"Then get to it."

"Bossy."

"I learned it from you."

He reached out and pinched her nipple. "I imagine so."

"Hey!" She jumped, both from shock and from the unexpected pleasure. "You can't just do that whenever you feel like it."

"Who's going to stop me?"

"Me."

"And what army?" Diesel stood up, throwing the ball

again for Wilma. "I'll go get the meat since you're dying for it."

As he walked past her, Tuesday smacked his ass. Hard.

Twisting her hair up into a makeshift bun, she stretched her legs out as he went into the kitchen. Her shoulders relaxed, but her smile didn't.

If this was what content felt like, she could get used to it.

"AT what point do you know that what you're doing is more than dating?" Diesel asked his uncle the question that had been on his mind for days.

It was a rhetorical question, since he was fairly certain that what he and Tuesday were doing had moved beyond an occasional dinner and a movie, but they hadn't talked about it. Was he supposed to talk about it with her? Hell, he didn't know.

They were sitting on his aunt and uncle's deck, watching Tammy and Pete's kids run around the yard, chasing Wilma. He had brought her over to give her some exercise, and as a good excuse to see his deceased cousin's kids. His aunt and uncle were babysitting for the weekend while Tammy accompanied Elec to Richmond for the Sunday race. His aunt Beth was putting together ice cream sundaes in the house so he figured this was his only chance to talk to his uncle without her hearing and sending the wedding announcement into the papers.

"You seeing her more than twice a week?"

"Yes." He'd seen her three nights this week alone since their lazy Saturday afternoon and they were going to the drive-in movie in an hour.

"You talk to her every day?"

"Not always in person, but texts, yes."

"Are you feeling like you want to buy her gifts or do some kind of a grand gesture?"

Funny he should ask that. "Well, I donated my car to her cancer benefit auction."

His uncle's jaw dropped, his beer bottle halfway to his mouth. "You did what? The '63? Are you serious?"

He nodded.

"Boy, you aren't just doing more than dating. You're in love."

That made him bristle. "It's for charity, it was the right thing to do!"

"Uh-huh." His uncle's voice was dripping skepticism. "I take it we're talking about Tuesday Jones?"

"Yep." All he thought about was Tuesday. Morning and night, she was crowding his thoughts. He wanted to be with her constantly, wanted to make her laugh, and craved her sharp tongue putting him in his place. He wanted her in bed, sliding her mouth over his, spreading her legs for him, letting him control her the way he never could anywhere else. He enjoyed every minute with her, and when he wasn't with her, he just wished he were.

Oh, my God, he was in love.

The realization shocked him to the core. He wasn't sure he'd ever been in love before and that it would show up now, in this form, was more than a little unnerving. He felt like he couldn't breathe all of a sudden. "So what the hell do I do, Johnny?"

"Well, you could turn tail and run. That I don't recommend. You could put a ring on her finger. Which I think is rushing it. Or you could just enjoy spending time with her, stop worrying and thinking about it."

That made sense. "That's true. So I should just enjoy it? Not try to define it or whatever?"

"Did you change genders when I wasn't looking? What man sits around trying to define his relationship." His uncle shook his head. "Christ."

Between his uncle and his friends, he was pretty much being told he was a girl. That was comforting. "What's wrong with wanting to know where you stand?"

"You're making me uncomfortable." His uncle was actually shifting in his chair. "For crying out loud, what is it that you want?"

"I just want to know that she's not going to date anyone else." Forced to cut through his confusion, Diesel was instantly relieved to know that was exactly what he wanted. He didn't need a declaration of love just yet because he wasn't sure he was ready to share *his* feelings. Nor did he want to skip five steps ahead and contemplate marriage.

But he did want to know she wasn't going to be getting boned by anyone else, because that just might make his head explode.

"Then tell her not to."

"Tell her? What decade are you dating in?"

"Well, okay, *discuss* it with her." His uncle rolled his eyes and waved his hand. "Just figure it out soon because you're starting to get on my nerves."

He could probably do that. He could casually broach the subject with Tuesday, feel her out about being exclusive. "First you want me to date, then you tell me I'm getting on your nerves?"

Johnny grinned. "Guess there's no pleasing me."

His aunt came out onto the deck just then, four ice cream bowls precariously balanced in her hands. "Tell me about it."

But despite all his grumbling at him about being a real man, Diesel noticed how his uncle stood up immediately to help his wife, taking two bowls from her and giving her a soft kiss.

He had to admit, he could see himself with Tuesday that way.

Yep. In love. Jesus, how had that happened to him?

CHAPTER
ELEVEN

TUESDAY was feeling incredibly awkward at dinner with her mother, which irritated her. Never in her whole life, even in her angsty teen years, had she been uncomfortable around her mother. Now all she could think about was her mother and Tom Richards falling into each other's arms, grateful all obstacles had been removed from their being together.

It made her want to throw up a little in her mouth.

"Are you okay?" her mother asked, tucking into her salmon.

Tuesday hadn't even touched her chicken parmesan, which definitely wasn't like her. She even passed on the bread, and she was a girl who loved a good carb. "Yeah, fine, why?" she asked defensively, then hated how the tone of her voice sounded.

"You're just quiet, that's all. You seem like something is bothering you. Does it have anything to do with Diesel Lange?"

"No." That she could say in all honesty. Diesel was . . . good. In fact, just hearing his name made her feel a little warm and fuzzy inside. It had been years since any man had done that to her. Since like junior year in college. It was embarrassing at the same time it was actually really nice. She enjoyed his company, both in bed and out.

"Do you like him?"

"Yes, or I wouldn't be dating him." God, she sounded snippy.

But her mother didn't get angry. She just frowned. "Is this about Dad? Do you want to talk about it?"

Tuesday put down her fork. Her appetite had disappeared entirely. "You know I'm not big on talking about my feelings."

"That's not true. You like to talk about your feelings, you just don't like to admit weakness." Her mother smiled at her knowingly.

Tuesday pulled a face. Trust her mother to both know her and to baldly point it out to her. "Okay, fine, that's probably true. So how am I supposed to ask you about Tom Richards without showing how pathetic I am? I mean, you should be able to hang out with whoever you want."

Her mother stared at her blankly, her water goblet in her hand. "What? What about Tom Richards?"

"Do you like him?"

"Well, of course I like him or I wouldn't be going to lunch with him. He's a friend."

"Just a friend?" Tuesday realized her words were ground out and that her nails were digging into her leg, but she had to know. She needed to get this over with.

Understanding seemed to dawn on her mother. "Ooh. Did you think that I was interested in Tom as more than a friend? That it was a date?"

She shrugged. "Maybe."

"Tuesday, Tom is just an old friend. He lost his wife five years ago so he understands what I'm going through. He's actually very recently remarried but he said it took him a long time to open up to the possibility of being with someone else. I feel the same way. Right now I can't even imagine it."

A lump had lodged itself in Tuesday's windpipe. She felt both immense relief and guilt for thinking anything otherwise. Then a different kind of guilt for realizing she wouldn't have been happy for her mother if she had found solace with another man. All the way around, it made her feel like a horrible person and daughter.

"I'm sorry. It just freaked me out, and you used to always say Tom was the one who got away."

"That was just to tweak your father. Tom's a good guy but he never lit my fire, if you know what I mean."

She did. Lord, did she ever. "Okay. I'm sorry. It's just so soon and I was being selfish."

But her mother waved her words off. "You'd have a right to be angry if I started dating again this soon. It's only been a month, good grief." She passed the breadbasket to Tuesday, who took it without thinking. "So when do I get to meet Diesel?"

Realizing that somehow she had taken a piece of bread

she hadn't wanted and was buttering it, Tuesday marveled at how mothers could manipulate the hell out of you. "I don't know, Mom. I'm not sure we're that far along in our dating to meet the parents." Which, now that she said that in the plural out loud, she realized didn't apply. Her mother was the only parent between the two of them. There was something really sad and unfortunate about that.

"How do you feel about him?"

Did she have to talk about it? Couldn't she just keep the way she felt locked inside her, where she could check on it secretly? "I like him."

"You like your dentist. Tell me about him . . . what's he like. What do the two of you do together?"

They had sex. A lot. But that wasn't it. They laughed together. "We grilled out. We play with the dog. We went to putt-putt golf, which he hated, but did anyway. I forced him to go wine tasting, which he also hated. And he made me go to the shooting range, which I actually really enjoyed and that probably irritated him." Come to think of it, she irritated him a lot. But he seemed to like it. "We're going to the movies tonight. Just normal stuff."

"Sounds nice."

"It is."

"So do you think it's becoming serious?"

Why did that question always have to come up? Why couldn't it just be that she was having fun in the now? Tuesday didn't want to think about the future, she didn't want to think about what would happen if she admitted that she was falling in love with Diesel. What if he didn't feel the same? What if he dumped her? What if she thought she'd found something special and she was wrong? That was all too damn risky. It was better to keep a tight lid on her emotions and just have fun. Hold back. Call it a crush and roll with it.

"I don't know. It hasn't been long enough to say one way or the other."

The waiter leaned over her just then, dressed in black and white, his name as Italian as the pasta on her plate. She normally loved this restaurant, with its hushed atmosphere, warm stucco walls, and hearty food. But this whole dinner had made her anxious, and her stomach had the knots to prove it. Even though the outcome of her mom's lunch with Tom had been what she would have hoped for, it still made her feel bad. Now she didn't want to talk about Diesel.

"Don't allow your grief to prevent you from enjoying this relationship."

Here they went. Tuesday chewed the piece of bread she'd bitten off and tried desperately not to roll her eyes. Couldn't her mother just understand she didn't want to talk about it? And when she did, she'd let her know.

"Mom. I love you. I appreciate you. But don't worry about me. I'm fine." She suddenly wanted a glass of wine, but she resisted the urge to flag down the waiter.

Bracing herself for another round of questioning or more advice, Tuesday shoved her pasta around on her place.

But her mother just stared at her for a long moment then said, "I know you're fine. You always are. But I want more than just 'fine' for you."

Suddenly, those words knocked the fight out of her. Tuesday's shoulders slumped and she was horrified to realize that tears were in her eyes. "It's too soon to be more than fine. And yet, here I am totally laughing and enjoying myself with Diesel. That's not right."

Her mother reached across the table and patted her hand, her dark eyes filled with love. "Of course it's right. Do you honestly think your father would have wanted you to be miserable indefinitely? You know he wanted you happy. And you know he respected Diesel quite a bit. He would be thrilled."

She would not cry. She would not cry. So she just nodded so violently her teeth clanked into each other.

"Now let's order some tiramisu and gloat over the fact that we don't have to fight the battle of the bulge."

Tuesday gave a laugh, followed by a deep breath. She could do this.

All of it.

DIESEL had thought he would feel awkward picking up Tuesday now that he knew the truth about his feelings for her. I mean, come on, he had just admitted to himself he was in love. The big *L*. That didn't happen very often. It was a big freaking deal.

He should be nervous. But the truth was, the minute she got in his car and smiled at him, wearing a short summer dress that showed off her long legs, he was immediately at ease. Well, not all of him. A certain part was instantly at attention.

Especially when without hesitation she just leaned over and gave him a sweet, delicious kiss, filled with both passion and tenderness. It wasn't how she usually greeted him. So far, his initial moments with Tuesday usually involved sarcasm and/or demands. But he had to say, he liked this a whole hell of a lot.

"Now that's a hello," he told her when she finally pulled back.

She just gave him a soft smile. "What's up?"

"My dick."

"I was trying to ignore that. Because if I pay attention to it, we'll never make it to the movies."

"Would that be such a bad thing?" That's what Netflix was for.

"No, I suppose not."

She didn't say it with any flirtation. In fact, she seemed a little distracted, so Diesel let it drop. He backed his car up out of her driveway. "I can hold out until after the movie. So how was dinner with your mom?"

"It was okay. I confronted her about her lunch date with Tom Reynolds and she told me he's recently remarried after having lost his first wife. They were just sharing grief stories."

He would have thought she'd sound more relieved than she did. "Well, that's good, right? Your mom isn't dating."

"Yeah, but I'm still a shitty daughter. I should have been happy if she was happy."

She was way too hard on herself. "I don't think anyone would be cool with their parent jumping right back into dating a month later. You can't beat yourself up for having totally natural feelings."

"Yes, I guess." But she didn't sound convinced. "What are we seeing?"

"They show classics at the drive-in. I thought we could see *The Exorcist* if you're cool with it." She didn't strike him as the kind of woman to be afraid of a horror movie. He could pretty much guarantee she'd already seen it.

"That sounds romantic." She rolled her eyes at him. "But actually, that's fine with me. I love that movie."

Of course she did. It was amazing to him how well he felt like he knew Tuesday already after just a few weeks. "You never said you wanted romantic. You just said you wanted to see a movie."

"Isn't it obvious that all women want romantic? Even when they say they don't?"

Was that a trick question? "I plead the fifth on the grounds that I might incriminate myself."

She laughed. "Oh come on, I didn't ask you if my ass looks fat. It was just the kind of question you're supposed to agree with."

"In that case, yes. I agree. And for the record, nothing could make your ass look fat. Your ass is perfect."

"Why thank you."

Then Diesel thought through what she'd been saying. So if all women wanted romantic even when they didn't say it, what did that mean? "Wait. So you don't want to see *The Exorcist*?"

She groaned, pulling her necklace out of her cleavage, where it had dipped. "No, I said it was cool. And it is. Don't overthink it."

It was a bit of a problem he had with her. Was it because he really wanted to make sure she was happy? Or was it because he was whipped? Either way, his friends were right— he needed to quit being such a wuss. She was the kind of woman who just said straight out whatever she was thinking, so there was no reason for him to sit there and try to interpret her words. They were exactly what they were.

Which meant he could relax. Just enjoy.

When they pulled into the drive-in, Tuesday read the marquee and gave a happy exclamation. "Okay, I changed my mind. They're playing *Lady and the Tramp*, too. We so have to see that. We can catch *The Exorcist* next week."

He liked that she was just assuming they would be spending the next weekend together as well. But he wasn't thrilled about the idea of sitting through a cartoon.

"You don't mind, do you?" She gave him a pleading look. "It's just so sweet when they share that piece of pasta and wind up kissing. I haven't seen it since I was a kid."

Whipped. He totally was. He could not resist those eyes of hers. "Sure, of course."

Forty-five minutes later, he was regretting his quick concession. He was so bored he was struggling to stay awake and the girl dog's voice was the only thing preventing it. Every time she spoke it was like razors to his eardrums. He'd eaten an entire box of candy trying to give himself something to do other than groan in agony. Tuesday had been remarkably silent the entire time, which he took to mean was her being absorbed in childhood memories and joy.

Until she suddenly said, "This movie blows. Why did I like this as a kid?"

He had no answers for that.

"I mean, Lady is like the most annoying priss ever. She's not innocent, she's just dumb, and that's not charming at all. Seriously, like what would Tramp even see in her? She has an old-lady voice on top of it all."

Diesel laughed. "I agree with you on all points, sweetheart. I don't know. Maybe it just seemed very Romeo and

Juliet when you were a kid. Those stray dogs probably seemed exciting."

"I remember being terrified by the rat at the end. Somehow I don't think that's going to live up to my expectations."

"It's meant for kids, not thirty-year-old women."

"Does that make me jaded? Cynical?" She looked a little frightened of that possibility. But she still managed to interject, "And I'm not thirty yet."

"You're not jaded. Cynical. Or thirty. You're a grown woman who knows that relationships don't work that way." People didn't fall in love in a day. It took at least three weeks. He should know.

"What, that total opposites could actually work?" Tuesday tossed a piece of popcorn into her mouth.

"No, that's not what I meant. I think sometimes opposites work out just fine." They were verbal opposites. She talked nonstop and he didn't. "I was thinking more about the fact that they decide to commit to each other and a litter of puppies when they don't even know each other."

"That's true. Not to mention he's patronizing."

Since his candy was all gone, Diesel reached over and stuck his hand in her popcorn bucket. This was a perfect opportunity to tweak her. "I think he's just being protective. She obviously needs a firm hand."

"What?" She totally rose to the bait and shrieked at him, smacking his hand. "And get out of my popcorn! How could you even say that—"

He chewed and grinned at the same time.

"You're an ass. You're just trying to get a rise out of me."

"Yep. Works every time." Diesel hit the button to make

his seat go back. "Now put your popcorn down and make out with me. That's why people really come to the drive-in."

"Good call." Tuesday put the popcorn container in the backseat.

"Why are you putting it back there?"

"Because we get rowdy when we make out. You know I'll end up kicking it if I leave it up here."

"You're always thinking, babe. That's why I—"

Diesel cut himself off. Shit, he'd almost said love. That's why he loved her.

"Why you what?" She looked at him expectantly, her eyebrows raised.

He coughed. "Sorry, I choked on the popcorn. What I was trying to say is that's why I worship you." He knew she would take that as humorous.

Which she did. "As well you should. I'm very worshipable."

"Then get over here and let me at it."

"Why do I always have to be the one to come to you?" she complained. "Isn't that patronizing?"

He could argue or placate or he could just lean over into her space and kiss her, which is what he did. She was midrant still when his mouth covered hers. Her squawk of indignation dissolved into a sigh. Diesel loved the way she acquiesced to him, the way she just gave up her position and embraced the passion that always sparked between them. Her protests were just token gestures anyway, she wanted him just as much as he wanted her. Which was every minute of every damn day, it seemed like.

Sliding his tongue across her bottom lip, Diesel coaxed her to open up her mouth.

"Mm, have I told you I love your beard?" she murmured. "It's soft. Sexy."

"Everything about you is sexy."

It was. God, he couldn't get enough of her. Diesel took her mouth again in a searing kiss. What had started out as just the need for some casual drive-in making out turned into a deep, urgent need to taste her, touch her. Consume her.

Her reaction met his and her hands raked his hair, her body leaning forward, seeking contact with his. The buzz of the movie sound track was to his left, but it couldn't distract him, not when his tongue was pushing into her mouth, and her hands were sliding down his chest, scraping along his pecs. He tugged at the bottom of her dress, wanting access to her smooth skin, and he was rewarded with a low moan in his ear.

Oh, yeah. He was going to score at the drive-in. A teenage ambition finally realized.

Until he saw movement out of the corner of his eye.

"Jesus." He moved back from Tuesday, quickly removing his hand from under the dress.

"What? Where are you going? Get back here."

Tuesday reached for him, but Diesel shook his head. "Look behind you, sweetheart."

"Huh? What?" Tuesday turned and let out a startled shriek. "Holy crap, we have a Peeping Tom."

There was a boy, about eight years old, standing outside their car, watching them with round, curious eyes, tearing a piece off of his licorice with his teeth.

"I guess we're the show." Diesel was amused. He could imagine he'd have done the same thing when he was that age. Little boys were curious.

"Okay, that's just disturbing." Tuesday glanced out the window again. "And he's not leaving."

The kid had backed up two feet, but he was still checking out Tuesday like he had seen an alien. A very appealing alien.

Diesel started laughing. "I think you've made a new friend."

Tuesday unrolled her window. "Hi there. I hear your mother calling you. You'd better get back to her."

That made him laugh even harder. "Seriously? Just leave the poor kid be."

The boy turned and sauntered off in no particular hurry.

"What? He needed to go. That was creepy. He was watching us make out."

"Well, we're not making out anymore. So let's get back to that." He dropped his hand to her knee. They had just been getting to the good stuff.

"Absolutely not." She picked his hand up and moved it to his own thigh.

He had no desire to be feeling up his own leg. "Why not?"

"I feel violated."

"It was a kid! Who cares?"

"More like a future Green River Killer. Where's my popcorn?" She reached into the back and recovered her box and started tossing pieces in her mouth, eyes trained on the movie screen.

His amusement evaporated. Not only was he not getting any he was going to have to sit through the rest of the cartoon. The characters were singing something warbly and off key, and while probably entertaining for a six-year-old,

Diesel was thinking he'd prefer a kick in the nuts to another hour of this.

"My suggestion of just skipping the movie was a good one," he told her. "I wish you'd listened to me."

She ignored that. "You know, this woman in the pound is who Tramp should have hooked up with. They have more in common. And really, Lady is just a puppy in comparison. Long-term she's not going to be able to hold Tramp's interest."

Why was he supposed to care? He needed more candy. It wasn't a replacement for sex with Tuesday, but it would keep his mouth busy.

Tuesday was keeping her mouth busy with running it.

"I mean, what is this obsession men have with innocence? They think they want it, then they get bored with it."

They did? "I have no idea what you're talking about," he told her in all honesty.

She turned to him. "What attracted you to me?"

Oh, damn. This was a bear trap waiting to snap. "It wasn't your innocence," he assured her.

She rolled her eyes. "That's not an answer."

What did she want him to say? He cared about her, he was attracted to her on a whole lot of different levels? But an open-ended question like that was overwhelming and he didn't want to risk pissing her off. "I feel like there's a right answer and a wrong answer here and I'm going to get reamed if I misstep."

She looked so astonished that for a second she didn't speak—always amazing when it came to the woman he loved.

"Really? Is that true? That a lot of times men don't say anything because they're afraid of saying the wrong thing?"

"Um. Yeah." Where the hell had she been? "It's like women have formed the answer they're looking for in their head and we can never match it."

"Interesting. So if I promise not to get mad at you, no matter what, how would you answer the question of what attracted you to me?"

He raised an eyebrow. "Sweetheart, I don't think you can guarantee you won't get mad. You're a bit of a hot-head."

"What? I am not."

"See your voice raised right there." It was tempting to laugh, but he held it back. The grin he couldn't contain.

She pulled a face. "God, I hate it when you're right."

"Then you must be hating all the time." Diesel reached over and touched her cheek. "No, in all seriousness, I was attracted to your smile, your laughter. You looked like you were having fun. And of course you're beautiful. Gorgeous."

He wanted to tell her more, and he searched for the right words. He'd never been particularly good at expressing his feelings.

"Thank you," she said. "I appreciate it. The wrong answer would be saying that you were attracted to me because I looked like an easy lay. Anything else I'm going to take as a compliment, so don't be afraid to flatter me."

That sounded like the Tuesday he had come to know and love. He wanted to get closer to the truth of his emotions, put something out there, and pull her a little closer to him if that was at all possible. "I'm attracted to you now for all those same reasons. But also now I know that you're smart, generous, loyal, and big-hearted. I think you're an amazing woman and I want to be with you, only you. I don't want either of us to be seeing other people. Just you and me."

There it was. Out there and he couldn't take it back.

But you never got what you wanted unless you asked for it.

Maybe he was too boring for her, maybe she would lose interest in him, but between now and then he would like to enjoy it knowing she was with him, and only him.

Tuesday clutched her popcorn and stared at Diesel. She knew she should say something, but she was stunned speechless. She hadn't turned the conversation in this direction because she'd been fishing for compliments. It had really just been her natural curiosity as she'd been watching the movie to ponder what drew people to each other. She had just wondered what had drawn him to her because truthfully, they were almost as much of opposites in temperament as Lady and Tramp were in personality. Tuesday was verbal and easily agitated, Diesel was neither. She dealt with her emotions poorly, he didn't deal with his at all. She liked to dance and talk and laugh and be the life of the party whereas Diesel liked to be an observer. He sought his thrills quietly, with a firm hand, in the bedroom and elsewhere.

She liked those qualities about him. He, too, was loyal, and generous, and intelligent. He meant what he said and nothing was hot air with him. So for him to say he was attracted to her and wanted to be with her, only her was something she trusted one hundred percent. It might mean that she wasn't the only one who was falling head over ass here. It meant that this man that she was falling in love with just might be falling in love with her as well, or might at least at some point in the future, and that made her speechless. Breathless. Her heart raced, her palms sweated, her chest felt inflated.

For the first time in her adult life, she didn't know what to say to a man. But he was looking at her expectantly, and she forced the words out past her tightened throat, the first ones that popped into her head. "I'm cool with that."

It wasn't good enough. She knew it immediately from the flicker of maybe disappointment in his blue eyes. Why was it so easy for her to rant and express agitation or dissect other people, but so damn hard to throw her own true feelings out there?

Diesel had been there for her, as a friend, as a lover. He deserved more. He deserved honesty, even if the thought of making herself vulnerable made her want to run and hide behind a steel door with a massive lock. She almost said something like, "You know I dig you," but stopped herself. That wasn't right either.

She was squeezing the box so hard, the popcorn was forced to the top and a piece tumbled into her lap, but she ignored it. It was scary to be real, but she swallowed hard, making eye contact. "I think you're a very attractive man, Daniel, both inside and out. You're thoughtful, loyal, responsible, kind, sexy as hell, and amazingly calm. I'm really grateful to have you in my life."

God, had she really just said that? Her instinct was to tack a snarky comment on to the end of it, but she resisted, fishing the popcorn out of her lap and eating it out of pure nervousness. Doing this right with Diesel mattered.

It earned her a smile from him, a genuine, wide smile.

"Thanks, sweetheart, I feel the same way. I care about you, you know."

Caring was good. That was how she felt. And wasn't caring a pit stop on the road to love? She was hoping it was. "I care about you, too."

"Good." He reached out and took a piece of her popcorn. "Now can we ditch this movie and go home?"

She glanced at the screen. "It's almost over."

"I'll let you pick what position you want to be fucked in."

Tuesday felt a kick of lust between her legs. Her choice? She never got a choice, mostly because he controlled what they were doing, and she liked it. But the idea of being the one calling the shots for once held a certain appeal. "Done."

"Put your seat belt on." He was already backing the car up, turning the radio off to kill the sound of the movie. "So what's your position pick?"

She made a sound in the back of her throat. "I'm running through all of them in my head." It was an arousing little exercise, picturing all the ways he could enter her. "I haven't decided yet."

"Ladies' choice isn't going to happen very often, so you'd better pick wisely."

But the truth was, Tuesday knew no matter which position she picked, it was going to be damn satisfying.

"I'll just show you," she told him.

He didn't answer, but his erection was answer enough.

CHAPTER
TWELVE

BACK at her place, Tuesday let Diesel push her up against the wall in her entryway, his hands on her waist, head bent over her as he slid his tongue across the top her breast. That was the wonderful thing about warm weather clothes—easy access.

It was amazing how hot he could get her with so very little effort. That was the beauty and the mystery of attraction . . . when you clicked with someone, the sexual sparks were lit as easily as dry kindling.

He pulled down the front of her sundress and her bra and pulled her nipple into his mouth. Tuesday felt the echo of the movement deep inside her womb and she held on to his shoulders for support. Part of her just wanted him to lift her dress and pound into her. Right now. Two steps from the door. Against the wall, hard.

If she wanted it, he would give it to her.

But that would still be him, in control, driving her pleasure.

What she wanted was for him to lose control. To completely and totally give in to his desire, his passion. He never lost that edge, never gave up any of his power during sex, and that was what she wanted.

Tuesday picked her position.

"Let's go to the bed," she told him, trying to gently pull his head away from her breast.

"Not yet." He went to the other breast, sucking and tugging at her nipple.

Despite the sharp kick of desire that brought her, Tuesday stood her ground. "You said it was my choice."

"We're not ready for sex yet. This is called foreplay, sweetheart." He looked at her with hooded, dark eyes, his beard tickling her cleavage.

Tuesday yanked harder on his head. "No. Now."

There was a pause where his eyes narrowed, then he spoke, his voice low and tight, filled with lust. "Well, alright then. If you want to be in bed, we'll go to bed." With a fake gallant gesture, he moved his arm in a swirl. "After you."

Feeling confident with her plan, Tuesday walked past him breezily, her breasts still popping out of her sundress. "Thanks."

Her bedroom wasn't as tidy as Diesel's but it wasn't a disaster either. There were only a few discarded clothing choices on the chair, so she bent over to grab them and toss them on the floor. "Sit down."

"Where? The chair?" He gave her a look that was both

lascivious and satisfied. "You're going to ride me on the chair? I like that idea, babe."

Let him think that's what she had in mind. "Take off your clothes."

To encourage him to do the same, she pulled the straps of her dress off her shoulders and shoved it down past her waist. Stepping out of it, she raked her hair back off her face and waited for him to strip off his T-shirt and jeans. He had the most incredible body. She loved looking at him, touching him, scratching her nails down his stomach and back. He shoved his briefs down.

Don't even get her started on that penis. It was a work of art. Sculpted for pleasure, just for her. As he sat down in the chair, Tuesday thought about another woman putting her hands on Diesel, of another woman sliding herself down onto that fantastic erection, and she knew that what she was feeling wasn't just attraction. She was in love with this man, and she only wanted him with her. Ever.

He was in the chair, looking tense and turned on, his erection straining upward.

He expected her to climb onto him.

That wasn't her plan.

Dropping to her knees in front of him, Tuesday bent over, her mouth open.

"What the hell are you doing?" he asked, stopping her forward motion with a sharp grip on her hair.

Looking up at him from under her lashes, she gave him a sly shrug. "This is the position I've chosen."

His eyes widened in shock, then he shook his head. "Doesn't count."

"Oh, yes, it does. You didn't define the terms."

This was what she wanted to do. He never let her suck him because he had to direct and control their sex. Every time she had tried to reach for him, he moved her away. He flipped her over on her back, pulled her up for a kiss . . . anything that kept her off his cock. Because for a man like Diesel, he was not prepared to let go of himself completely.

Today she was going to suck him until he did.

One hand on the bottom of his shaft, she enclosed him with her mouth.

"Tuesday." It was half groan, half protest.

She ignored him and took him fully into her. When she pulled back off, she made sure to leave a nice slick trail behind her, which made the next downward motion smooth and effortless.

His hands were on his thighs, balled into fists. He was tense, his breath short and clipped. He was containing himself.

Not for long. She found a nice, slow rhythm, her hand gripping his cock tightly, following behind her mouth as she stroked up and down on him.

With her free hand, she cupped his balls, enjoying that for the first time, she had all of him in her hold. She picked up the pace. His breathing increased, short, urgent pants that whistled through his clenched teeth. His fists opened and his fingers dug into his thighs. Tuesday thought he tasted delicious, her own body responding to the thrusting parody, her inner thighs soaking wet with desire. But she didn't even think of conceding, of climbing onto him. This was her choice and this was his turn.

Without warning, his hands went into her hair and he took over the rhythm for her. He pounded her mouth down onto his cock, his groans bursting out with satisfying volume.

She had him. He had let go.

It was immensely gratifying to know that he trusted her completely and that she got him so hot, so aroused, that he was willing to give in to that passion.

She could feel his balls tightening in her hand, his legs tensing. He was going to come. Bracing herself for the explosion, she felt the definite feeling of triumph sweep over her. It would be impossible to ever feel this way with any other man. She was certain of it, high on that knowledge, and she was going to let him burst into her mouth, something she never did.

But Diesel had different ideas. He moved so fast, she almost fell backward, but he steadied her after he pushed her off of him. Then before she could react or gauge his intent, he had her turned around. With a tug, he tore her panties with a snap of the side string.

Holy shit. He had torn her panties. There wasn't anything hotter. And when he pulled her back down toward him, she understood his intention, and sucked in a sharp breath of anticipation.

A second later his erection was pushing into her, her body dropping down onto him from gravity, and it was a hot, delicious collision, the angle forcing his cock to stretch her open for him.

"Oh, Diesel," she told him, reaching blindly for the arms of the chair for stability.

He slapped her ass cheek. "Up and down. Come on, baby. Fuck me."

You didn't have to ask her twice. Tuesday put her feet on his and lifted herself up and down onto him, the position pulling her down with a nice hard bounce each time. His hands gripped her waist and he aided her movements.

Then he did something that he'd never done before. He bit her shoulder and came as he pounded into her, like he was bearing down on a leather strip during nineteenth-century surgery. He had never come before her. Ever. He always made sure she'd had two, three, sometimes four orgasms before he came. But now he just gripped her with teeth and hands and exploded inside her. It was so powerful she almost lost her balance, but she held on, and knowing what she had done to him sent her hurtling into her own orgasm.

It was so intense from the angle that the room actually went fuzzy in front of her, light-headedness forcing dancing spots in front of her. For a second she thought she was actually going to faint, the pleasure ripping through every inch of her, taking her somewhere she had absolutely never been before, in and outside of her body all at once.

When the spots receded and her body settled down into little spasms, Tuesday shook her head, shocked. Diesel's head was against her back, his slick forehead between her shoulder blades.

"What the hell was that?" she finally asked with a little laugh.

His cock jumped a little inside her and she shivered from the aftershocks.

"That was perfection," he told her. He kissed the spot where he had bitten her. "Sorry, I left a mark."

"I don't care." She didn't really care about anything but him at the moment.

His hands were running down her sides, and it felt sweaty and intimate and important. She wouldn't, couldn't do what she had just done with anyone else.

Standing up carefully, she pushed the remnants of her underwear to the floor and reached back for his hand. Pulling him out of the chair, together they stumbled three feet to the bed and laid down on it face-first.

"Mmm," was his opinion, his hand on her waist. "That was good head, sweetheart."

How bizarre that his praise for her oral sex skills made her want to blush with pride. "Thank you."

She draped her hand across his chest, her eyes fluttering, not sure if they wanted to stay open or close. They should go under the covers, but it seemed like too much work to move, and she was feeling very, very content.

Sleep was closing in on her when Diesel murmured in her ear, "Would it make you run if I said that I love you?"

Her eyes flew open. He was watching her, steady, calm, just like always. Yet there was something else . . . the truth behind his words was in his eyes.

Holy shit. He loved her.

Even as her heart started to race and she felt giddiness creep over her, she matched his casual tone. "No. Would it make you run if I said the same thing?"

"Nope."

"Cool. Because I do. Love you."

"So we're on the same page then."

"Yes."

"Perfect." He kissed her forehead and closed his eyes. "Goodnight, sweetheart."

"'Nite, Daniel."

He was in love with her. She was in love with him.

Tuesday lay there, her body pleasantly sore from their powerful lovemaking, and marveled at that.

They were in love.

How awesome was that?

DIESEL stood there, dressed and staring down at Tuesday as she slept. At some point during the night, she had pulled up the comforter they'd fallen asleep on and had wrapped the right side over her so it looked like a bun holding a hot dog. Her one shoulder was peeking out, her breath steady and even.

He needed to leave and let the dog out, but was stuck there, staring at her, feeling amazingly happy. She'd said she loved him.

Women had said that to him before and sometimes it had exasperated him, sometimes it had pleased him.

Never had it made him feel like this.

This was something different.

Better.

Leaning over, he kissed her forehead. "Tuesday."

Her eyes popped open. "Hmm? What?" She blinked at him, startled.

"I need to go. I'll call you later."

The shock of being woken receded and her eyes started to flutter back shut. "Okay," she said, voice full of sleep. "You're not going to get a haircut, are you?"

He laughed at the randomness of her question. "No."

"Good." She yawned. "Bye, sexy."

When Diesel stopped to linger in the doorway and stare at her yet again, she was already back asleep.

There was something overwhelming about understanding you loved someone.

He wasn't sure what to do with it.

But it occurred to him as he left to go take care of his dog, that if he lived with Tuesday he'd never have to crawl out of her bed and leave her.

TUESDAY finished up her blog then glanced at the thumb drive sitting on her desk still. She couldn't avoid it forever. It wasn't fair to her boss or her father. The benefit plans were completely under control thanks to Kendall's assistant, and Tuesday couldn't believe it was only a week away.

It had been almost two months since her father had died.

She hated that.

Yet at the same time, she understood now when people had told her that she would get used to it. She didn't think about it all the time. She accepted it. But then there were moments where it slapped her in the face and she was overwhelmed by the grief. Hence the reason she'd been avoiding the thumb drive. She hadn't wanted to read her father's notes.

But today she felt capable of handling it. She was in love with Diesel. It was the most unexpected, weirdest damn thing, but it was true. She was in love with him, and it made everything else in her life just a little bit better, easier.

He was a good man, and while she never thought of herself as the kind of woman who would enjoy staking a claim, Tuesday felt a bit like announcing that they were together to whoever would listen. She didn't, obviously, but it was tempting.

Picking the drive up, she inserted it into her computer, taking a deep breath. Hopefully it would be an easy subject, and she could knock out the article in the next few days.

What she saw when she opened the folder made her jaw drop.

Her father's last article, outlined in front of her, had been about Diesel Lange.

There were notes from an interview, Diesel's driving stats, and details on his accident.

She should have known. She should have talked to her father more. Diesel should have mentioned it to her. Somehow, even before knowing about his cancer or having met Diesel, she should have known that the two men were communicating. She should have been a part of it, and she felt left out and . . . lonely.

Unsure where to begin, or what to open first and read, Tuesday saw there was also a video of Diesel's accident. Her heart pounding, she clicked on it.

It had been at Pocono, the Tricky Triangle, as the track was referred to. She recognized it immediately when the camera panned over the track, and the announcers confirmed that as they chattered over the roar of the engines.

Diesel was running in fifth place and Tuesday studied his powerful black car, like somehow she could see him, the man, behind the windshield and the net and the helmet.

She'd seen him drive dozens of times in the past, but she had never thought twice about it. She'd never met him. Now he was her boyfriend, as much as that ridiculous word made her want to squirm. Boyfriend sounded so high school, but that's what he was. He was *hers*.

It happened so fast, the camera missed half of it. One minute the sportscaster was commenting on leader laps, the next there were cars spinning out in the infield, smoke, exclamations of concern, and Diesel's car in the wall.

"That was a hard hit, Rob," the one announcer said. "Diesel Lange went straight into that wall at almost one hundred and forty miles an hour. Did you see that debris? It went straight up into his windshield. I don't know what it was, but we heard the spotter, and he tried to avoid the twenty-three car, but the turn was right there, and he had no visibility."

"Yeah, this is a bad one. I don't see him climbing out of his car yet, Phil."

Her stomach flipped and she felt the hot taste of fear in her mouth, even though she knew the outcome. That was two years ago. Yet, still, it made her sick to think that Diesel could have died.

His car was completely crunched in and there was an ambulance streaming across the infield already. The network had obviously cut to a commercial, but whoever had made the video edited in the EMTs taking Diesel off the track on a stretcher. His helmet was off and it was clear he was unconscious.

That was it, all she could take. Tuesday smacked her keyboard to stop the video.

God, she was shaking.

She read the details of his accident, outlined in her father's notes. Punctured lung, two broken vertebrae, shattered kneecap, dislocated shoulder . . .

No wonder he was in pain. No wonder he didn't want to drive that vintage car.

She read through the interview her father had conducted with him. As she stared at the words on the screen, she could hear them both, the two men she knew the best. She could hear her father, recognized his phrasings, choice of words. The same with Diesel. They had known each other, met, talked, and laughed, and for some reason tears came to her eyes. Both with relief that they had had the opportunity to meet while her father had still been alive, and shock to realize that in some ways, her father had known Diesel better than she did.

For all she believed that he loved for, he hadn't told her anything about the accident, about his injuries, about the impact it had had on his life. It was an off subject, not allowed. If she raised it, he changed the subject.

Yet he had reflected on the life-changing event with her father.

It was there in the notes, a direct quote.

"I don't know, Bob. A lot of people want to believe that everything happens for a reason, because it brings them comfort. But I think down that path lies the torment of trying to interpret what you were supposed to learn from something that was painful and unplanned. But you know, I think sometimes horrible and random things happen, and we just have to deal with the outcome. I had a great career as a driver. Now I don't. It's called an accident for a reason . . . yet I'm still the same guy. Nothing more, nothing less."

Tuesday reread everything in the files again. She watched the video three times, each time her gut twisting into army knots. She made a list of questions she had for the article.

Then she started to write.

DIESEL was standing in his driveway with Johnny, admiring the car he had restored as they loaded it onto a hauler.

"That's one fine-looking car, son. You should be proud."

He was. It was damn satisfying to be seeing the very obvious results of his labor, time, and money.

"Thank you. I think I just might consider myself an honest-to-goodness grease monkey now."

"You might just be greasy." His uncle clapped him on the shoulder. "Hey, your girl just pulled up in the front of the house."

His girl. It was something he still couldn't get over even a week after their talk in bed. Tuesday was nuts enough to agree to be with him and he was feeling pretty damn happy about it. She got out of her car, a manila envelope in her hand, sunglasses on her face. Wearing narrow jeans and high-heeled sandals, with a form-fitting shirt, Diesel thought she was that perfect combination of hot and classy.

"Hey, baby, what's up?" He leaned over and kissed her, enjoying that he had the right to show her affection in front of his uncle, the haulers, and anyone else who happened to be around.

For the last few weeks, he'd been running on kind of a

perpetual high, between all the sex and his growing feelings for Tuesday. Since he didn't plan on giving up either of those things anytime soon, he was thinking he was in for a very pleasant fall and winter.

"Hi," she said with a smile. Leaning around him, she waved to his uncle. "Hi, Johnny, how are you?"

"Good, good. How's that for a beautiful-looking car?"

"I know, it's amazing." She beamed up at Diesel. "I think it's amazing that you restored this car all by yourself."

He had a bit of an "aw, shucks" moment. "It wasn't that hard." Just four months of his life and twenty-five grand of his cash, but who was counting?

"I think you're amazing," she murmured.

Her eyes were covered by her sunglasses but he recognized that tone of voice. It was the one she used when she wanted to hide genuine emotion behind lust. "Well, you're pretty amazing yourself." Diesel wanted to kiss her again and was about to when his uncle cleared his throat.

"Are you both trying to make me sick to my stomach? Good Lord, write the woman a poem and read it to her in private. Don't subject the rest of us to your mutual adoration."

Tuesday laughed. Diesel rolled his eyes at her and admonished his uncle. "Mind your own damn business."

But he knew his uncle wasn't really criticizing him any more than he was his uncle. His family was pleased for him. Johnny was giving him lots of knowing grins and Beth was already dropping hints that she was available for ring shopping.

It made him feel even better to know that his aunt and uncle liked Tuesday. He wouldn't be able to deal with it if they disliked the woman he loved.

"So are you just here to check on the car? Or you missed my pretty face?" he asked her.

"Neither."

He appreciated that Tuesday never bothered to stroke his ego.

"I'm here to show you the mockup of the magazine article. They're running it with the new issue next week."

Diesel tried not to groan. She had told him that the racing magazine she freelanced for wanted to go ahead and run the interview he had done with Bob Jones six months earlier. Doing the interview in the first place had been an impulse, a moment of weakness where he hadn't been able to say no to the man who everyone knew most likely had terminal cancer.

But then he had thought it would never see the light of day, and he wasn't entirely unhappy with that prospect. He didn't like to talk about his previous career or his accident, and that was what everyone wanted to know about. It was the only thing interesting about a retired driver who had never won a championship.

Tuesday had tried on at least three occasions to discuss the article with him, ask him more questions, picking at him for more details but he had put her off. He didn't want to talk about it.

"Oh, yeah?" He took the envelope she was thrusting at him. "Thanks."

"It's great timing. It hits the shelves just a few days before the auction, which is fantastic exposure for the car. I had a picture included."

Diesel stared at her, suddenly feeling really uncomfortable. Why did he have a feeling he was about to be thrust into the spotlight in a way he wasn't going to like? "When did you get a picture of the car?"

"I went out in the garage and took it. You were sleeping and I was bored."

That seemed reasonable. Yet somehow he felt like she should have asked permission. "You could have told me. I would have pulled it out of the garage."

"I like it with all the clunky garage junk around it. It looks real."

Johnny had moved away to say something to the hauler and Diesel was grateful because for some reason he had a feeling like they were skidding down the track about to crash into an argument. "It might have been nice if we had discussed it."

She just shrugged. "Aren't you going to look at it?"

"I'll look at it later." He really didn't want to see it, read it, in his driveway in front of her. It was going to make him uncomfortable.

"I worked hard on this. It was hard for me to finish my dad's last article." An edge crept into her voice.

"I know that," he said in exasperation. "I'm sure you did a fine job. But it's hard for me, too. I don't like people poking into my business."

"I'm not just 'people.'"

"No, you're not. But everyone reading it is." How could she not understand that he wanted his life to remain private? It was the one good thing to come out of his accident. The media left him the hell alone.

"Argh, you're so frustrating sometimes. You don't tell me anything, so how am I supposed to know what's going on in your head?"

"If anything is important I'll say it. Don't get all worked up." He wasn't sure how they'd gone from embarrassing eye-gazing to sniping at each other, but he didn't care to continue.

Her forehead went up at his words. It was so pronounced her eyebrows lifted above her sunglasses. "Okay, I think I'll leave now. I have some errands to run before dinner tonight, and after this conversation one of those errands might be picking up a jug of wine."

Unfortunately, she probably wasn't kidding. "Oh, come on, you don't need a drink. It's two in the afternoon and we're just having a discussion. You go run your errands. I'm going to finish up with the car here and then I'll go in the house and read your article."

She reached up and gripped his chin. Scratching his beard and sighing, she told him, "You're stinking cute, you know that?"

Apparently they weren't going to argue. That worked for him.

He kissed her. "Hell, yeah, I knew that. But you're foxy."

"Foxy?" She laughed. "Alright, I'll see you tonight." She backed up and blew him a kiss. Then she waved to his uncle. "Bye, Johnny."

His uncle strolled back over to him and Diesel watched Tuesday get in her car and pull away. "I was thinking maybe I'd ask Tuesday to move in with me. What do you think?" The idea had been kicking around in his head for a while, and the more he thought about it, the more he liked it. Having her with him, every day, sharing a bedroom, sharing meals together, it was really appealing.

"As long as she's not the type of woman to be insulted by that. Some girls still like a ring first."

"I don't think she's that type."

"Then go for it. But expect your aunt to have a word or two to say."

He imagined Aunt Beth would lecture him, but it seemed a natural step to him. They weren't ready to get married, but living together would make what they were doing even better. "Oh, I'm sure."

"But just so you know, I'm happy for you. She seems like a fine woman and she's put a grin on your face, which is all that matters to me. Now let me have a look at that article." His uncle held his hand out.

Diesel could have said no, but chances were his family was mentioned. Because Diesel and Pete were cousins and had both had a similar accident, Pete's resulting in his tragic death, they were forever be linked together in racing stories. Since Pete had been Johnny's only child, he deserved to see anything that might involve his son.

In Diesel's opinion, Johnny had always done a fine job of keeping his son's memory alive without being obsessive about it. He had faced adversity and loss with strength.

Diesel wasn't sure he'd done as well, but he'd managed. He gave his uncle the envelope and went over to discuss the final details with the hauler, who looked about finished loading the car. It was going over to the practice track for a few days to be on display, then a big-box retail store, and finally to the hotel where the benefit was taking place.

He was damn proud of this car. It was his idea of art, a finely tuned machine that was fifty years old and could still go around that speedway track at one-thirty.

"Did you see the picture of the car?" his uncle asked him.

"No." Curious, Diesel leaned over to see the magazine

spread. "I wish she would have told me what she was doing. I would have pulled the car out of the garage."

The photo looked cluttered to him, like the focus wasn't really on the car but on his mess surrounding it. "I'd have washed it, too. It's all dusty."

"Did you see this picture?"

Following his uncle's finger, he saw the last car he'd driven, mangled after the wreck. Nice. "She didn't tell me she was printing that either." Maybe because everytime she'd brought up the article, he'd shut her down. He didn't like seeing his failure in glossy color, and now he was regretting brushing her off. "Do you mind if I have a look at that?"

He suddenly had a bad feeling . . . like he wasn't going to be thrilled about any of what was printed on that page.

"Knock yourself out."

Five minutes later, he definitely wasn't happy. The tone of the article was verging on critical of him. At least that's how he took it. And last time he'd checked, it was his girlfriend who had written it.

In the two years since his accident, Lange has neither pursued the possibility of returning to the track, nor has he become an advocate for stricter safety measures, two traditional routes we've seen injured drivers take over the years. He lives instead in relative obscurity on a large property with no wife or kids, or any evidence of his stellar but short-lived career inside his spacious home. The garage is the only room that indicates any connection to racing, and after viewing the litany of car parts scattered around, most people would assume he had been a chief mechanic, not a driver.

What exactly was she suggesting? So he didn't have a bunch of pictures of himself on the walls or awards displayed. It didn't match the décor. Plus he didn't need a constant reminder of what he'd had and lost by losing control out on the track.

"Johnny." He called to his uncle, who had stepped away to let him read the article and was tossing the tennis ball to Wilma.

"Yeah?"

"Do you think I should have become an advocate for stricter safety measures after Pete's crash and mine?"

His uncle's eyebrow went up, like he was wondering where the hell that question had come from. But he didn't ask, he just shook his head. "No, of course not. Nothing could have been done to change the outcome of what happened to both of you. It's a risk you take, plain and simple. We can't bubble-wrap the sport any more or it won't be racing."

That would be his opinion as well. His accident had been a combination of unexpected circumstances and human error. "This article is kind of pissing me off."

"Business and pleasure don't mix, son. They never have."

He definitely wasn't feeling any pleasure toward this business.

CHAPTER
THIRTEEN

DIESEL put the chicken skewers on the grill and tried not to worry. A storm was brewing and he didn't mean over Lake Norman. Tuesday was clearly pissed at him and he had to admit he wasn't feeling so pleased with her himself.

"Okay, I've been here an hour now and I think I've been patient enough."

Yep. Storm coming. Diesel took the grilling tongs in his hand and messed with the skewers, adding more spacing between them. "Patient enough about what?"

"You haven't said one word about my article."

She could sense she was leaving the chair she'd been sitting in, but he still didn't turn around. He wasn't prepared to have this conversation. "I told you it was a nice article." Which he had.

"That's lame and you know it."

"What am I supposed to say?"

"Something that says you care about me and know it was hard for me to write the thing."

He turned, feeling his anger spark a little. "I do care about you. I do know it was hard for you. It was hard for me to read it."

"Why?" she asked him baldly, standing a foot in front of him, her hands on her hips. She was wearing jeans and a T-shirt and the gesture had her shirt riding up, exposing her stomach.

"Because it was." Diesel knew that was a frustrating answer but he couldn't make himself say anything else. He couldn't tell her how sometimes he felt like a total loser. That he had let down his uncle and his team owner and sponsor and himself.

That he had never come close to achieving the success he had worked hard for in his twenties.

"Are you kidding me? That's all you're going to say?"

"What am I supposed to say?" He couldn't take the way she was staring at him, irritated, her eyes pleading with him. He couldn't stand the thought that he was inadequate to Tuesday.

"You're supposed to tell me how you feel."

"I feel fine." Diesel went back to the grill, turning the skewers.

Her arms wrapped around him from behind, snaking around his waist. He closed his eyes as she laid her cheek on his back. Maybe he should tell her he was angry about the article. Maybe he should tell her that he didn't like the way she'd portrayed him, as a racing hermit locked in his house.

"You can tell me anything, you know. I care about you."

"Yeah, I know." He did know and he was very grateful for her in his life. "I care about you, too."

He loved her.

Yet he didn't want to fight and he didn't want her to regret she'd chosen him.

So he still said nothing.

"ARE you okay?" Kendall asked her. "You look a little stressed."

Tuesday was more than a little stressed. She was supernova mega-stressed and she was alternating between wanting to throw up and cry hysterically.

So she'd taken what she thought was a smarter route and was drinking a glass of wine. "I'm totally stressed. What if this benefit is a massive failure?"

Kendall rubbed her arm in a gesture of comfort but Tuesday hardly noticed. She was glancing around the room, looking for anything that could be improved at the last minute, making sure everything was in place and the serving staff was poised for the crowd who was about to enter.

"Hey, it's not going to be a failure. You've done a fantastic job. The room looks amazing, there are a ton of donations to be auctioned off, and there are a crapload of people attending. Relax."

Relaxing was not going to happen. Not until it was eleven o'clock, the last guest had left, and she had some indicator of success. "Thanks, but I'm just going to worry. It's the way it is."

"I get that. Where's Diesel?"

"I don't know. He's around here somewhere."

They had hardly seen each other all week and they'd driven to the benefit separately. Tuesday had been so busy with final details that she'd barely had time to text him, let alone hang out or spend the night with him. Not that he seemed to care. If she weren't so insanely worried about tonight, she would have been worried about the fact that he seemed remote, like something was bothering him. She would worry about Diesel tomorrow. Tonight she had to pray that she actually raised money and didn't let cancer patients and survivors, and all the friends and sponsors who had so generously donated to the auction, massively down.

It didn't exactly surprise her that the man would retreat right when she needed him the most. Diesel wasn't big on emotional vulnerability.

She took another big swallow of her wine.

"Are you sure you should be drinking?" Kendall asked her.

"Yes." She didn't even hesitate. She wasn't going to survive this without her old friend Merlot. For the first time she paused and actually looked at her best friend. "I can't believe you're wearing heels."

"I think this exceeds my limit for the year," Kendall said. "They hurt like hell."

"Well, thanks for wearing them. You look fantastic." Kendall was in a red cocktail dress and nude pumps. It was a good look on her. Tuesday fiddled with her necklace. She was wearing black, which initially had just seemed easy and smart. Half her wardrobe was black and it was spill-proof. Now its mourning hue seemed appropriate. This event was going to kill her. Or it was going to die, a horrible unsuccessful failure of a fund-raiser.

"So do you."

"I have sweaty armpits." Which made no sense because her dress was sleeveless. She drained her wineglass. "Okay, I need to find a waiter to get another drink, then we can open the doors and let in what are hopefully the masses."

She headed for any man wearing a black uniform who could supply her liquid courage.

KENDALL went in search of her husband, hoping she might spot Diesel along the way. She wanted to warn him that Tuesday needed to be monitored. She would never forgive herself if she got drunk at this event, and Kendall knew all too well Tuesday could lose count when she'd skipped dinner and was tipping the glass back out of nerves.

Evan was actually talking to Diesel by the doors, so she managed to kill two birds with one stone. Taking a split second to admire how hot her husband was, Kendall approached them.

"Hey, baby." Evan kissed her cheek.

Kendall loved being married to him. He was her first and her last love. They may have taken a wrong turn and spent ten years apart, but they were more than making up for it now. Even something like an unexpected pregnant one-night stand hadn't been able to drive them apart once Kendall had contemplated a future without him. "Hey. So what are you going to buy for me tonight?"

"Anything you want," he said, sweeping his arm in the direction of all the many beautiful auction items.

Kendall laughed. "Yeah, right. You'll change your mind

when I want you to bid on a twenty-thousand-dollar trip to Bora Bora."

"Yeah, that might be out. But only because of our schedule, not because I wouldn't buy you the world if I could."

Someone really wanted a piece of ass later. Kendall rolled her eyes.

Diesel made a face. "Laying it on a little thick, aren't you, Monroe?"

Evan grinned. "It's the truth."

"Uh-huh. Thanks, babe." Kendall turned to Diesel and lowered her voice. "Hey, uh, word to the wise, Tuesday's already on glass of wine number two. You might want to keep an eye on her."

Something flickered in his eyes. "She's a grown woman. She can have a glass of wine if she wants one."

His response surprised Kendall. She would have thought he'd understand what she was saying. She had thought he'd shown a very protective nature toward Tuesday, something she had really appreciated seeing. Her best friend might be independent and snarky, but she needed someone looking out for her just like anyone else did. Kendall thought she'd seen the potential for that person to be Diesel. Tuesday certainly seemed happy with him and they'd been spending a ton of time together.

"I just meant that it would be a good idea if she doesn't go beyond three glasses and I don't want to say anything to her mother. This event is going to be hard enough for her."

Diesel sighed. "Yeah, I know. I've got an eye on her, don't worry about it."

"Thanks," Kendall said. But she felt a tinge of concern.

Tuesday had been dismissive when she'd mentioned Diesel. Now he looked annoyed at having to watch Tuesday.

Something was not right and Kendall didn't like it.

TUESDAY had a nice buzz going. She wasn't drunk at all, she was just happy and relaxed and making the rounds of all her many guests with aplomb and a big smile. The auction was going well. The items were receiving on-par bids, some going even higher than she had anticipated. The waitstaff was doing their job well circulating with finger foods and champagne, and everyone seemed to be enjoying themselves.

Diesel's car was front and center in the middle of the ballroom. It had been getting a great deal of attention from both current and former drivers and stock car enthusiasts. She was so proud of him she wanted to just kiss the snot out of him in front of everyone. Seriously, that was her boyfriend, and he rocked. He'd taken a piece of junk and made it the envy of everyone with a penis in the room. And Kendall. She probably dug it, too.

He was the center of attention by the car, looking smoking hot in his suit, hair in his eyes as usual. Tuesday had teased him about gelling it back but he'd made his opinion on that very clear. He didn't use hair products past shampoo. End of story. She had found herself the perfect man, really. He was manly, yet sensitive, protective, and not a slob. If he was a little anti-social, hey, there were worse things. And if he refused to talk about his accident with her she wasn't going to force him to relive something so awful.

Tuesday smiled at a driver's wife whose name she had

forgotten. Which was ridiculous because she never forgot names and she shouldn't have forgotten this one in particular. It was Jonas's wife, the blonde with breasts not found in nature.

Whatever her name was, she said to Tuesday, "Gawd, I almost wish I knew how to drive a stock car. I think that antique one is so sexy . . . and every guy here wants it, which makes me want it."

Where was her wine? Tuesday grabbed a glass off a passing waiter's tray and blinked at the blonde. She was having trouble following her and she wasn't about to point out that the car didn't exactly qualify as an antique. "I know, it's cool, isn't it? We're closing the bids on it in just a few minutes."

"I guess I'd really rather have the Hermès bag. Besides, I think that old guy really wants it. Which is stupid, because he doesn't know how to drive it any more than I do." She pointed toward the car.

Diesel was talking to a guy who was probably all of fifty, which clearly qualified him as old in this woman's book. But Tuesday knew who he was and the fact that he might be interested thrilled her. He was the CEO of a Fortune 500 company and owed a piece of the speedway, which combined to make him filthy, stinkin', bid-as-high-as-he-wanted rich. It had been a coup just to have him attend. If he bought Diesel's car, he would more than likely pay top dollar for it.

"Does he? Excuse me," she told the blonde. "I need to go make some announcements."

An idea had jumped into her head. It was brilliant, the absolute bestest way to secure a bid from Roger Hanover, Mr. Gazillionaire. She took a monstrous sip of her wine, dribbling a little down her chin. Wiping it off, she straightened her skirt and headed for the podium.

DIESEL was trapped with Roger Hanover, listening to him go on and on about all his accomplishments and travels. Diesel basically wanted to slit his wrists and go home to Wilma, but he had to stay through the whole damn auction for Tuesday. He wanted to support her. He also wanted to make sure she didn't pass out in the chocolate fountain.

Last he had seen her she was talking to Nikki Strickland and snagging yet another glass of wine. Now a quick glance around as he nodded politely to Roger proved her nowhere to be found.

"So as I was saying . . ."

Blah, blah, blah. God, Diesel hated doing the pretty. He wasn't good at sucking up or being the center of attention, and tonight he'd had to do both. Since he'd walked in the room, there hadn't been a single second where someone hadn't wanted to shake his hand, thank him, take his picture, or ask him questions that were none of their damn business.

"Right, right." He nodded, surreptitiously trying to find his girlfriend. They'd had a shaky week, but tonight he'd wanted to clear the air. He wanted to explain to her why that article bugged him. He wanted to ask her to move in with him.

But he was getting crankier and she was getting drunker and it didn't look like tonight was going to end with his telling her he loved her in any meaningful way.

He should have known she would reach for a glass of wine tonight. She was nervous, and he should have stuck closer by her side. Except all the exposure she and her PR team had given his car had ensured he was trapped next to it for the last three-plus hours. His knee was killing him and he'd yet to have even one of those damn puff things circulating on serving trays of waiters.

"Excuse me, can I have everyone's attention?"

Tuesday's voice can streaming over the microphone, louder than was necessary and full of an exuberance that immediately raised alarms in Diesel. She was at the podium, leaning over it, her dress falling a bit forward, her hair looking a little less polished than it had several hours earlier. There was a wineglass in her hand and no particular reason for her to be up there. She wasn't scheduled to speak. He knew that. She'd gone over the whole event out loud so many times, he could have run it.

"I hope everyone is having a wonderful time. I'm so grateful to everyone who came tonight, and keep those bids coming in."

So far, so good. She sounded coherent, appropriate, and she wasn't slurring her words.

"So we have a very special item here as you all have seen, this wonderful 1963 Chevrolet restored to the condition it was in when it won the championship that year. I have a special treat for whoever is the high bidder on this item."

Uh-oh. There wasn't supposed to be a special treat. Diesel took a step forward, knowing he was too far away to stop her, but afraid of what she might say. He did not want her to embarrass herself.

"The man who has restored this stock car treasure will

be granting a driving experience to whoever wins the car tonight . . . that's right, you'll be in the passenger seat while Diesel Lange takes you around the track."

The guests started clapping, cheers went up, and Roger made an exclamation of surprise and pleasure, but it was all secondary noise to the buzzing that had just started up in Diesel's ears. She had ambushed him. Sold him out. Done exactly what he had fucking asked her not to do. He didn't want to drive. Couldn't drive.

Why the hell hadn't she respected that?

He managed to smile and give one last handshake to Roger before excusing himself, his head suddenly throbbing as badly as his knee. He made his way to Tuesday, who was making a wobbly descent from the stage.

"Hi," she said with a loopy smile, eyes bright. "Wasn't that an awesome idea?" She leaned in to whisper, "I think whatshis-face will up his bid for that. Brilliant, huh?"

So getting a few extra grand was worth throwing him under the bus? Blatantly disregarding his request?

He was so pissed he took a deep breath before he spoke. Then another one.

She frowned. "Are you okay? Is your knee bothering you?"

Yes, but that was the least of his concerns. "Can I talk to you somewhere private?"

"Just for a minute. I have guests, honey bunny."

If she were sober, he would appreciate the term of endearment. As it was, it just irritated him further. Diesel took her hand and led her through a door next to the stage, which led to the kitchen eventually. They were in a secluded hallway, no staff in sight. He pushed the door to the ballroom closed behind him.

"Why would you tell the whole damn room I'll take the winner on the track?"

She just looked at him blankly. "I just told you. I thought it would increase the bid."

His stupid shaggy hair was in his eyes and he raked it back off his forehead. "I told you straight out when I gave you the car—a twenty-five-thousand-dollar investment on my part—that I would be happy to donate it but I wasn't driving it. Plain and simple. My one stipulation. And you just ignored that."

For a minute, she looked horrified and contrite, like she'd just remembered he had said that. Which was very possible. But then her bottom lip jutted out. "Oh, come on, don't be mad. What's the big deal?"

"It's a big deal because I asked you to respect my feelings and you haven't." God, this was pointless. She was bombed and he was an idiot.

"Maybe it's something you just need to do, you know, like getting back on a horse."

"To what purpose? And that's my decision, not yours!"

She raised her wineglass to her lips and started to drain the liquid.

Diesel lost it. Without even any thought behind the action, he reached out and yanked it out of her hands. "Lay off the fucking wine."

"Hey!" Her face contorted into fury and she reached for it. "Give me that back. You can't just take that away."

"And you can't just announce that I'll drive that race car, but you did. And I most certainly can just take this glass away. I just did." He held it up over his head, knowing she couldn't reach it, knowing he was letting his anger force this conversation in a terrible direction, but he was just so hurt, so frustrated. He didn't understand her sometimes and this was one of them.

"Give me that." Her voice was steely cold and she reached out and shoved him in the chest.

Diesel was caught off guard. He stumbled and his knee buckled. When embarrassment was added to his anger, the last of his control shattered. Turning toward the wall, he hurled her glass at it, feeling a sick sense of satisfaction when it exploded in a spray of glass shards and deep red liquid. As pieces rained down onto the carpet and the wine trickled at a slower pace through the beige paint, her shriek of shock penetrated his momentary triumph.

Damn, what the hell was he doing?

"I'll just go get another one," she told him.

Diesel turned back to her, suddenly weary. "I know. What I don't know is why."

Her look was one of belligerence, defiance. "Well, I don't know why you won't share any of your feelings with me. Maybe I wouldn't have offered for you to drive if you had just taken the time to explain it to me. I had to learn about your accident from watching a goddamn YouTube video."

"You found out enough to call me out in that magazine article."

"I didn't call you out! I was reporting from an unbiased angle. People want to know what happened to you, how you've moved on. I want to know, and I'm your girlfriend!"

"I don't recall you ever asking me outright about the accident." He took her by the elbow and moved her back away from the broken glass, knowing that what he was saying was unfair. She had asked him to talk to her on more than one occasion and he had blown her off, unable to show her any signs of weakness.

"You're a liar. You just didn't want to tell me. You don't care about me enough to share your feelings with me."

He knew Tuesday was struggling with her grief, knew that she loved him. But he was frustrated, afraid of losing her, either to wine or someone else when she saw clearly how unexciting he and his life were. But he still heard the insult and reacted in the worst possible way. "It's just all about you, isn't it?"

That was probably poking the bear. Especially given the bear was drunk. But Diesel was hurt, he was tired, he was embarrassed by the attention of the night, all the damn questions about his accident. He wanted to have it out. Clear the air. Have them both say what they meant.

Except sometimes you get exactly what you intend, and you don't like it.

Tuesday's expression changed and he expected drunken anger. That's not what he got. She had retreated, pulled back into herself. "Oh, really? I didn't know that's how you felt. And if you do, I question why the hell we're even together."

Diesel couldn't meet her eye. At the moment he wasn't sure why they were together. There were issues she needed to deal with and he couldn't fix them for her.

But she wasn't finished. Though she wobbled a little on her heels, her words weren't slurred. They were just harsh. "I did try to talk to you a few times and you shut me down. You can stand here and say I'm the only one with a problem, but I'm not. You don't know how to share your emotions. And if you think for one goddamn minute that you have dealt with the repercussions of your accident, or hell, even your mother's and brother's deaths, then you're kidding yourself. You've just locked it all in a box inside of you marked Don't Touch and told yourself you're fine."

He wasn't about to agree with that, even if somewhere inside him it struck a chord of truth so powerful he was suddenly afraid. "I'm dealing just fine."

"And if you think everything in our relationship was about me I'd argue that it was the exact opposite. It was about you. What you wanted."

That pissed him off. "We're not talking about sex, and that was a dynamic you liked, don't deny it."

"I'm not talking about sex either," she said disdainfully. "You're right, I enjoy you being in charge of what happens in the bedroom. I'm talking about the fact that when you withhold your feelings, yet expect them from me. That's selfish."

It was so unexpected, he could only stare at her in shock. No one had ever called him selfish before.

Tears filled her eyes. "Tonight, I just needed you to support me. And you made it about what you didn't want to do. I wasn't trying to put you on the spot, I was just trying to get through the night."

When she put it like that, he felt guilty, and that made him angry. "I wanted the same thing. Just a little support and understanding. Instead you splashed my business all over. I think maybe we need to take a break here, spend a little time apart and see where we're at."

Her jaw dropped. "You're breaking up with me in the middle of the cancer benefit?"

Again, when put like that . . . "No, of course not! I just

think we need to take a step back and think about some things. Talk when we're calmer. When you're sober."

Her lip curled in disgust. "A break is a break-up and you know it. Thanks for ruining my night." She pushed the door to the ballroom back open and tossed her hair back as she wiped the tears from under her eyes. She looked vulnerable, but she had straightened her posture and steeled her voice. "Have a nice life, Daniel."

A steel pipe to his knee would have hurt less.

He watched her go, wondering what the hell he had just done.

CHAPTER
FOURTEEN

TUESDAY got trashed at the cancer benefit to honor her father. After her fight with Diesel, she had stalked the waiter and had made him rustle up an unopened bottle of wine for him, which she then proceeded to drink in an hour. She was conscious of the fact that she wasn't walking entirely straight and that her tongue had gotten too big for her mouth. When a reporter she knew asked her some interview questions, she had a hard time thinking up answers and she giggled way more than normal.

But she didn't really realize exactly how loaded she was until her mother pulled her into the hallway. "You need to go home," her mother told her.

"Why?" Tuesday tried to lean over and hug her mom but she stumbled a little and got distracted. Her mom looked beautiful, elegant, and classy, and she'd given a brief speech before Tuesday had gotten trashed after the argument and breakup with Diesel. Had she and Diesel really broken up?

God, that sucked.

Tuesday felt tears rise in her eyes. "Diesel and I had a fight."

"I know, he told me when I asked him to take you home. I don't think I should leave and he pointed out he probably shouldn't either. It looks better if he and I continue to show our faces all night. So he said he asked Kendall to take you home."

Yeah, she was definitely drunk because none of this was making any sense to her. "Why do I have to go home?"

"Because you're embarrassing me," her mother said quietly and firmly.

That shocked her. She was embarrassing her mother at her father's cancer benefit? Tears filled her eyes.

Without warning, all the wine decided to make a reappearance and Tuesday turned and threw up into the pot of a fake palm tree in the lobby.

When she stood she was vaguely aware of eyes on her, then the night went black.

TUESDAY remembered coming to in the cab and bawling on Kendall, then proceeding to drink two more glasses of wine at home before she passed out for the night.

Now the next morning, she had a pounding head and a broken heart. And a deep, deep shame that she had embarrassed both her mother and her father's memory by acting like a drunken idiot at the benefit. Fighting the urge to throw up, she fumbled for her cell phone and dialed her best friend.

"Hey, are you okay?" Kendall asked by way of greeting.

"I guess." Taking stock, she counted a throbbing head, a swollen nose, an earache, a stomach that was alternating between knots and nausea-inducing flips, sore shoulders, aching feet, and a mouth so dry licking sand would improve its moisture content. Not to mention a pain in her chest so severe it took her breath away, and even after being awake for five minutes, she'd already had repeated attempts to fight back tears. She pretty much wanted to die, but she was assuming the physical pain would recede. The heart was going to take a while to heal, if ever.

"Did I say anything really inappropriate last night? How many people saw me puke?"

"You ranted about Diesel, but no one heard that. You were obviously drunk, but you didn't say anything awful. I'm not sure how many people saw you puke, but I'm guessing at least one or two. I came out right after and I knew you needed to leave. But you managed one more glass of wine before I could haul you to the car. You have ninja skills when you want a drink." Kendall said it lightly.

But Tuesday just sighed. "Thanks. You're the best best friend I could ask for. I can't believe I ditched out on my own benefit."

"Diesel just broke up with you. I don't blame you. No one would blame you."

"It just proves I'm completely weak. I hate that. I want to be in control." She fought with that every day. She tried to control her life and the environment around her and when she couldn't, she went off the rails.

"Everyone does. But honey, there are just some things beyond our control."

"I know." She looked at her nightstand, wishing a glass of water would magically appear. Diesel had asked for a break and she had definitely given him one—he hadn't had to deal with her drunk ass the night before. "I need to learn to let go. Diesel once asked me what my issues were, and I think it's safe to say that's it . . . I want to control everything and when I can't, it's bad."

"There are definitely worse issues to have, and if you know that about yourself, you can work on it."

"Yeah. I want to." She closed her eyes, hoping the pounding would recede a little. It didn't. "I always thought men were the problem, not me, that they were selfish. But who wants to be generous emotionally or otherwise with someone who has a steel vice on their own feelings and the relationship in general?"

"I think you're being really hard on yourself. You're right, you shouldn't have had so much wine last night. That wasn't cool. But Diesel needs to give a little, too."

Maybe it was time to be hard on herself. This wasn't how she wanted to live her life. "I went up to the podium and told the whole room Diesel would do the very thing he said he didn't want to do. I humiliated my mother. I flubbed an interview. And I barfed in a bush. I don't think it's possible to be too hard on myself."

She closed her eyes, trying to blink back the tears. God, she was a mess. A complete disaster. "Did that interview air?"

Kendall hesitated. "Yes."

That wasn't encouraging. "It's bad, isn't it?"

"It could be better. It could be worse."

Tuesday hauled herself into a sitting position and reached for her laptop. She hit a few keys, searching for the interview on the local news.

"Tuesday, I don't think you should . . ." Kendall's voice was filled with concern.

"Oh, my God." Tuesday put her free hand over her mouth as she saw herself on the screen, wavering on her heels, her hair out of place. Her eyes were narrow and she had a lazy grin on her face. It was more than obvious she was drunk.

"Maybe you shouldn't watch that," Kendall told her.

"Shh." She had to see, to hear how she had presented herself the night before.

"So what kinds of items are available tonight at the auction?" the blond interviewer asked.

"Oh, all kinds of shit." She waved her arm around. "Meet-and-greets with drivers, restaurant gift cards, wine. Too bad I can't win the wine." She laughed, an obnoxious cackle that screamed she was bombed on Merlot.

As she watched, she saw herself stumble and grab the reporter for support. "Oops, sorry."

The woman smiled tightly. "I don't think you need to win the wine."

Onscreen, she laughed like it was the funniest thing she'd ever heard in her life. Tuesday hit the stop button. She'd seen enough. Swallowing hard, she made a decision.

"So, do you know a good therapist? Someone who specializes in alcohol abuse?"

"What? Are you serious? No, but I can definitely help you find someone. You really think it's that bad?"

Tuesday didn't even have to glance in the mirror to know what she looked like, and her physical symptoms were completely familiar to her. She had humiliated herself the night before in front of all her friends and co-workers. Her mother and her boyfriend, the two most important people in her life. That made it a problem. "It's not beyond repair, but I need to get a grip before it gets worse. You know, I lost my dad to cancer. I just lost Diesel to my own stupidity. That fight could have gone a different way if I hadn't been drinking. Hell, we might not have had the fight."

The tears spilled out and a little sob escaped before she could stop it.

"Hey," Kendall said softly. "Who's to say you've lost him? It wasn't entirely your fault, you know. He could have chosen a better time to initiate a conversation that was emotionally charged. He made it all about your drinking and that wasn't fair. He brought his own issues to the fight."

She nodded, even though Kendall couldn't see her. She knew that was true. Everything she had said to Diesel was true, even if the way she had said it was awful and bitchy. He wasn't necessarily dealing with his grief any better than she had. He just suffered internally, whereas her method of coping was external, on display at the bar. Neither was going to serve them long-term. But she supposed, no matter how much she loved him, that was his problem. He needed to decide to deal with it or not deal with it. It hadn't been fair, the way she had been poking at him, insisting he talk to her.

Love was supposed to be patient. It was something she needed to learn tenfold.

She was going to deal with her problems head-on. She never should have tried to be the strong one, pretending she could handle her father's death. It was a big deal, a catastrophic loss, and most people couldn't just forge ahead on their own. There was no shame in needing someone to talk to, or finding a positive outlet for her grief.

In lieu of that she had turned to alcohol and that had been the worst possible choice.

"It doesn't matter," she told Kendall, even as her voice caught. "It's over, and it's probably for the best. I need to get my shit together before I'm involved with someone. It's not fair to Diesel otherwise."

"Maybe a little later, after you've both had a chance to think and process everything, you can be together."

A part of her desperately wanted to cling to that hope. But a break was a breakup and she couldn't pin her future on something that had very little chance of happening. "I don't think so. We both said some rough things." Her stomach tightened miserably and the tears came freely. "But I do love him, Kendall. I really, really love him."

Maybe she should have told him that. In a way that wasn't roundabout and flippant.

"I'm sorry, sweetie, God, this sucks. And you know that I'll help you in any way you can. If you want to do inpatient therapy let me know. And I can help you out financially, you know I'm happy to do that."

"Thanks, Kendall. I really appreciate that." Then she knew she needed to get off the phone. "Oh, damn, I'm going to be sick, I'll call you later." Tuesday hung up the phone urgently.

While the pain in her heart swelled, her stomach did likewise, and clearly in an effort to make her as utterly miserable as possible, hurled up all of last night's wine all over her white down-filled comforter.

CHAPTER
FIFTEEN

DIESEL studied the window of the car, his helmet in his hand, driving suit on. He was ready to go. All he had to do was climb in. But that was what was worrying him. What if he couldn't get in? There was a ton of people milling around and if his knee gave out on the way into that car, he'd be humiliated. Then once he was in, what if he couldn't get back out? What if his leg was too weak to control the car?

Well, he could stand there indefinitely or he could find out.

If he couldn't do it, he couldn't do it. So there might be some sympathetic glances from the crew and the media, but no one was going to call him a pussy. He was the only one doing that.

In the week since the benefit, he'd only tried to call Tuesday once. She'd hit the ignore button on him, and he didn't blame her. He had blindsided her at that benefit as much as she had blindsided him with her announcement onstage, and shittiest of all, he hadn't checked up on her the next day. He had waited until Monday to call her, when his anger had simmered down a little, but by then she was probably even more pissed at him, and he couldn't blame her.

Reflecting on whether or not to cancel this charity drive with Roger, who had pulled out the highest bid on the car, Diesel had reflected on a lot of things. Tuesday had made some fair points in the course of their argument even if she had hurled them at him in anger and alcohol. He hadn't dealt with his accident. He hadn't dealt with the fact that sometimes he didn't feel quite as much of a man as he had before. He had been stingy with his emotions. Hell, he loved the woman and he'd never really told her that. His delivery of such a powerful sentiment had been lame and after that first time, he had only told her he cared about her. He had never said straight out, "I love you."

So he was going to get his ass into this damn car and then he was going to tackle the rest of his life. He would conquer his fear, then he was going to apologize to Tuesday. He was going to open up, tell her how he felt, and make a total nuisance of himself until she agreed to give him a second chance.

He could live without racing.

But he couldn't live without the woman he loved.

He wanted to help her with her own grief, work through it, without wine or walls up between them.

Together.

Taking a deep breath, Diesel climbed into the car, receiving only a slight twinge of protest from his knee. He was going to take the car around the track solo a time or two before Roger rode shotgun with him.

It felt good sliding down into the seat, like seeing an old friend again. He put his helmet on and secured his harness. When he flipped the switch to start the engine, he turned and grinned at Jesper, his old crew chief who had come out to back him up.

Jesper gave him the thumbs-up and said into his radio, "Hell, yeah. How's that feeling, Diesel?"

"It feels fucking awesome." It did.

Jesper laughed. "Have fun out there, bro."

"I will." Diesel hit the gas and pulled out onto the track. After a few seconds, he opened her up, enjoying the rumble beneath his legs, enjoying the power of the car. He had built this car, and that made it even more satisfying.

As he took the first turn, all the instincts, all the training, all the years of driving came right back to him, and he felt in control. He felt exhilarated. Free.

So he couldn't drive for a living.

It didn't mean he couldn't have fun.

He'd been denying himself this because he was afraid of failure, afraid of embarrassing himself.

None of that mattered anymore.

As the lady in black rose up before him, the heat of the September sun making waves on the surface, he drove into his future.

TUESDAY squeezed her mother's hand as the final hymns of the mass rang through the church, but not out of concern, out of love. When her mother glanced over at her, they shared a smile. It had been surprisingly peaceful to be back in church, something she didn't make a habit of, and she'd stood there next to her mother as they had dedicated the mass to her father, and she'd felt grateful, not the overwhelming sadness she'd been anticipating.

Grateful that she'd had Bob Jones as a father. Grateful that she still had her mother. Grateful that she had done justice to her father's memory and the fight against cancer, despite her personal appalling behavior. In the end, they had raised money, and the driving community has praised her father's memory. Out of respect for him, she hadn't gotten much heat in the media for her drunkenness that night, which she had to admit was classier than the way she would have handled it. The old Tuesday Talladega would have torn apart in her blog anyone who had shown up at an event blitzed.

That was not the person she wanted to be. Either the drunk or the bitch. She wasn't that person anymore. She hadn't had a drink in four weeks and she was doing well in her counseling sessions.

The grief from her father's death was still there, but not raw and weeping on the surface anymore. It was a beautiful day in late September. Birds sang outside, babies cooed inside, and she had survived both the loss of her father and the first man she could have seen herself actually marrying.

To have the hurt of her father be replaced by the sting of losing Diesel had been like an electrical jolt, especially knowing she had done the latter to herself. She had spent two days in bed, vomiting long after the results of the wine, and crying repeatedly. Then she had dragged herself out of bed, called a therapist, and dug deep for that strength she constantly touted to herself and others as having so much of.

She had screwed up with Diesel and she had paid the price. He had called her on Monday, but she'd still been throwing up, and too embarrassed to talk to him. She didn't want to hear the truth, which was that she had probably ruined any feelings he had ever had for her. Eventually, she was going to return his call, to apologize for her part in their failure as a couple. She owed that both to him and to herself, but she had been waiting until she could speak to him without falling apart. She needed to do it soon before her apology no longer held any weight.

"You ready?" her mother whispered as the last notes died down.

She nodded, and they filed out of the pew and started the slow shuffle down the aisle with the rest of the congregation. She was about to invite her mother to lunch when she looked to her right and came to an abrupt stop.

There was a man wearing a Diesel Lange T-shirt. His face was right on the guy's chest, right there in church. His hair had been shorter when the picture had been taken several years ago but he was wearing the half smile she recognized so well.

She looked back at the altar, where the priest had solemnly dedicated the mass to her father earlier.

Heart beating wildly, Tuesday decided it was definitely a sign. Today was the day she needed to apologize to Diesel. She had just been thinking about it and now there was

Diesel's face in front of her. What were the odds of that? As soon as they were out of the church she turned to her mom. "I need to call Diesel. I need to apologize."

Her mother's eyebrows raised but then she nodded. "I think that's a good idea, honey."

Now that the idea had popped into her head, she had to pursue it immediately. Pulling her phone out of her purse, she called him standing in the parking lot. It went to voice mail. She debated leaving a message, but his phone was clearly turned off, so she didn't bother. Instead, she called his uncle.

"Hi, Johnny, it's Tuesday Jones . . . how are you?" She paced across the sidewalk, barely aware of the warm air swirling around and the flowers still blooming, despite the coming fall.

Diesel's uncle was obviously surprised to hear from her, but he just said, "Good, good, how are you?"

"I'm better, but I need to clear a few things up. I'd like to talk to Diesel but he's not picking up. Do you happen to know where he is?" She knew it was a long shot. Diesel could be doing any number of things.

But his uncle answered right away. "Sure do. He's at the track. Giving that businessman his ride today."

Again, that struck Tuesday as a sign. That today would be the day he was fulfilling the promise she had rudely made on his behalf . . . she needed to apologize plain and simple.

"Oh, okay, great, thanks, Johnny." She hesitated. "How is he?"

"He's fine, but he misses you, girl. I wish the two of you would patch things up."

Her throat tightened. "Me, too, but I'm not sure Diesel

wants that." But a glimmer of hope rose in her. "I guess I'll let you know."

Another minute and she was on her way to the track in high heels and a pencil skirt.

When she got there, for a minute she was worried she wouldn't be able to gain access without any of her press credentials. But one of the guards recognized her and let her in.

Diesel was climbing out of his car, favoring his knee only a little bit. She stood on the edge of the track, overcome with emotion at the sight of him. When he pulled off his helmet, she saw he'd trimmed his beard. It wasn't so unruly and mountain man as it had been. She wasn't used to seeing him in riding gear. He looked sexy, like he was born to drive, which he had been. He was grinning, ear to ear, like he had just torn up the track and enjoyed every mile.

God, she loved him. How could she have ever let him go? How could she have said the horrible things to him that she had?

When he spotted her, he stopped walking and the grin fell off his face.

Tuesday forced herself to walk over to him, her heels clicking on the asphalt. "Hi," she said, her voice low and husky.

"Tuesday. Hi. Are you here for the drive?" He looked wary of her, hands clenching his helmet against his chest.

She shook her head rapidly, not trusting herself to speak, the emotions she'd been busy processing all rushing to the surface at once, threatening to pull her under. "No," she squeaked out. "I'm not here for the drive. I came to talk to you."

"Oh."

When she didn't say anything, unable to figure out what to say he added, "How have you been? Are you okay?"

The answer she would have given in the past would have been that she was fine. But she no longer needed to cling to the façade of strength when none was needed. What they needed was the truth between them. "No, I'm not okay. I'm doing better, and I'm going to a counselor, and I've quit drinking, but, no, I'm not completely okay . . . not yet. I will be though."

"I'm glad to hear that you've stopped drinking. That's a good thing, sweetheart, a real good thing."

The term of endearment emboldened her. She forged ahead. "I came here to apologize to you."

"What?" Diesel glanced him around. "Do you mind taking a walk? I'd like to talk in private."

"Sure, of course." Tuesday fell in step beside him and without even thinking she reached for his hand and squeezed it, just like she had with her mother. She didn't keep it there, though, and as glorious as it felt, it only made her more acutely aware of how difficult it was to no longer have the right to touch him.

She wasn't sure what to say, where to start. She wanted to choose her words more carefully than she had in the past. "I'm sorry," she said finally. "I was awful that night at the benefit. I can't believe I made that announcement saying you would drive after you told me you didn't want to . . . that was inexcusable. I did it because I was drunk and it made sense to me at the time and that just makes it even worse." Tuesday stole a glance at him to see how he was reacting to her apology. She wasn't sure if she should just shut up or keep going.

He was staring down at her intently. "I miss you, sweetheart," he told her. He stopped walking and cupped her cheek with his hand. "I love you."

Oh, God. That was the first time he'd ever come straight out and spoken those words to her and it thrilled and devastated her. But it had her tossing caution out the window and there was no thinking about her response. She just said it.

"I love you, too. So, so much."

Then she threw her arms around him, because if this were it, if this were the last time she was going to see him in any meaningful way, she wanted to feel him, hold him. His arms came around her and he held her tight, his lips brushing along her temple.

"I'm sorry, too," he told her. "I'm so sorry. You were right, I was holding back, I could have shared more. But I was afraid, I was afraid you would think I wasn't a real man. And attacking you about everything that night at the benefit was the worst selfish timing."

"What?" She pulled her head off his chest. "Why the hell would I think you were less of a man?"

"Because I can't do this anymore." He gestured behind him to the track. "Because I'm not an advocate for better safety measures. Because I sit in my house with no awards, no evidence of my career. Because I walk with a limp."

Tears flooded Tuesday's eyes. "God, I never thought any of those things. I had to write that into the article, it was a reporter's speculation. But I don't care if you drive or not. I just care that you're happy. I should have listened to you better when you did talk."

She stared into those pale blue eyes and what she saw there had flicker of hope sparking into a bonfire.

"I want to be with you." He kissed her, the softest, gentlest kiss he'd ever given, one that spoke of love and promise and a life together. "I love you, and I want to work on whatever we need to. I was really damn happy with you, Tuesday. The happiest I've ever been."

"Me, too, me, too." She kissed him back, not caring who was watching, not caring where she was, just wanting him to feel what was inside of her. "I love you, Daniel."

Thank God. Diesel hugged Tuesday tightly in relief, knowing they were going to be okay. They were going to be fine. They were going to be better than anything either of them could have anticipated and they were going to be happy.

They already were.

Suddenly he found himself impulsively going down on one knee, his bad knee, too, of all stupid-ass things. But here before all these other people on the track, before a photographer and Jesper and Roger Hanover, he was going to toss his idea of living together and go for the real deal.

"Tuesday."

Her hands had flown up to her mouth and her eyes were huge. Tears glistened in her brown eyes.

"Will you marry me?"

She nodded without hesitation, up and down rapidly, multiple times.

Euphoria exploded inside him and he grinned. "Did I finally make you speechless?"

With one final nod, she burst out, "Yes! Holy shit, yes!"

He laughed. "I have always loved your enthusiasm."

She jumped up and down a couple of times. "Oh, my God, we're getting married!" She turned and waved violently to Roger, the billionaire, who was standing by the car he'd bought, looking bemused. "Married. Really? Are you sure, Diesel?"

As a matter of fact, he had never been more sure. "Yes. Totally sure." But then he winced when he tried to stand up. "Now help me up."

"My pleasure." Without hesitation she held her hand out to him, her smile as wide as any he'd ever seen her sport, and he didn't feel like less of a man when she gave him support.

He felt complete.

And together, they were going to both go from just fine to absolutely amazing.

"So let's go get you a ring. And a cookie."

She laughed. "Sounds like a plan, Dan."

WEDDING BELLS

One by one the eligible bachelors of racing have fallen to the lure of matrimony and it's happened yet again, people. Former driver, Daniel "Diesel" Lange, the sexiest damn driver to ever grace the circuit was smart enough to propose to ME. I said yes, of course, because Daddy didn't raise no fool, and when you find love you need to hold on to it with both hands. Like a steering wheel. See, I can fit racing in if need be . . .

You're all invited to the wedding. Not.

I'll write from Bora Bora unless I'm otherwise occupied.

Kisses,
Tuesday Talladega

Turn the page for a special preview of
Erin McCarthy's next Fast Track Novel
Coming summer 2012 from Berkley Sensation!

NOLAN Ford wasn't listening to Eve Monroe as she chewed him out. It wasn't that he was trying to be disrespectful, but Lord, the woman could start an argument in an empty house.

Besides, the top button on her blouse was straining, and each time she lifted her arm and waved it around, he held his breath, waiting for it to pop. He'd had something of a crush on Eve for years, always aware when she was around the track or the garage, stomping around in her heels and severe office clothes. She thought no one noticed that she was a woman, and seemed to work damn hard to make sure it stayed that way, but Nolan had always noticed.

Eve was hot. Full-on, smokin', jalapeño pepper hot. From that lustrous deep brown hair with a hint of red, to her gold-flecked eyes, down past an amazing chest, to slim legs and a perky behind, she was all that and a bag of chips, in his opinion.

"I mean, seriously, I don't care what kind of underwear you wear, just wear some!" she said, making a sound of frustration. "I mean, really, let's show a little decorum."

Nolan fought the urge to grin. She looked so serious when talking about his underwear. Or lack thereof. But he knew if he so much as curved the corner of his mouth up, her head would blow off her shoulders. Eve was not happy about the little incident during the race the other day. "Well, ma'am, it's hot in those crew suits. Some particular parts need air circulation."

She drew in a deep breath, obviously struggling for control, but it only made her blouse pull tighter. Nolan stared in fascination as the button slipped halfway through the hole. If that thing gave, he was going to see her bra. He wasn't sure he was capable of not getting a hard-on if that happened.

And since he wasn't wearing any underwear today either, she would probably notice.

"Stick a bag of frozen peas in your drawers. Just wear them." Her hands went up to rake her hair back off her head. "Don't pretend you don't understand that this is a big deal. You have been in the business for years. Sponsors want a friendly, wholesome image for the sport their name is attached to. As do the team owners, and the powers that be in stock car racing. When a jackman goes over the wall and rips his suit, the whole world doesn't need to see his back end."

Nolan had to agree with that. He certainly hadn't intended to tear the seat of his pants going over the wall into pit road when Evan's car had stopped for a tire change. Or for his ass to end up on YouTube. But it had. So what were you going to do about it? That was his philosophy in life—don't sweat the small stuff. Or bare butts.

"I do understand, Eve. I'm proud to be a member of Evan's crew and I take my job seriously. It was an accident. I believe they even have a term for that—wardrobe malfunction."

She started talking. He stopped listening again. As her arms waved, the button gave up the good fight and parted ways with the hole it had been in. Her blouse sprung apart. He was assaulted with the sight of lots of pale, creamy flesh bursting out of a hot pink bra, the cleavage high and perky. It was a gorgeous surprise, all that breast she'd been hiding under her crisp tailored shirts.

But then that was what he thought of Eve in general—that she was hiding a whole lot of woman under the attitude. It was a thought that had intrigued him more than once as he'd seen her typing furiously on her smart phone, clipboard in hand. What would it be like to see every inch of her naked body, to get her to totally come undone . . .

"That's just an excuse," she was saying. "Wardrobe malfunction. Give me a break. Are you even listening to me?"

Nolan nodded. "They do happen, you know," he drawled, really savoring the moment of triumph. Forcing his eyes off her chest, he let his grin win out. "You seem to have one happening right now."

He pointed to her blouse, wide open and catching the breeze.

She glanced down and turned as pink as the lace bra she was wearing.

"I think they call that tit for tat," he told her.

THE CHASE
A Fast Track Novel

When racing for the checkered flag . . .

Kendall Holbrook is determined to make it to the top,
even with the challenge of being a woman in the male-
dominated racing circuit. She doesn't have time for
romance—especially not with racing rival Evan Monroe,
the man who nearly crushed her dream years ago. Forced
into meeting up with him, Kendall is experiencing all
those old feelings again—and she can't deny that they still
have more than enough chemistry to set fire to the track.

. . . expect a few speed bumps.

After getting dropped by his biggest sponsor, Evan is
watching his racing season go up in flames. The only
replacement available is completely humiliating: a co-
sponsorship for his-and-her deodorant with Kendall
Holbrook—the girl who once broke his heart. Acting like
Kendall doesn't still get him all hot and bothered is bad
enough, but the biggest challenge awaits him on the
track—where Evan has to decide if a second chance at love
is more important than making it to the finish line . . .